"Let me get this straight,"

Ben said. "You're saying you want to come with me?"

"Let's just say I'm *willing* to come with you," Kelsey replied.

"And exactly what is all this altruism of yours going to cost me?"

"I want an in-depth profile on you," she shot back. "The price of my cooperation will be for you to open up to me."

"If you come with me voluntarily, Kelsey, you could be charged with aiding and abetting an escaped felon."

"I can always say that I was only trying to prevent anyone from getting hurt by driving more safely than you could."

"Or that you're just a reporter covering an important story," he added, his voice sharp and dry, "and wanted to be there when they took me in."

"Okay. That too." Which, of course, was exactly the case. She wasn't about to make a fool of herself by admitting anything else. All sorts of feelings about Ben Carlyle had been bubbling through her since meeting him. It seemed safer not to examine them too closely.

Dear Reader,

Hot days, hot nights and hot reading—summer's really here! And we truly do have a hit lineup for you this month. For example, our American Heroes title is by Naomi Horton. *Hell on Wheels* is a very apt description of the hero, as well as the name of the truck he drives. But when he meets our heroine... Well, all I can say is that they'd both better prepare for a little taste of heaven!

Award-winner Justine Davis checks in with *Target of Opportunity,* a sexy bodyguard story with a hero who's absolutely scrumptious. Lee Magner's *Standoff* is set in the rugged American West, with a hero who's just as rugged—and a whole lot more romantic. Frances Williams brings in *Passion's Verdict,* with a hero on the run and a heroine who's along for the ride of her life. Christine D'Angelo's title says it all: *A Child Is Waiting.* But for the heroine, finding that child is going to take the help of one very special man. Finally, welcome new author Victoria Cole, whose *Mind Reader* has a psychic heroine and a skeptical hero on the trail of a missing child. Something tells me that you'll want to get hold of each and every one of these books!

And in months to come, look for more great reading from favorite authors such as Emilie Richards, Marilyn Pappano, Suzanne Carey and Linda Turner, to name only a few of the talents contributing to Intimate Moments, where excitement and romance go hand in hand.

Enjoy!

Leslie Wainger
Senior Editor and Editorial Coordinator

PASSION'S VERDICT

Frances Williams

Silhouette®
INTIMATE MOMENTS®

Published by Silhouette Books New York

America's Publisher of Contemporary Romance

SILHOUETTE BOOKS
300 East 42nd St., New York, N.Y. 10017

Books by Frances Williams

Silhouette Intimate Moments

Easy Target #223
Night Secrets #287
The Road to Forever #378
Shadows on Satin #455
Passion's Verdict #508

FRANCES WILLIAMS

was born in Montreal, Canada, and now lives in the Washington, D.C., area. Fran loves reading romantic suspense and thrillers. In fact, the one drawback to writing, she maintains, is that it doesn't leave a lot of time for a book addict to read. She has been nominated for the *Romantic Times* Reviewer's Choice Award, and she has won the Georgia Romance Writers' Maggie Award, the Delaware Romance Writers' Diamond Award and the *Romantic Times* Award for New Romantic Suspense Author.

For Johnny, Keith and Rit

Chapter 1

Two men burst into the small country diner on a roiling gust of wind and rain. Kelsey swiveled on her high chrome counter stool and grabbed for a menu kicked into flight, along with a handful of paper napkins, when the door opened. She snatched the menu out of the air, but the napkins fluttered to the grimy black-and-white-tile floor.

She glanced up at the men standing at the diner entrance, and her gaze lingered as she straightened and slid the single-page menu back on the counter.

The taller man, somewhere in his mid-thirties, wore a navy blue suit darkened with rain across the shoulders. Strange, she thought, that a man who could afford the finest wool and most expensive tailoring would wear a suit two sizes too big. Curious, too, that he wouldn't invest in a decent haircut. His rumpled black hair, glossy with rain, curled over the tops of his ears, and one wet shock slashed down across the clean, sharp arch of a dark eyebrow.

Her journalistic antennae pricked up.

Unlike the older, heavyset man who gripped his arm, he was tieless, his white dress shirt open at the collar. The ruggedly carved lines of cheek and squared-off jaw were arrestingly attractive, but hardened by the tight, rigid line of an unsmiling mouth. He and his companion had just run through a torrential downpour to the shelter of the diner. The older man let out an audible puff of relief. The younger showed no reaction.

A hard man, she decided.

And he looked familiar. She couldn't place him, but she knew him from somewhere. Her gaze skipped down to the hands he held so curiously crossed in front of him.

The sight of the handcuffs jarred her. The man was manacled not with the new plastic cuffs that looked like garbage bag ties, but with rings of serious, heavy-gauge gray metal.

The prisoner lifted his hands to wipe the rain from his face and the others in the restaurant saw the shackles. The same joking comments about another boarder for Noah's ark that had greeted Kelsey's appearance in the diner died off into murmured apprehension. The friendly young redhead in a black *bustier* and skimpy red shorts, who'd come over to settle herself on the stool next to Kelsey, picked up her cola and moved farther away from the door.

"Hey, man!" The grizzled counterman who'd been quick to offer her coffee wiped his hands nervously on his soiled apron. "What's going on here?"

"Nothing to worry about, folks." The older man fumbled for a wallet inside his jacket and flipped it open to display a badge. "Sergeant James Whittaker, prison security. This man is in my custody. I'm returning him to Moundsville. Like the rest of you, we're temporarily stranded by the storm." He shoved the wallet back into his pocket. "Bring us a couple coffees, will you, Mac? And a piece of that apple pie. Want some, Carlyle?"

The prisoner gave a curt shake of his head.

Carlyle. Of course. She hadn't been assigned to cover his sensational murder trial, but like everyone else she'd avidly followed it. Benton Carlyle had provided hordes of media people with a triple bonus. He was wealthy, photogenic and talkative. At first he'd corralled every reporter in sight to protest his innocence. That ended the first day of the trial, when he punched out a particularly aggressive journalist on nationwide TV.

"Carlyle," the counterman repeated. "Yeah!" He jabbed a pudgy finger toward the prisoner. "I recognize him now. Seen him on television. That's Ben Carlyle. Family had a place up in these hills somewhere. Guy got drunk and wasted his old man a few years back."

"Naw," one of a couple of bearded pickuppers hollered from a booth. "He didn't get drunk. Had a fight with his pa. Bashed his head in with a poker."

Crudely put, Kelsey thought, but essentially correct. However, the weapon of choice had been a golf club, not a poker.

The defense had put Carlyle on the stand. It might have worked. At first the man's straightforward, unflinching testimony had made a good impression on the jury. Then the prosecuting attorney's stabbing questions had succeeded in provoking the defendant's damning anger.

To her, that anger could as easily have been the panicked flailings of a man trying desperately to stave off the deadly trap closing around him. But Carlyle's furiously defiant outburst had demonstrated to the jury exactly what the prosecutor had set out to prove: When antagonized, Benton Carlyle had a temper that could fly out of control—perhaps enough to kill. Without premeditation, perhaps. But still, to kill.

By the time the trial ended, she had agreed with the jury's verdict—guilty as sin.

"From what I heard," the redhead called, "Henry Carlyle deserved it. My sister worked at the Carlyle plant. She says the big boss was a hard old buzzard. Always complaining about the workers not meeting their quotas. Always accusing everyone of stealing."

"Cop or no cop," the counterman protested, "don't want no murderer in my place." He waved the intruders away. "Get the guy outta here."

His customers shouted their agreement.

Kelsey didn't. While the others obviously weren't happy with the prospect of being holed up—perhaps for hours— with a convicted murderer, for her the idea spiked a rush of excitement. An interview with Benton Carlyle was exactly the kind of material that could prove to her editor she could handle harder-edged news stories than the slush he'd given her so far.

Carlyle might have been deaf for all the reaction he demonstrated to the argument swirling around him. He stood stiff and straight, staring directly ahead, his face impassive. He said nothing.

"Calm down, everybody!" The guard's loud command cut through the rising clamor. "No one's in any danger." He hauled up his charge's hands to show the heavy metal chain imprisoning them. "Carlyle's not a problem. He's cuffed, and I'm armed."

The policeman's assurances did nothing to mollify the counterman.

"The guy's vicious. Don't want him around."

"Look, if it'll make y'all feel any better I'll cuff him to me." The officer fished out a key from his pants pocket and locked the prisoner's right hand to his own left one. "See? He's not going anywhere without me. And no way we're heading back out in that storm. Can't, anyway—the bridge is out. They're turning everybody back. So just go about your business, folks. Storm like this, we're all gonna be here for a while. And you—" he gestured toward the diner owner "—bring the coffee to that booth in the back."

Kelsey had no problem admitting that she was nosy. Always had been. Maybe that was why she'd become a reporter. People interested her, especially unusual people—and a man who walked into an isolated restaurant in the mountains of West Virginia in handcuffs, a man who'd killed his father, was surely that.

The two men strode toward her, the guard slightly in front, the prisoner still holding to that unwavering, straight-ahead gaze.

Carlyle walked with tensed alertness, like a fighter in the ring, ready to spring at an attacker or drop into a crouch. As he passed her in the narrow aisle, his leg brushed against her bare knees. The warmth of the man's body swept a surprising wave of heat up her thighs, as if she were wading into a warm pool.

A steel gray gaze whipped down on her, a stronger, more disturbing connection than his inadvertent touch. Her body tightened. Carlyle's free hand jerked up, fisted in front of him.

For an instant his eyes lost their shuttered look and opened, not with expected ugliness or a killer's rage, but with a look of such fierce defensiveness she thought he might backhand her away. Instead, his arm fell to his side, and blank, purposeful withdrawal slammed back down over his eyes. He turned away, forced by the handcuffs to follow his guard.

The sergeant motioned the prisoner into the faded orange leatherette booth and eased himself in beside him. Frowning, the diner owner walked over to slap down mugs of coffee and a slab of pie before his unwanted customers. Then he scurried back behind the relative safety of his counter.

"Anything else, miss?" he asked, refilling her mug.

Kelsey didn't need to read the soiled menu she'd rescued from the gust of wind. A greasy memory of every hamburger and fries and every eggs and bacon ever cooked in the place lingered on the walls. Her kind of place. Having the perfect excuse to indulge in food that her sister Cara, with the irritating authority of a physician, was always on her case about, she ordered a double cheeseburger and fries.

A strand of her short blond bob, still damp from the mad dash through the rain from her car, dipped low into her eyes. With a glance into the blue-tinted mirror on the wall behind the counter, she tucked her hair behind an ear.

The mirror, she discovered, afforded her a view of Carlyle and his guard. She studied him, her mind busily dredging up memories of the trial and running through different angles she might take with a story.

Even the prisoner's size, a little over six feet and broad of both shoulder and chest, so big relative to his father's slight build, had worked against him in court. The man she saw now had changed considerably from the vigorous, talkative individual the world had seen on TV, much too ferociously passionate in his own defense.

Not too surprising that she hadn't immediately recognized him. A year behind bars had left Ben Carlyle about twenty pounds leaner and...what? *Subdued* wasn't exactly the right word—not with that toughness carved into his face. More like totally self-contained. As if he carried around his own personal force field nothing could penetrate.

What would it take to shake that iron control? she wondered.

Unaware that he was being watched—more like spied on, Kelsey admitted, but hey, that was her job—he finally dropped that unyielding eyes-front look. Behind the shield of his coffee mug, he took stock of his surroundings. Not carelessly and openly as she'd done when she'd entered the diner. Scarcely moving his head, he flicked his gaze around the room in a series of takes, careful, quick and intense. As if it were vital to extract every last ounce of information about whatever that gaze fell on. Just as he'd done in such an unsettling manner with her.

She'd never seen anyone so wary. It occurred to her that in prison, where a glance at the wrong man at the wrong time could provoke a dangerous confrontation, an inmate might need to develop such excessive caution as a survival trait.

Carlyle's second glance her way may have lingered a moment or two longer than it had on the others, but not much.

Oddly, the prisoner, and not his guard, seemed the most commanding presence in the room—at least to her. Strange that such a man wore no hint of his evil on his face. Nor had she seen any in his eyes. She prided herself on her ability to read people, a necessary talent in a reporter. But all she could discern, molded into Carlyle's blankly closed-off features, was control—inflexible control. He gave nothing away. If the curiosity, not to mention the outright hostility, of everyone in the room bothered him, he didn't show it.

She probably hadn't really glimpsed that brief break in his barriered eyes at all, she decided. Just her usual tendency to overdramatize. A weakness she struggled to keep in check when writing factual articles.

She broke off her study of Benton Carlyle. Not because of the rules of politeness her college-professor parents had ingrained in all three of their children—a training sometimes incompatible with her job—but because the cook blocked her mirror view of the prisoner by appearing before her with a heavily laden plate.

The hamburger tasted much better than she'd expected, and the french fries were crisp and delicious. That the most delectable of foods were also the most artery-clogging seemed one of nature's most irritating laws.

As she pushed away her plate and reached for another paper napkin, her gaze strayed to the mirror and down the length of the diner. Again it snagged on the person of Benton Carlyle.

He seemed to have forgotten that he'd raised his mug halfway to his lips. He stared out into the rain hammering against the window beside him as if he'd never seen a storm before. Maybe he hadn't for a long while, she realized. Locked within the sterile confines of a prison cell, he probably never even saw much of the changing seasons, let alone experienced snow or rain on his face. That he didn't often get to walk in the sun, she could see from his pallor. The idea brought with it a quick rush of sympathy for the man. No human being deserved to be shut away from the sun.

Carlyle suddenly swung his head around and caught her staring at him.

Even buffered by the mirror, his gaze provoked a ripple of unease. Despite her eagerness for a story, she couldn't help feeling sorry that her interest in him had robbed a man, not in a position to enjoy many pleasures, of the small distraction of watching a storm. But not only would a man as hard as Ben Carlyle probably be shamed by her pity, such a criminal merited no one's compassion.

Evidently much less interested in her than she was in him, he flicked his eyes back to the window. She was ready to tackle him, she decided. She'd let the interview itself present her with the best slant on her story.

She dug into her roomy canvas handbag to find her press ID and the small notebook she always carried with her.

Ben saw the watery reflection of yellow and white approaching in the window glass and braced himself. If he focused his whole concentration on how the rain spiked off the asphalt in the parking lot, he might be able to hold his gaze away from the young woman who'd caught his attention the moment he'd pushed through the door.

God! What a jolt to his system when he'd accidentally brushed against her legs. And another when her eyes, the clear vivid blue of the sky denied him in his cell, flashed up at him. His insides were still quivering from the sharp red bolt of desire that had jagged through him before he'd even seen it coming. Though she couldn't know it, she'd given him a gift more precious than she could imagine when she'd faced him with eyes not colored with the same contempt or fear as those of the others.

Dangerous to chance almost losing it again, he warned himself. Once already she'd robbed him of the self-discipline, as strict as a monk's, that kept him both alive and sane. That is, if he were still truly sane after what felt like a lifetime of being caged like a wild animal.

In a few short hours that iron door would slam shut on him again. He never thought he'd find himself wishing to get back to his cell sooner. But spending much more time in the presence of that exciting woman would make it sheer torture to be thrown back into the harsh world of men. She reminded him too much of the sweet, soft things he'd forced himself not even to think about, let alone want.

The erotic fantasies that occasionally snaked through his mental defenses into his dreams were always of sultry women fashioned of lush, ripe curves and great tumbling masses of dark hair. This real woman, with large golden hoops dangling playfully from her ears, was reed slender and wore a yellow top that hugged small but perfect breasts. Her white walking shorts bared legs not as curvaceous as those of his dream women, but with a strong, athletic shapeliness to them. There was no point in wondering if his hands could span her narrow waist. He'd never have the chance to find out.

Her shining hair, not dark and long, but cropped almost as short as a boy's, seemed spun of silk and sunshine. And there was absolutely nothing boyish about the delicacy of the oval face or skin the color of pure cream. But it was the sight of the tantalizing mouth, pink and petal-soft, and only excruciating inches away, that had knotted his groin.

Without doubt, she was the most beautiful woman he'd ever laid eyes on. Open and clean and free. Everything he wasn't.

And utterly beyond his reach.

It would be less of a torment, he decided, not to drink in any more of her loveliness than to carry back to his cell a picture, already too achingly clear, of what he would never have. That she'd so easily robbed him of the control he prided himself on maintaining angered him. He wouldn't allow her to do it again, he promised himself.

To make sure his hands did nothing crazy like reach out to touch her, he locked them around his coffee mug. Though he made sure to betray no sign of it, he was totally aware of her arrival at their booth. His ears strained for the sound of her voice.

"Kelsey Merrill, Sergeant."

Her voice was stronger than he'd expected, and rang like an angel's song to a man unaccustomed to hearing a woman speak. He recognized the click of plastic—an ID, he guessed—on the table.

"I'm a reporter and I'd like to talk to you."

An ironic laugh scraped into his throat. He quickly choked it back. Somebody up there sure had it in for him. The first woman, aside from his mother and sister, that he'd touched since they'd locked him away—and she was one of the loathsome breed that had torn him apart even before the justice system took its devastating shot at him.

"Sure, Ms. Merrill," his guard said. "Sit down."

Kelsey slid into the other side of the booth and flipped open her notebook. "You said your name was Whittaker?"

"Yeah. James Whittaker. Everyone calls me Jim."

She dutifully recorded the name. Evidently she wasn't going to encounter any difficulty in getting an interview from the affable policeman. He needed no buttering up; she could get right to the point.

"Why is a convicted murderer not in his jail cell?"

"No need to worry, miss. Carlyle can't hurt you."

Whittaker jerked on the handcuffs, pulling the prisoner's hand away from the mug. The action, though no more than a small indignity to a man who'd consigned himself to much worse, bothered her.

"No. That's not what I mean. You said you were taking him back to Moundsville. But why is he out on the streets when he's supposed to be doing twenty years in the West Virginia state pen? What are the two of you doing here on a back road in these mountains?"

"Family has connections with the higher-ups. They gave the guy compassionate leave to see his mother. She died a couple of days ago. Cancer."

Kelsey winced. She'd forgotten that Carlyle had a family. A brother who'd staunchly maintained Ben's innocence to interviewers and a teenage sister quick to provide the tears the media loved. She didn't remember seeing his mother in news footage of the trial. But she must have been there, doing the obligatory turn. *My son's a good boy. Never gave us any trouble. Can't believe he did this.*

It was far easier, she was learning, to maintain undiluted contempt for a criminal when he was no more than a distanced image on a TV screen than when a man of flesh and blood was sitting only two feet away from her. A man whose humanity had been made astonishingly real to her in a single touch. A man who'd just suffered the loss of his mother. Did murderers cry? she wondered.

"I'm sorry, Mr. Carlyle," she offered. She started to move her hand toward his in sympathy, but the ice shell around him discouraged the touch.

Expressionless gray eyes flicked toward her. Carlyle hadn't even bothered to look her way when she'd sat down. "No, you're not. No reporter gives a damn about anything but a story."

The dark richness of his voice resonated in some strange way down the rungs of her spine. She'd remembered nothing of his voice from TV interviews and had wrongly expected it to be as hard as the face. Oddly enough, he'd delivered the stinging words without rancor, in a calm, observational tone. He looked anything but relaxed, though. The officer had settled himself comfortably against the back of the bench. Carlyle never slackened his stiff posture. And if his grip on that coffee mug got any tighter, the mug would crack.

It always irked her when anyone denigrated reporters. The world teemed with horrifying examples of what happened to countries without a free press. It wasn't her place to argue with a story source, but she was unable to hold back.

"That isn't true of most reporters. It certainly isn't true of me. But I admit I'd like to do a story about you, Mr. Carlyle. Readers might be interested in the prison experiences of a man who was once a celebrity of sorts."

"No."

The irritating quickness of his response made her more determined than ever to get what she'd set out to achieve. She never quit after one refusal. Often a person who at first brushed off a reporter went on to reveal something about himself.

A quick motion of her head flipped her hair out of her eyes. "Why not? A story wouldn't hurt you and might even work to your advantage. Your case is still under appeal, isn't it? I might be able to help you. I can't promise anything, of course, but the case of a man in the public eye might rate a closer look, might be reviewed with a little more urgency."

"I'm not fool enough to think that you or any other reporter has the slightest interest in helping me. After my father's death, you people tore into me like sharks in a feeding frenzy. I'm not about to let you do that to me again. I can't even attend my mother's funeral for fear people like you will turn it into a media circus."

She understood that he was only looking at her as a member of a group he evidently despised. Perhaps, she admitted, with some cause. By her standards, some of the press coverage on him had been brutal. Maybe she could overcome that by making him see her as a reasonably sympathetic individual with whom he might make some connection.

"Look, Mr. Carlyle, I—"

"You look," he cut in, his tone still flat. With a rigid set to his jaw, he lifted his fisted hand the few short inches from the table the confining manacles would allow. "I can control painfully little about my life now, and the law has already done a lot to me. But not even the law will force me to talk to you."

The guard shrugged. "Sorry, lady. He doesn't have to talk to you if he doesn't want to."

She had no choice but to give in, for the moment. "Okay, Mr. Carlyle. As you say, I can't force you to give me an interview. But just for the record, I have no interest in forcing you or anyone else to do anything. And the law hasn't done anything to you that you didn't bring upon yourself. Like all the rest of us, you have to bear the consequences of your actions."

He hissed in a breath, and she thought him on the verge of responding. But he just pressed his lips together tightly. If she hadn't been actively watching for it, she might never have caught that brief look of flat desperation that speared into his eyes. A look so bleak she had to sheer her eyes away. When she lifted them again, Carlyle had gone back to watching the storm.

Was he aware, Kelsey wondered, that the emotions he worked so successfully to keep from showing on his face or in his voice broke out sometimes in his eyes? She guessed not. She refused to let it play on her sympathies. Prison was no picnic, but a killer deserved it.

"*I'll* be glad to talk to you, Ms. Merrill," the sergeant offered.

"Thank you. Maybe later." The story she wanted had to come from Carlyle himself. Without him, a policeman's comments would hold little interest.

She wasn't about to give up. The storm showed no signs of letting up anytime soon. If anything, it was getting worse. Nightfall on a late afternoon in May was still hours away, but the green-and-red-neon beer sign not far from Carlyle's head glowed brightly against deepening gloom. And rain slapped so noisily on the roof of the one-story building that conversation was becoming difficult.

Thunderstorms in the mountains, though sometimes violent, were usually brief. These had rolled through the area for hours, and she was beginning to think the diner's orphans of the storm would be forced to stay here through the night. Even if the downpour stopped, it would be a while before flooded roads became passable.

Restaurant booths weren't built for comfort. Spending long hours sitting in them could get boring for anyone, even a man who played his cards as close to the chest as Carlyle did. He might soften his stance later on just to break the monotony. He wouldn't talk to her, he'd maintained. But he already had. A simple "no" to her query would have sufficed. He'd gone much beyond that. Antagonism toward the press didn't mean he wouldn't speak to her eventually. She hoped he would.

The objectivity she'd enjoyed on first seeing him had slipped away to strong curiosity—even a measure of compassion for a man in chains.

Her suggestion that a sympathetic story might help his appeal was valid. Well, maybe not exactly sympathetic. But she'd focus not on the killing—old news—but on his mother's death, on what had happened to his family since his incarceration. And a man as well-educated as Carlyle should have engrossing insights into the prison system gleaned from life on the inside.

Her earlier compulsion to study him had been sparked by no more than professional interest, of course. But this electric awareness of him that prickled over her skin, even now, when she'd blanked him out of her field of vision, was something different. And her compulsion to take another look at his eyes—not metallic after all, more like rain-colored—certainly lapped over into the personal. She'd once toured a nuclear power plant. Lying in bed miles away that night, she fancied she could still hear the giant facility's intimidating thrum. Carlyle's presence was having a similar effect on her.

Neither she nor Ben Carlyle were going anywhere. She could wait.

Apparently the pickuppers had already grown bored. Announcing that their four-wheel drive could handle anything the storm could throw at them, they got back on the road.

Kelsey ordered a piece of the apple pie that the sergeant had demolished with such gusto. She transferred it and her tote to a table a couple of booths down from the prisoner and his guard. After eating, she stretched her legs out on the bench and leaned back against the wall to nap.

The sudden sharp clatter of hailstones battering walls and roof snapped her alert. As it had done everyone else, she guessed, judging from the startled cries around her.

"Do you think we'll be all right here?" She recognized the frightened high-pitched voice of a gray-haired woman who'd fearfully clutched the arm of the old man with her when Carlyle appeared in their midst.

"Now, Mother, don't start your worrying again," the woman's companion admonished. "We'll be fine."

Kelsey couldn't blame the woman for the quaver in her voice. A midnight darkness was encroaching on the outside world. The redhead sidled over, as much for the comforting closeness with other people, Kelsey guessed, as to look out nervously at the torrent of rain slashing across the parking lot.

The counterman whistled. "We're in for it, all right."

A roll of thunder crashed down directly overhead, rattling the whole building. Across the road, lightning flashed over trees whipped unnaturally low by wind that had just exploded into a howl. Outside, everything not nailed down—trash cans, litter, torn-off tree branches—was careening through the air. The diner's lighted roadside sign swung wildly. With a metallic screech and a frightening shower of sparks, the heavy sign tore from its moorings and smashed to the ground.

Kelsey reared back. The woman's fearful question didn't seem so foolish anymore. The storm that had posed only an irritating inconvenience earlier now lashed their haven with a fury that frightened her.

"Everybody away from the windows," Sergeant Whittaker ordered. "Come on, Carlyle. Let's get the hell out of here." Both men slid quickly from their booth.

"The storeroom," the diner owner yelled, pointing toward the closed door at the opposite end of the restaurant. "Get into the storeroom. No windows there."

Kelsey grabbed her handbag and joined the rush to the back of the room. Before they'd made it to safety, a deafening wind roared down on them. The lights flickered and snuffed out. A window shattered inward spewing a fearsome whirl of rain and wind and shards of glass through the diner.

A woman screamed. Men shouted curses.

Stark white flashes of lightning like the strobing light on some crazy dance floor lit the stumbling bodies around her. Someone in back of her shoved her the last couple of feet into the storeroom.

She tripped over an unseen box on the floor and flung a hand into the darkness to keep from falling. The shelf she'd grabbed onto gave way. A man's arm hooked around her waist and yanked her up against him. Instinctively she clutched at him and crouched close as he bent protectively over her. Benton Carlyle, she sensed. She didn't care. All that mattered was that the solid windbreak of his body would hold.

The building shrieked and shuddered.

She was going to die, Kelsey thought. And there wasn't a thing she could do about it. The feeling of utter helplessness was almost worse than the fear. Raw, swirling energy tore at her, threatening to rip her away from her human anchor. Praying that Carlyle didn't lose his iron grip on her, she squeezed her eyes shut and clung to him.

If only the horrible noise scouring her mind would stop. Trying to shut out the paralyzing roar, she burrowed one ear against his chest and pressed the heel of her hand over the other. Under the raging noise she could hear the faint thump of his heartbeat, rapid, but compared to her own heart's erratic race, remarkably slow and steady.

The fact that he evidently wasn't as terrified as she buoyed her courage. Maybe they stood some chance. She tried to focus all her awareness on the comforting rhythm, felt more than heard, of his heart.

Thump ka-thump ka-thump.

Some heavy object brushed by her and crashed to the floor.

Her protector struggled to hold his footing. His arm still clamped around her waist, he fell forward. His weight was too much for her. She crumpled to the floor beneath him.

Chapter 2

Her back hurt and it was hard to breathe.

Remembrance flooded back. Her eyes fluttered open onto a heavy, inky sky shot through with streaks of eerie yellow light. She was grateful for daylight, however weak, after the howling darkness.

Daylight, she realized with a start, because most of the roof above her was gone. Torn away by the storm. Water dripped heavily from the roof's jagged edge, but the rain had stopped. She threw her awareness to her arms and legs and found that she was able to move them a little without pain.

The long, hard length of Benton Carlyle's body lay like a dead weight on top of her, his left arm still wrapped around her waist. His head, eyes closed, rested on the floor a couple of inches from hers. Praying that the man who'd shielded her with his body still lived, Kelsey pushed at him gently.

"Mr. Carlyle?"

Nothing. A moment's panic overcame her before she realized that she could feel the slight movement of his chest against hers as he breathed. She tried to extricate herself but couldn't, hemmed in as she was between toppled metal storage shelves and Carlyle's body. She worked her hands beneath his chest and pushed again, harder. He stirred.

"Wake up, Mr. Carlyle."

Carlyle moaned, and the long leg sprawled across hers jerked upward. He lifted his head a little, then dropped it again.

"I can't move my arms," he mumbled.

"Your left arm is caught underneath me. I'll try to lift myself so you can pull it out." With his weight pressing down on her, it wasn't easy, but she managed to raise her back off the floor a little.

Ben moaned again when the woman beneath him arched an inflaming softness against his middle. He'd awakened not to the usual hardness of a narrow prison cot but to the soft warm curves of her body, his nostrils filled not with the stink of prison, but with her intoxicating feminine scent. Before his mind had gathered itself together enough to make sense of the situation, he'd already slipped into the beginnings of arousal. His effort to stop it by the quick movement of his leg hadn't helped much.

Kelsey felt Carlyle's arm tug free of her back. He braced himself a little above her. Not much, because his handcuffed right arm, flung out beyond her head, still held him down.

"Are you all right?" he asked.

"I think so. How about you?" He turned his head and she saw the blood. "You're hurt," she said in quick alarm. "Your head is bleeding."

She wasn't one to faint at the sight of blood. The adventurous Merrill kids had suffered more than their fair share of scraped knees and cut lips. But seeing the blood trick-

ling from the three-inch slash on Carlyle's forehead made
her feel queasy.

He lifted his hand to probe gingerly at the right side of his
forehead and winced. "So I am," he said, inspecting his
blood-smeared fingertips. "But since I can talk and move,
it can't be too bad."

Without his full weight on her chest, Kelsey could lift her
head, but still couldn't see much beyond Carlyle and the
metal storage unit beside her.

"What about the sergeant?" she asked.

Carlyle angled his head back to check. "Doesn't look
good."

Kelsey twisted to see. Whittaker lay on his back at an angle to them. Only his legs were visible. The wooden beam
that pinned him to the floor had missed striking Carlyle's
head by no more than an inch. Some of the flying debris
accompanying it must have grazed her protector, causing the
wound. His manacled arm trailed under the beam, although the heavy roof support didn't actually touch it.

Carlyle pulled on his shackled arm. It gave only a little.

"Can you slide out from under me?"

"I'll try."

He managed to kick the shelving away a few inches. She
started to wriggle her hips against him in an effort to skid
herself out. She was already uncomfortably aware of the
warm, soft bulge pressing against the top of her thighs. Her
attempts to free herself were making that bulge grow hotter
and harder.

"I'd appreciate it, lady," Carlyle said through gritted
teeth, "if you'd get yourself out of that position a whole lot
quicker."

She agreed. Carlyle could hardly be blamed for the en-
forced intimacy, but he wanted it ended no more quickly
than she. No longer concerned about hurting him, she
heaved herself to the side. She had to snake herself down his
body to find enough room to get to her knees.

She looked around and gasped, shocked at the destruction. It was a miracle that anyone had survived the room's explosion. Debris of all kind, upended boxes and scattered cans of food had tumbled everywhere. A large bottle of ketchup lay smashed in a bloodred puddle by the old man's legs.

Tornadoes didn't often hit in the mountains, but it sure looked like the place had been struck by one. Or perhaps a sudden violent downburst of the kind that sometimes slammed planes out of the sky had whomped down on them.

Felled bodies around her started to move, shaking off dust, scraps of wood and material from the collapsed roof. Given a little more space to maneuver in, Carlyle managed to pull his arm and the guard's from under the beam and sat up. Someone whimpered in pain. The teenager in the sexy top and shorts started to cry. "Help me, somebody. My leg hurts."

Carlyle nodded toward the girl. "I'm okay for the moment. Why don't you check on the others. The little redhead is bleeding a lot heavier than I am."

Kelsey forced herself to ignore the sharp ache across shoulder blades that had taken the brunt of the falling weight of two people, and hoisted herself shakily to her feet. She picked her way through debris. The girl had good reason to cry. She had a long, ugly scrape along her shin. But because the line of the bone seemed straight Kelsey didn't think it was broken.

"I'll take care of that as soon as I find the first-aid kit," she assured the girl. "There's got to be one around here somewhere." If it hadn't already sailed off into nowhere like so much else. She helped the young woman sit up against the wall.

The elderly couple were shaken up and nursed several scratches and bruises. The woman complained loudly when Kelsey helped her to sit up, but was unhelpfully vague about exactly where she hurt. She was more frightened than injured, Kelsey decided. The diner owner worried her. Except for a few small cuts he didn't seem to be seriously injured, but he still hadn't spoken a word. He just sat staring blankly at what was left of his business.

She returned to Ben Carlyle, still linked fast to Whittaker's motionless body imprisoned under the beam. "Is he . . . ?"

Carlyle knew what she was asking. "I can't really tell if there's a pulse."

The beam that cut across Whittaker's chest was angled up at one end and precariously balanced on a low metal storage box of some kind. She stepped over the beam and carefully lifted a broken sheet of drywall from the policeman's head. His face was a ghastly shade of gray.

"We've got to get this thing off him," Carlyle said. From his sitting position, he wrapped his arms around the beam and tried to lift it. The thick length of wood didn't budge.

"No good. I can't get a strong enough grip on it this way."

Kelsey could see that with one hand shackled to a helpless man Carlyle's efforts would remain useless. His steady gray eyes fastened on hers, but he said nothing. He didn't have to. She knew perfectly well that he was asking her to find the key to the handcuffs and unchain him from his guard.

Kelsey hesitated. Had she the right to set the prisoner free? To tell the truth, for the last few minutes she'd forgotten that he was a convict. They'd only been two people struggling to deal with a bad situation.

But she and Carlyle seemed to be the only two in decent enough shape to help the others to a less dangerous spot. They'd already had to duck a couple of loose shingles that dropped to the floor. Large pieces of the roof, swinging free in the dying wind, could fall at any moment.

Her muddled feelings must have shown on her face.

"I won't hurt anyone," Carlyle said. "Regardless of what you believe, I don't hurt people."

An immediate vision of the news footage of him decking the obnoxious reporter—an action most viewers probably cheered—flashed through her mind.

"And I give you my word I won't just cut and run. You need help to take care of the others. From the looks of things, I'm it."

Carlyle was right about that. She didn't think the elderly couple would be of much help. The old woman was whimpering, her husband trying to comfort her. The owner still looked to be in emotional shock, and the girl sat holding her leg and moaning.

"I promise you I'll do what I can," Carlyle said. "The key is in his right pants pocket."

Maybe if she were handcuffed, she conceded, she too would be acutely aware of the location of the key. She tended to think he really might help. He'd already been concerned enough about their companions to urge her to look to them instead of to him.

She had no other choice, Kelsey decided. If they didn't get the massive beam off the trapped man, Whittaker, if he weren't already dead, soon would be. She fished into the pocket Carlyle had indicated.

The small metal key scraped in the lock and the prisoner jerked his wrist free. He sat up and rubbed at the angry red welt where the metal bracelet, its chain twisting as both men fell, had cut into him.

"Thank you, Ms. Merrill," Carlyle said quietly. "Okay, let's have another go at that beam. It'll take the two of us to get Whittaker out. If I manage to lift the beam, you pull him out. Don't be nice about it. Just take hold of his legs and yank him out as quickly as possible. I don't know how long I'll be able to hold up the weight."

"But it might fall back down on you."

"I'll be careful. If I can't hold it, the beam should just fall back into place on that box."

Not if he moved it forward even a little, instead of straight up, Kelsey thought. The man was taking a big risk with his own safety. If that heavy beam crushed down on his head...

Carlyle called over for the old man's help. His wife offered a quick objection, but he came over and grasped one of the guard's ankles. Kelsey took hold of the other.

"Ready?" Carlyle asked.

"We're ready," Kelsey answered.

Carlyle shouldered himself beneath the raised part of the beam and struggled to get his knees under him. Without the leverage of his strong legs, the weight would be beyond him. Beneath the jacket that provided little enough protection against rough and splintered wood, the muscles of his shoulders and back bunched and knotted with strain. The beam moved only a discouraging fraction of an inch. A grunt rumbled up from deep in his chest. He heaved upward. Cold fright raced down Kelsey's spine when the beam wobbled. But it moved up an inch. Then another.

"Now," he gasped.

She and the old man pulled Whittaker out an instant before Carlyle wrenched himself free and the beam crashed to the floor. He sat hunched over beside it, hauling in great gasping lungfuls of air.

The old man stooped to finger the policeman's face. "This feller's in real bad shape." At his wife's tremulous call, he nodded to Kelsey and returned to the old woman.

Carlyle struggled to his feet. He swayed, and Kelsey moved quickly to clasp her hands around his upper arm to steady him. The rock-hard muscles beneath her fingers still quivered from exertion. His face streaked in sweat, he pressed a hand to the side of his head. His brows drew together tightly over closed eyes and she caught his muted groan. The man was in more pain than he let on.

"Are you sure you're all right? That gash on your head might be more serious than you thought." She prayed that he, too, wouldn't join the ranks of the incapacitated.

He dragged the back of his hand across his eyes, then opened them. "I'm fine," he said, blinking a couple of times without looking at her. "Just got a little dizzy there for a minute."

"Maybe you'd better sit down and rest."

He shrugged off her concern. "Let's see what we can do for this man."

The answer was, all too clearly, not much. Carlyle knelt over the unconscious man to pull off his tie and unbuckle the belt holding a holstered snub-nosed revolver. Kelsey had a quick moment of apprehension. But Carlyle only worked the belt from its loops and slid belt and weapon away along the floor. He did the same with the handcuffs still attached to the man's wrist.

Unmindful of its sticky bloodstains, Carlyle unbuttoned Whittaker's shirt, as rain-soaked as their own clothing. Kelsey winced at the poor man's torn and bruised flesh. Carlyle's hands were large and she'd already seen evidence of their strength, but they moved over the injured man's chest with surprising gentleness.

"At the very least," he told Kelsey, "he's got several broken ribs. His breathing's not real strong, but it's there. Just as well he's out cold. He'd be hurting like hell if he weren't. The man needs a hospital, Ms. Merrill. And fast."

"Kelsey," she said, not knowing quite why, except that for some reason she wanted to hear him speak her name. "My name is Kelsey."

Carlyle lifted his head and looked at her across the guard's body. That hard, dark gaze of his always seemed to hit her with heart-stopping force.

"Kelsey," he repeated. The deep voice gave it a curious softness. "Yes, I heard you tell the officer earlier. Kelsey. I like it. I've never known a woman named Kelsey before."

"Oh," she said, lamely. Not surprising, she thought, that her mind had grown a little sluggish after her ordeal.

"I'm Ben."

"I know."

"Yes. Of course you know." He cut his eyes back to their patient and folded Whittaker's shirt carefully over the damaged skin. "You're a reporter. You know all about me." The comment, delivered in the same flat tone he almost always used, sounded to her like an accusation.

Carlyle ended the conversation, which was starting to make her uncomfortable, by standing up. "Let's take a look at what we've got here."

They found that sections of the roof had been ripped off this end of the diner. The far end was largely intact. At least they'd have shelter of a sort until help came. But that could be a distressingly long time. The phone was gone. Not just out, ripped off the wall.

Most of the counter area was a jumbled mess. She and Carlyle swept broken glass out of a couple of booths, cleared the floor around them and helped everyone but Whittaker from the storeroom. The quiet strength with which the prisoner worked did a lot to tamp down everyone's shock and fright.

She and Carlyle fashioned a makeshift stretcher from a large piece of plywood and carefully worked it under the policeman's body. When they lifted the heavy burden from the floor, pain jagged through Kelsey's back. She let out a soft cry.

Carlyle shot her a worried look. "Can you handle this, Kelsey? Maybe we should try to get some of the others to help."

"It's a little heavy, that's all. It won't help to stand around gabbing. Let's move this guy." They carried Whittaker out and laid him down on the driest, most sheltered spot on the floor.

Carlyle's search of the cupboards beneath the counter unearthed a reasonably well-stocked first-aid kit. Together they worked to clean the sergeant's wounds. She hoped the antiseptic she sprayed over his chest would fight off infection until trained medical personnel could take over. Ben tore the paper off a sterile gauze pad and handed it to her by a corner. She carefully laid it next to the others over a long gash in the man's flesh.

Whatever she may have expected a convicted criminal to be like, Ben Carlyle sure wasn't it. His face seemed to have softened in some subtle way while they worked. His mouth was no longer a tight slash and his lips were slightly parted. Buried beneath the cold, hard exterior that armored him lay concern and compassion for others. She saw that in the sensitive way he worked over the guard, his hands smeared with the blood of the man whose duty it was to return him to prison.

She no longer had to work out an interesting angle for a story about the prisoner. The storm had handed her the perfect slant, along with plenty of material to center a good story around a convict who turned out to be a hero.

No matter that an impartial jury had decreed it, she didn't like to think of this brave and caring man facing more long, dreary years behind bars. She was losing her necessary objectivity about him, she realized. She had to be careful of that. The bottom line remained that Benton Carlyle had killed his own father. The jury had come to that conclusion *beyond a reasonable doubt*.

She added the last piece of adhesive tape to the guard's chest and sat back on her heels. Carlyle reached over and folded his fingers around hers. If she'd thought about it first, she'd never have done it, but at the impact of the warm, enticing touch, her fingers curled reflexively around his.

"You've done a good job with this man," he told her. "Maybe you should have been a nurse."

If that quirk at one corner of his lips was his version of a smile, it needed work. Whatever, it made her want to go on talking to him. "There's already a doctor in the family. My sister Cara is a physician on staff at a Baltimore hospital."

"Sounds like there are two impressive offspring in the Merrill family."

"Three—although I certainly wouldn't call myself impressive next to my brother and sister. Both are much more accomplished than I. Stephen is with the State Department. He's just received a commendation from the Secretary."

"I have a sister, too. I hadn't seen Bonnie for a long time before going home a few days ago." The wistfulness in a criminal's voice didn't come as much of a surprise as it would have done only a few hours ago.

The roughened thumb rubbing gently back and forth over her knuckles was uncurling a strange, cottony warmth inside her. She shouldn't allow it to continue, but it felt comforting after the frightening events they'd just undergone together.

"Bonnie doesn't come to visit you in...uh..."

"In prison." He easily spoke the word she'd been trying tactfully to avoid. "No. I won't allow it. My sister's very young. The trial alone was too upsetting for her. She couldn't handle a prison visit."

Ben smoothed his thumb over the back of the small, feminine hand clasped in his. He marveled both at the softness of it and the surprising strength he could feel in the silky-skinned palm and elegantly tapered fingers. The warmth of it spread through his whole body, relaxing strained muscles and even taming somewhat the pain that raged above his eyes.

He'd tried to keep himself from reaching for the hand that had skimmed so temptingly close to his while they'd worked over his guard. Lord, how he'd tried. But he'd had no more luck in holding himself back now than he'd had when he was six and trying mightily to keep away from the closet where his mother hid the presents that last Christmas in that dingy house in Keyser.

He'd expected Kelsey to pull away. Better for him if she had.

Touching her reminded him so painfully of all he had lost. But for the life of him, he couldn't let go of the hand that felt so good in his. Holding it almost made him feel like an ordinary man, like any man on the outside who had the right to approach this woman, to enjoy her company on an evening out.

But he wasn't like other men. He was marked as an outcast, judged unfit to function in society, unfit to touch any woman, let alone a woman as beautiful, as intriguing, as this one. Her world—the world of ordinary men and women—was closed to him. And he couldn't allow this stirring in his blood to make him forget that. He could do it, he told himself. Prison had given him plenty of practice in self-control.

But the thought of going back to the inhuman life that lay in wait for him twisted his gut.

"Ben," she said. "I want you to know that…well, I want to help you. The story I write about how unselfishly you helped deal with this situation should weigh heavily with the parole board when the time comes. I hope they'll let you out sooner than—"

Ben cursed softly and dropped her hand. "You can keep your pity, lady," he spat out, sweeping to his feet. "I've no use for it." Prison had already taken enough of his manhood. He sure as hell wouldn't give away any more of it—not even to the woman who set his head reeling every time she came near.

Kelsey had seen the flare of anger in his eyes. The cold, impersonal justice system, she suspected, hadn't conquered this man's passion, only buried it. "I'm sorry. I didn't mean—"

"The cold water faucet still works," he said, cutting her off. "We can wash up there.

"The redhead's leg needs looking after," Carlyle reminded Kelsey as they held their blood-soiled hands in the cool trickle. "You'd better do it. She cringes whenever I come near. I guess I can't blame the kid for being scared silly of me."

He'd thought he'd gotten over the shame and humiliation of having people stare at him as if he were a freak. During the argument about his presence in the diner he'd found out that he hadn't.

The teenager might be afraid of Ben Carlyle, Kelsey thought, but strangely enough, she felt no fear of him.

"The redhead can wait. It's your turn." His red-rimmed eyes held a watery sheen, and she hadn't missed how often he'd squeezed them shut. "Is the cut on your head painful? It's starting to swell."

"Nothing I can't handle."

After what he'd been through, Kelsey thought, pain probably *was* the "nothing" he'd just labeled it.

"Sit down on this box so I can reach your head more easily."

"I'm all right."

"That cut needs to be looked after. Come on, Ben. Please sit down." It amused her that such a big man might be afraid that having his injury treated would hurt. "I'll be careful about touching the sore spot."

She laid her hand on his shoulder to encourage him to sit. His whole body tightened, and he immediately dropped to the box. As gently as possible, she brushed her fingers across his forehead to lift his hair away from the wound. He moaned softly.

"Oh! I'm hurting you. I'm sorry."

"Just get on with it," he gritted.

Ben wished the ache in his head were even worse. It might keep that painful spurt of heat from leaping into his groin every time she touched him. She dabbed at the cut with an antiseptic pad, and the soft warmth of her breast brushed against his arm. He groaned again and heard her murmur another apology for hurting him.

The kind of pain she was giving him was a long way from actual hurt. And she was doing him a kindness by taking care of his injury. But he was about to repay her by handing her real pain, real fear. He was about to drag her out of her nice, safe world of caring and trust, into the ugliness of his.

"I can finish up here alone," Kelsey said. "Go sit down in a booth for a while and rest." She was pleasantly surprised when Ben followed her order without argument.

What were Stephen and Cara doing right now? she wondered as she passed around cans of soft drinks and the dry box of crackers she'd found. She doubted that either of them would be stranded, as she was. Her sister had left Baltimore early to reach the family's summer place in the mountains by the agreed-upon hour of noon. Her brother, too, had probably made it from his home in the Northern Virginia area before the worst part of the storm hit.

She'd set out from Pittsburgh in plenty of time, hoping, for a change, to be the first to arrive for their yearly reunion. She'd been the last to make it last year. And the year before that. But a truck accident on the road had blocked traffic long enough for the storm to overtake her.

She was twenty-seven years old, but as the youngest, she always seemed to be playing catch-up to the accomplishments of her incredibly competent siblings. She smiled to herself. This time neither of them would be able to top her adventure.

When they all finally got together, her meticulous sister would immediately start issuing gentle orders about who should do what in the way of household chores and when. It didn't matter. They'd all end up giggling like kids in the kitchen, anyway. As they'd done since high school when they'd been given the job of opening up the mountain cottage each spring.

She finished up on the teenager, and night had fallen in earnest by the time she dabbed the diner owner's cuts with antiseptic. When she knelt by the guard's body to check the dressings, she had to do it by the feeble light of the flashlight the old man had fetched in from his car. She didn't like the way blood was already starting to seep through the bandages. She liked even less the growing worry that they might lose him despite Ben's dangerous rescue.

She heard Ben's footsteps crunching down on the broken glass on the floor behind her.

"We can't do any more for them, Kelsey. We've got to find a working telephone and call for medical help."

Kelsey nodded. "Yes. I'll go."

"We'll both go."

A sudden chill streaked over her. The flat, hard sound of Ben's voice snapped her gaze up to him.

Her stomach lurched.

In all the confusion, she hadn't given the policeman's weapon a second thought. The prisoner certainly hadn't forgotten it. The cone of light from the flashlight laid on a stool picked out the ugly black shape of the .38 clutched in Ben's right hand. Only a small motion of his arm would aim it directly at her.

The teenager let out a wail.

"Hush, girl," the old man ordered.

"But... but you promised," Kelsey protested, knowing the remark was foolish. "I trusted you."

The blank, closed-off look had once more clamped down over Carlyle's face. "I told you I'd help with the injured. I've done that. Now I've got to think of myself."

Word games. Maybe he'd never actually said he wouldn't escape, but they both knew that was how she'd taken it. Real stupid to have trusted the word of a convicted criminal. She felt his action as a personal betrayal. And it hurt.

"Don't do it, Ben," she warned, her mouth gone dry.

"The subject is not up for discussion."

No. She didn't expect it was. A man with a weapon called the shots. The last thing any of them needed was to be shut up with a murderer waving a gun around. Actually he was holding it motionless at his side, but the idea was the same.

"All right, then," she bit out. "Go. We can't stop you."

"I said we're both going."

The tiny hairs on the back of her neck prickled upright. "No," she flashed. "No. I won't go."

Carlyle bent and whipped one side of the handcuffs onto her right arm. He jerked her to her feet, and the second metal bracelet he locked around his own wrist.

Chapter 3

Kelsey bit down on her lip, willing herself not to give in to terror. The man who'd worked so hard to help them all only minutes ago had disappeared. The man who'd just chained her to him looked lethal.

"Please, Ben," she begged. "Don't do this. It will go much harder for you when they catch you, if you do this." She kept tugging futilely at the metal ring that imprisoned her and trying to twist out of it. It was horrible to feel herself tethered without escape to a criminal with a weapon.

"Get this straight, lady." Carlyle's voice was harsh, his eyes a cold, gunmetal gray. "It can't go much harder for me than it already is. I have nothing left to lose. Back where Whittaker was taking me, I don't even have a name. Just a number."

"But you don't need a hostage. Just go." She stopped trying to scrunch up her fingers tightly enough to drag them out of the cuff. She was only hurting herself and her efforts were doing nothing to pull his bent arm and its iron-ringed fist away from its locked position at his shoulder.

"Get your car keys out of your purse," he ordered.

She could see from the hard-set look on his face that further argument would be useless. Recognizing her defeat, Carlyle finally extended his arm to allow her to do as she was told. Clutching the keys, she hooked her handbag over her shoulder, hoping the tote held something she might be able to use against him at some point.

Carlyle waved the weapon in the general direction of the four huddled in the booth. The diner owner paid no attention to the frightening drama going on next to him. "I'll have to take the keys to all your cars so that you'll stay here and not set the authorities on me for a while."

"I can't give you my keys," the redhead whimpered. "I've lost my purse."

"I'll need 'em," the old man said forcefully, apparently uncowed by the armed convict. "I'll have to drive somewhere for help. That guy ain't gonna make it if he don't get a doctor soon."

"The keys," Carlyle insisted. "I intend to stop at the first working phone we find and call for an ambulance."

"And that's a promise, right?" Kelsey bit out, as he scooped up the keys the man had flung on the table. "Just like your last one."

Carlyle ignored her sarcasm. "If the guard wakes up, don't let him move. Too much chance of having a broken rib puncture an internal organ. I'll throw your keys in the parking lot. It's too dark out there to search for them tonight, but you should be able to find them in the morning. And I'll leave the flashlight out there. You might need it to take care of Whittaker. After we drive away, one of you can go out and get the light."

"You had this all planned, didn't you?" Kelsey didn't try to hide the bitterness she felt.

Evidently the convict wasn't interested in anything she had to say. "Let's go," he commanded, shoving her toward the door. Outside, he swept the flashlight's weak beam through the blackness. "Which is your car?" She pointed it out. "You drive," he ordered, making her get in on the passenger side and scramble awkwardly over to the driver's seat.

She tugged at the cuffs. "I can't drive while handcuffed to you like this."

"You'll manage," he said, resting his fingers next to hers on the wheel. "With an automatic shift, practically all you have to do is steer. Drive deeper into the mountains." It was the only direction left them, what with the police turning people back from the washed-out bridge.

They'd only been driving a few minutes when rain started again, turning the narrow road snaking into the hills into a watery black mirror that swallowed up the brightness of the car's headlights. Kelsey clamped her hands tight on the wheel and tried to steer a safe course between bramble-covered slopes and sheer drop-offs.

Calm down, girl, she ordered, forcing herself to take deeper breaths and slow her panicked breathing. *Marshall your defenses.* Her thoughts had been racing ahead in a frightened jumble ever since Carlyle had locked her to him. If he did this—she could do that. She made a conscious effort to slow down her thinking and not let her mind run around in ineffective circles. Right now he was doing nothing of immediate threat to her. She was more or less safe, she concluded, as long as they were driving.

She slid a glance at the man crowding the space beside her. Etched in the dashboard's faint blue light, Carlyle's face looked carved from stone. Was he thinking along the same lines as she? she wondered. Planning his moves? Deciding what to do with her?

He no longer gripped the gun, she noted out of the corner of her eye, but was holding it loosely on his lap. The mental scenario she quickly ran through on how to grab for the weapon provided no way for her to reach it before his hand tightened around it.

No point in wasting energy on being afraid of what might happen in the future, she decided. Better to focus on the present and be ready to act quickly when the chance came. For the time being, the handcuffs prevented her from leaping out of the car and dashing into the forest to hide. But sooner or later, please God, he'd take them off and she would act.

"Damn." She heard her captor's quiet curse.

"I can't go any faster," she snapped, tired of being ordered around, "unless you want us to end up wrecked. It's hard enough trying to drive through rain and darkness even at this slow speed."

He made no answer.

"Okay," she bridled. "If you think you can do any better, why don't you drive?" He'd have to free himself from the handcuffs to do that, in order to switch them around so that she'd be on his right side. Her chance to break and run. Maybe the only chance she'd get.

"You're doing fine," he said. "I know the road is treacherous."

Ben silently cursed himself again for terrifying a helpless woman. The look of dazed unbelief that had flashed into her face when he'd brought out the weapon still tore at him. She'd never seen it coming. He felt like he'd deliberately blindsided a kid.

Though his frightened prisoner didn't know it, the gun he'd commandeered was strictly for show. No way would he ever pull the trigger on her or any other innocent bystander. He hated himself for doing it, but for the moment he had to use the tool of her newfound fear of him to work for his own survival. Though he hadn't corrected her mistaken assumption that he'd taken her as hostage, his need for her was a lot more basic.

She was his eyes.

He'd like nothing better than to disappear into the night by himself, but that was impossible. If he tried to drive, he'd most likely smash into the nearest tree.

He'd done a good job of hiding the fact that Jim Whittaker wasn't the only victim of the storm in strong need of medical assistance. His vision had grown steadily worse since he'd exerted himself so much in lifting the roof beam. Blurred vision was a sign of serious head injury, he knew, but he didn't dare seek a doctor or a hospital. Better to take his chances with an injury than to risk recapture.

He knew, too, that Kelsey had spoken only the truth when she'd told him that in reaching for freedom, he'd also thrown it away. When they caught him, there'd be no parole. Very likely they'd tack more years onto the eighteen years of hell left him. He'd considered that dire outcome when he'd made the choice—a choice that was as difficult as it had been unexpected. As an innocent man, should he wait to be returned to prison? No contest. When handed a chance at the freedom he longed for during every tortured waking moment, he'd had to grab for it.

To enjoy blessed freedom—for no matter how agonizingly short a time—to walk again in a green, living world, would surely be worth the price. But he hoped for much more. While there was some possibility that his conviction might be overturned on appeal, he no longer held any faith in the justice system. Freedom gave him some chance, however slim, of finding out the truth about his father's death. Prison offered none.

A glance at the dashboard clock told Kelsey they'd been driving for thirty minutes. It felt like hours.

"Where are we going, anyway?" she demanded. Not that she was in any hurry to find out. The road that kept them both occupied had to be safer than any ultimate destination. But Carlyle's long silences made her nervous.

Where were they going? Ben thought. Damn good question. But he hadn't a clue. When given the opportunity, he had just run, almost literally blindly and without plan. He glanced at the gas gauge. From what he could make out, the indicator seemed closer to full than to empty. He didn't need to worry about them running out of gas for some time yet. "I'll let you know when we get there," he told her. "Just stay on this road until I tell you differently."

He had to hand it to Kelsey Merrill. Despite everything that had happened to her over the last few hours, she'd never given in to hysterics. And she wouldn't, he suspected. When they'd talked in the booth, he'd noticed that there was something about the directness of her gaze and the formidable tilt to her softly rounded chin that suggested she wasn't quite as fragile as she looked. Her actions so far had proved him right.

Kelsey kept her eyes glued to the road and wondered how she could have been so mistaken about Ben Carlyle. How could she have been so misled in judging a convicted criminal to be sensitive and caring? Obviously the rapport she'd sensed between them in dealing with the injured man hadn't really been there at all.

"Stop if you see a roadside telephone." Carlyle's startling words brought her angry musings up short.

"Huh?"

"Stop at the first outdoor telephone we come to."

"What?" She couldn't believe he was saying it.

"Having trouble hearing, Kelsey? I told you to stop at a phone."

Lord! Benton Carlyle confused her. She'd been convinced that his promise to send help to the people back in the restaurant had been nothing but talk.

She absently lifted her hand to rake back her wet hair, which left Carlyle's large masculine hand dangling in front of her eyes. His hand followed hers back to the wheel. To a certain extent he'd imprisoned himself when he'd imprisoned her, she considered. The difference was, of course, that he could get free of her anytime he wanted.

Following his orders, she stopped the car at a telephone kiosk outside a small grocery store closed for the night. He pulled her out of the car and toward the phone.

"You dial," he ordered as they stood in the chilly drizzle. He hovered over her as she spoke to the operator, the hand that held the gun resting lightly above the cradle. She wasn't surprised when he cut her off the moment she'd finished giving detailed instructions on where the injured people could be found.

A convicted murderer kind enough to think of others while he made his escape from the law? What the heck kind of complicated puzzle of a man had taken her hostage? How was she supposed to figure out a person who seemed to be two different individuals—the convicted murderer she knew him to be, and the man who kept muddling up her clear judgment by helping others.

The hard, frightening fact remained, though, she thought, as he forced her back behind the wheel. Benton Carlyle had taken her captive at the point of a gun, and kept her helpless by chaining her to him.

Think positive, Kelse, she ordered, swerving to avoid another fallen tree limb in the road. There was no advantage in considering the possibility that she might not make it out of the situation. Better to believe that she would.

"You must be aware," she ventured, "that when all this is over you'll have provided me with one heck of a story." A much more up-close and personal story of a convicted murderer than she'd ever wanted.

Carlyle didn't answer. But because it gave her the feeling of having some degree of control in the situation, she kept on talking. "The feature I'll write on this will carry a byline that will make my name with the most important newspapers in the country."

She chewed on her lip and waited. Still nothing.

"Frankly," she plowed on, "a Kelsey Merrill byline has never yet appeared over an important story. So you're giving me my shot at the big time."

Despite her fear about the price she was paying for it, she lusted for the big story that would elevate her to the level of accomplishment of her older sister and brother. Almost as much, she thought wryly, as the man sitting next to her lusted for escape. In a way, she could understand his running from the prison that waited for him. In his place, would she have meekly waited around to be hauled back there?

Forcibly taking her hostage, though. *That* she could neither understand nor forgive.

"Maybe you should thank me." Carlyle's words came quietly out of the darkness.

Kelsey congratulated herself on finally succeeding in making him respond to her. She'd read somewhere that hostages who established some sort of personal link between themselves and their captors stood a better chance of making it.

"Maybe I should," she answered. "I'll thank you even more if you'll just let me go. Right here, right now."

Nothing. Well, she hadn't really expected him to grant her wish. But the man sure had a lot to learn about the art of conversation. She gave up trying to get him to talk to her, at least for now. She needed to focus all her attention on the road. In the now-sheeting rain, the car's furiously slashing wipers were losing the battle to keep her windshield clear.

It seemed like they were driving in circles. On several occasions, after she'd followed his instructions to turn down a new road, they'd had to reverse course because of flooding or a dead end. And the effort of maintaining strict vigilance on treacherous roads was tiring her. Once or twice she'd almost driven off the road.

"Look out!" Carlyle grabbed at the wheel.

Kelsey slammed on the brakes just before the car smashed into the trees at the sharp turn she'd failed to negotiate. The car fishtailed on the slippery pavement and jerked to a halt. They both lurched forward against their seat belts.

Her already strained nerves were pulled even tighter by the near miss that could have left the car wrapped around a tree and both of them seriously injured—or worse. "Well, what do you expect?" she lashed out at her captor. "No sensible person is out driving under these conditions."

He couldn't argue with that, Ben allowed. And it was becoming obvious that the tension caused by the storm and its aftermath, along with the frightening situation he'd placed his driver in, had taken a dangerous toll on both of them. Since lifting the beam off his guard, his shoulders and back felt as if he'd been run over by a cement truck. And not only did he feel as exhausted as the woman hunched over the wheel looked, being out on roads unfit for safe driving was surely inviting a personal warning from any police car happening by. So far he'd been lucky.

He pressed his hand to his throbbing head. If he didn't lie down soon, he was afraid he might pass out. And he needed time to gather his thoughts. To avoid a quick recapture, he had to carefully map out his next course of action.

"Those lights up ahead," he said, after they'd turned off onto yet another road. "Looks like a motel. Not much of one, but it'll do. Pull off. We'll spend the rest of the night there."

The goose bumps of fear that had slackened off since the near accident prickled over Kelsey's skin again. Oh, God! she worried. A motel. A room where they'd be alone together. Thoughts of what he could have in mind for her there made her shiver.

As she bumped her Toyota onto the partly flooded parking lot, she deliberately blotted out any thought other than the possibility of escape. At the very least, she'd have a shot at alerting someone of her dangerous situation. If he left her chained to the steering wheel while he saw to the room, she could lean on the horn without fear of him using the gun on her. If he took her inside the registration office, she might be able to leave some kind of message.

"This is what we're going to do," Carlyle said, his voice flat and hard. "I have to remove the cuffs. They'd be seen too easily on your bare arm."

Hope leaped in her heart.

"But that won't help you as much as you're thinking it will. I still have the gun. I promise you it will be in my hand when we walk into that motel office and you sign our names as Mr. and Mrs. John Smith."

Ben hoped the obviously fake names would lead the motel manager to fit the two of them into a ready-made mental niche and deflect suspicion. He hoped even more strongly that he could hold himself steady on his feet for another few minutes. The manager might dismiss any wobbliness on his part as too many drinks. Kelsey would not.

"If you don't want anyone to get hurt," he cautioned, "you won't do anything foolish." A toothless threat, but she didn't know that.

With her captor pressing at her back and looking over her shoulder, Kelsey dared do nothing but scrawl the fictitious names and pay for their night's lodging in cash, as he'd ordered.

Wait a minute, she thought, as they drove up to the end unit of the squalid old motel. Why didn't Carlyle dial the telephone and sign the register himself instead of giving her any opportunity whatsoever to inform someone of her plight?

He'd fumbled for the key the motel manager had placed on the countertop, she remembered. He'd fumbled, too, at the telephone and at the door of the car, much the same way as her mother fumbled and dropped things while in the throes of her occasional migraine attacks. Could his head injury be giving him more trouble than he let on? she wondered, with growing excitement. Could the man actually be a little less intimidating than he looked?

That was it, she was sure. If his pain was as severe as she suspected, he might not be thinking clearly. Maybe the possibility that she could somehow outsmart him and get away was a lot stronger than she'd dared hope.

"May I bring my suitcase in?" she asked, seemingly all innocence as she pulled up the hand brake. "These clothes are soaked through and I'm cold." The hair dryer in her bag would furnish a weapon of sorts.

Carlyle nodded, and she popped the trunk.

As Kelsey pulled her bag from the trunk, she glanced up at her captor. Gun in hand, he stood with his head slightly tilted, apparently engrossed in the music and laughter pounding from the open door a couple of units down.

The storm had driven several others to break their journeys to mountain vacation spots and spend the night at the motel. Apparently some of the stranded had gotten together to raid a case of beer and start their long weekend of partying right here.

She'd noticed the group, of course, but her interest had been focused on how she might contact them. Ben's attention seemed fixed on the music and laughter. Also, she suspected, on the freedom enjoyed by the young men and women having fun together. He squelched the twitch that idea caused in her heart when he turned and slammed down the trunk. At the door of their unit, he handed her the key, confirming her suspicion that he was hiding serious head pain that might even be affecting his vision.

He shoved her into the room ahead of him and kicked the door closed behind them. But he hadn't clicked the lock, she'd noticed. Had his pain made him forget that? She hung back, deliberately covering the door lock. Maybe if he didn't see it, he wouldn't remember to twist it into place. He took a step away from her. A little more distance and she'd fling her case at him and whip out of the room without having to lose precious seconds fiddling with a locked door.

He didn't give her the chance. His hand closed around her upper arm and he pulled her away from the door. "Put your bag on the bed, Kelsey," he ordered tiredly, tossing the key on the cheap pine dresser nearby. She complied without argument. At least her ploy with the lock had worked.

Unfortunately she didn't have as much luck with her plan to brain Carlyle with the hair dryer. He never turned his back as she took out a pair of jeans and a short-sleeved cotton shirt from her case.

"I'd like to change clothes in the bathroom, please," she requested with a meekness that would have startled her friends. "Alone."

For a long moment he studied her through an assessing squint. Then he led her to the bathroom and gave the door a slight push. It swung back a few inches. Adrenaline surged through her.

"I'll need my handbag," she said timidly, as he reached to take it from her. She lowered her eyes modestly. "I have...uh...feminine necessities in there." If Ben Carlyle was anything like her brother, he wouldn't want to deal with any such necessities.

"Don't think you can just lock the door and hide in there, Kelsey. I assure you I'd have no trouble kicking it in."

As she drew the door closed behind her, her gaze flew around the tiny room, and her hopes plummeted. Carlyle had no doubt seen what she hadn't. The windowless room afforded no escape.

What were her other options? she thought frantically.

She could scream. But with two doors between her and the rest of the world, and with the boisterous party going on, would anyone hear? Carlyle certainly would. And how long would it take him to carry out his threat to kick in the door and silence her?

She still had the one small advantage she hoped might have escaped him. Maybe he was fastening that bolt on the room door right now while she was in the bathroom. Then again, maybe he wasn't.

A rapid search of her handbag yielded a second weapon of sorts. The metal nail file would inflict no serious damage when she stabbed at Carlyle's arm, but a few moments free of him was all she'd need to race out of the room and up to the party only a short distance away.

Quickly she shed her damp shorts and top and pulled on the dry clothing. She would have preferred to stay in the bathroom, separated from her captor by a door, as long as he'd let her. He might even expect her to do that. But the element of surprise would work in her favor. She grasped the file tightly in her right fist, holding it like a tiny dagger. Slowly and quietly she turned the knob.

Before she'd taken a second step, an iron grip closed over her wrist and Carlyle yanked the make-do weapon out of her hand. He'd been waiting by the door, as if he'd fully expected her to try something along the lines of what she'd just done.

In an instant, he imprisoned both her hands firmly behind her back and hauled her up hard against him. Alarm shot through her. He was naked from the waist up. She went stiff and tried to pull away. In a single step, he backed her up against the wall and caged her intimately close within his arms in a hold she couldn't break.

He allowed her no breathing space. Every small movement she made against him to free herself only brought him closer. From her shoulders to her knees, the length of him, hot and hard and threateningly male, pressed against her.

Surprise exploded in Ben's mind. He'd made a mistake—big time—when he'd subdued his wildcat prisoner by wrapping his arms around her. He'd acted instinctively. She'd been ready to stab him in a vulnerable spot like his face or neck, just as he would have done had he been in the same position. And her attack might easily have worked. *If* he'd believed her sudden switch to innocent timidity. He'd already learned a few of Kelsey Merrill's personality traits. Meekness and timidity weren't among them.

But his mistaken method of suppressing the woman's understandable assault on him left his body welded hotly along hers. Pure torture.

And he couldn't, for the life of him, let her go.

The feelings her scorching closeness unleashed in him were too sweet, the intoxicating scent of her too compelling, the softness of the breasts crushed against his bare skin too pleasurable. Thank God she'd changed out of the T-shirt whose wet transparency molded those breasts and their beautiful rosy little nubs so invitingly. As it was, his hands gripping her slender wrists shook with the need to spread themselves wide and stroke over the alluring curves of her body. And his lips tingled with the desire to learn of hers.

All his long-starved senses craved more.

It would be so easy to take more. Just a little more.

His aching arousal needed no conscious order to press itself into its natural warm niche at the top of her legs. The hot shaft of pleasure shuddering through him didn't quite succeed in blotting out his mind's insistent hammering that he was a civilized man.

"That was not smart," he gritted, unable yet to loosen his hold on her.

Her captor's voice came dark and dangerous to Kelsey's ears. She could feel its vibrations traveling through the soft tissues of her breasts pressed against the hot steel drum of his chest.

"Remember who you're dealing with," he rumbled. "For two long, cold years I've been locked away from any relationship whatever with a woman. Don't provoke me into doing to you exactly what I've wanted to do since I first saw you in the diner."

The strong fingers vised around her wrists let go only to slide down to the curve of her bottom to anchor her even more firmly against him. "Shall I spell out for you just what that means?"

He didn't have to, Kelsey thought. His arousal speared hot against her in a blatant sexual threat. She bit down on her lip and shook her head.

"You would do well to bear that in mind." He lowered his head. His mouth hovered an inch above hers. His warm breath fanned across her lips.

She squeezed her eyes shut and pressed her lips tightly together. But instead of feeling his mouth on hers, she felt herself spun around and her wrist once again encased in metal.

His face grim, Carlyle towed her behind him to the bed.

"Lie down," he commanded.

She swallowed. Hard.

"No." She struggled to hold her voice even. Maybe some semblance of calmness on her part would rub off onto him. He didn't seem a totally unreasonable man. And he'd only threatened her sexually after she'd forced him to defend himself. "I'll sit up for the night."

He scooped her off her feet and dropped her onto the bed. She bounced on the squeaking mattress. Why hadn't she clawed for his eyes when he'd freed her hands? His strong body had kept her trapped against the wall, but she could have done something—anything—with her hands.

He bent over her.

Her heart pounding furiously, she set her face in stony lines and dredged up the command tone that had successfully discouraged unwanted male attention in the past.

"Gun or no gun," she spat out, "you lay a finger on me, mister, and you'll find yourself in for the fight of your life."

He gave a quick, hoarse burst of humorless laughter. "I don't doubt it for a minute."

He leaned closer. She shrank back, ready to defend herself with tooth and nail and everything else it would take. And she vowed never to let him see how frightened she was.

But all he did was click the handcuff around the narrow bedpost in the small space between the headboard and the mattress.

Carlyle was breathing hard when he looked down at her, his eyes chips of gray ice. "Remember what I said," he warned. "Don't try my patience, or my self-control, any more than you already have."

He reached for the bedside telephone, fumbling it so badly that the receiver slid off its cradle. He replaced it and moved the instrument to the end of its long cord—too far for her to reach.

The sharp knock on the door startled them both. "Hey, you two," a woman outside the room called. "Want to come up to the party?" Kelsey's eyes flew to the rattling knob. She opened her mouth to scream for help.

Before she'd even taken a breath, Carlyle hurled himself upon her. His hand wrapped around her handcuffed wrist. His strong, bracketing legs held her immobile.

She heard the door scrape open. "Hi, folks. Come on—"

Ben's mouth crushed down on hers.

Chapter 4

The hard, hot prison of the open mouth bonded over hers caught her muffled cry. She tried uselessly to twist away. Ben's expertly camouflaged kiss followed. His free arm pinioned hers to her side.

She beat on his back with no more than the short, ineffectual motions of her forearm his hold allowed her. She tried to kick and succeeded only in wrapping her leg around his.

She heard their unexpected visitor's embarrassed gasp and knew her movements must look less like a woman's struggles to escape the half-naked man stretched out on top of her than they did the writhings of a lover. Exactly the effect her captor was striving for.

A sharp thud signaled the shutting of the door. The party-goer had wasted no time in leaving the loving couple on the bed to their own passionate devices.

Ben froze for a moment, apparently waiting to see if the intruder had gone for good. A loud burst of laughter erupted from the party, signaling a no doubt colorful report on the amorous couple too busily engaged to join the festivities. Ben slumped against her, breathing hard. His mouth peeled from hers and dragged hotly across her cheek as he dropped his head next to hers on the pillow.

She sucked in a mouthful of air. Ben's highly effective maneuver had scarcely allowed her to breathe. Having lost the well-disguised battle of wills to his superior strength, she felt the surge of adrenaline trickling away.

For the last couple of minutes she'd been completely focused on trying to free herself, to scream, to push him away. The strong masculine body stretched over her, the hard mouth covering hers, had been no more than barriers she'd fought unsuccessfully to remove.

Now, despite her conscious order to her relaxing muscles to remain alert, other perceptions started to creep into her mind: The light pressure of his hand trailing up slowly from her confined wrist to the inside of her elbow. The soft sound of his breathing, curiously dampening the party noise. The wild pounding of his heart against hers.

The air in the room seemed suddenly hotter, stickier. The scent of him curled into her brain. Not the sharp, institutional odor she'd expected when he'd first caught her in his arms at the bathroom door. He'd come, not from prison, but from his home, where he'd had access to long, hot showers with good shampoo and expensive soap. The clean woodsy scent mingled with male perspiration and the smell of rain lingering in his still damp hair was nothing less than enticing.

An electric sexual awareness of him that hadn't been there a moment ago jolted through her. She tried to ignore it. When that didn't work, she tried to counter it by reminding herself who he was and what he'd done.

The stiffness and tension in Ben's body underwent a subtle shift. He didn't move from his vanquishing position on top of her, yet the unyielding hardness that had just defeated her seemed to ease into her softness. The action re-

fused to register on her mind as a threat. She didn't
understand it. Was it mere exhaustion, some uncharacter-
istic resignation on her part, that was driving all thought of
fight from her mind?

The feelings rising within her weren't at all what they
ought to be. Only one reaction to this man made any sense—
that of fear and loathing. But even after everything that had
happened between them, she couldn't bring herself to loathe
him. And while fear of him remained, it wasn't the chilling
fear prompted by her first sight of the gun.

She never flinched from facing with total honesty situations she might not like. And that honesty compelled her to
admit that the apprehension threading through her now was
different. She was afraid he had the power to lead her into
surrendering to the strong emotional response he'd called
from her at his first touch. A response she'd been struggling to keep tight hold of.

The uncompromising truth remained: Stronger than the
simple sympathy called up by the haunted look in a man's
eyes, or the understandable interest any woman might feel
for an attractive male before he posed any threat, pulsed a
magnetic pull that so far had yielded to none of her efforts
to break it.

A moment ago she'd been trying to shove him away with
her fist. Now, without conscious direction, her hand slid
open to curve comfortably against the firm, warm skin of
his back. No matter that her mind remained a jumbled mass
of confusion about Ben Carlyle, her body seemed to have
made its own decisions about him.

His warm, roughened fingertips moved slowly along her
arm, producing a sensation she struggled to suppress. They
stopped to gently circle her upper arm. She couldn't keep
herself from trembling.

That she could actually be enjoying the man's touch
frightened her even more than had his earlier brutally frank
warning. Maybe she was slipping deeper into the Stock-

holm syndrome, a victim's strong identification with a captor, that she'd tried to use against him in the car. But right now she didn't feel like a victim. And Ben didn't feel like a man who threatened her life. The lean, hard body stretched over hers felt disconcertingly like that of a caring lover.

The hand that had lingered at her arm moved on to finger the spot on her ear where the gold hoop pierced a lobe. Her already drumming heart jogged into a faster race, pumping not fear, but hot energizing blood, through her veins.

Like a blind man intent on searching out its shape, he lightly traced the line of her jaw, the curve of her cheek, the bridge of her nose.

The careful gentleness, almost reverence, of his sensing fingers evoked a shivery sweetness within her that blanketed any thought but that of satisfaction. It was as if on some deep level she had been waiting for just this kind of touch from him. He drew the tip of his index finger slowly across her lips. The delicious spike of pleasure the delicate action produced sped another tremor through her. Another minute and she'd forget how it all started. Another minute and she wouldn't care how it all started.

His hand skimmed downward and came to rest over the curve of a breast. Her whole body constricted. Not with revulsion—far from it. With a flaring heat that brought the tips of her breasts to tingly sensitivity. She could clearly feel the searing imprint of the three fingers held straight and close together and of the little finger a half inch from the others slowly circling the fullness of the soft mound.

Ben Carlyle had never in his life felt anything as wonderful as the sensations sweeping over him. Kelsey's exciting perfume had his mind reeling, blanking out pain and weariness. The soft curves of her body called every last part of him to shivering life. The warm, moist silkiness of her lips captivated his fingers and urged his mouth to take their enviable place. His previous assault upon her mouth had been a battle tactic, not a seduction. And he'd been so preoccupied with deceiving the intruder he hadn't stopped to consider the erotic implications of his self-protective act.

Maybe the small, tentative motions of the slender fingers that once beat angrily against him were intended as some form of protest, but they were succeeding only in searing tiny arousing circles into his bare skin.

He'd give anything if the tremors he could feel running through her meant something other than fear. He wished he could read her eyes to discover what she was thinking, what she was feeling. It would do him no good to try. He'd see only the doubled blue smudges he'd been able to discern earlier when he'd held her so arousingly close.

She had awakened at a stroke his manhood, his longing for softness, for beauty, for a woman's gentle touch. Her entrancing nearness was dissolving years of controlled defenses like an ocean wave rolling over a sand fort.

He couldn't allow it to go on.

He couldn't bring himself to stop it.

Ben's strangled moan brought Kelsey a new thrill. Their intimate closeness obviously was having its effect on him, too. She should fear it. She didn't. His mouth, once pressed so unforgivingly hard over hers, softened against her cheek. He held his lips only a tantalizing hairbreadth away from her skin as they made slow progress across her face.

His eyes were closed, she saw, and some trick of the dim light gave their shadowed lids a pained, bruised look. A senseless pang shot through her. She caught herself. She had no business wasting any sympathy on this man. He wasn't the vulnerable one here. She was.

Trouble was, she didn't feel all that vulnerable—at least, not in the way she'd felt before. She hoped he couldn't sense her crazy longing to have his hovering mouth touch hers again. Whether he did read her desire, or whether his own longing forced him to it, he lowered his mouth to hers.

The contact threaded a hot ribbon of arousal through her. Following their own impulses, rather than the orders her spinning mind was weakly trying to dictate, her lips softened and pursed to his. How could a kiss so gentle produce such magic? she wondered, astonished. Never before had she felt this instantly rising glow of passion. Never before had she yearned like this for a kiss to go on forever.

No. That couldn't be. She wanted it ended before she lost any more of her mind.

She moved slightly, only to achieve a more comfortable position, but the action allowed the muscular thigh that had imprisoned hers earlier to slowly slip between her legs. The pressure of him hard against the bottom of her abdomen surged a heavy, moist warmth through her that left her whole body limp.

The soft cry of protest that rose in Kelsey's throat sounded to Ben so much like a cry of pleasure that it made him give up the impossible effort to keep himself from running the tip of his tongue along the soft velvet joining of her lips. Desire, white-hot and lightning sharp, jagged through him.

Something primitive inside him flashed to life: A craving to plunge his tongue into the intimate recesses of her mouth and feast on the sugary taste of her. A burning need to press himself into her softness and let loose all the hunger built up over endless, lonely days and even more endless nights. A wild desire to do to her all the sweet, throbbing things his heated body raged at him to do.

It would be so easy to give in to the fiery, mind-clouding desire. She no longer fought him. Not after he'd so graphically demonstrated she couldn't best him.

He could feel the woman beneath him quivering along his length. The soft, exciting touches so pleasuring him were only rousing her disgust, he realized. She was accepting them without protest only because he'd scared her and she didn't want to antagonize him. She'd already showed him that she had extraordinary courage. She'd do whatever she believed she had to do to survive, even let him—

God! No. He fought the frenzy of his sexual hunger for rational control. His actions sickened him. If prison had made him so much an animal he'd thrust himself on a helpless woman, he deserved to remain locked up.

He tore himself away from her with a strength he wasn't sure he possessed until he'd done it.

Kelsey's sanity only snapped back into place when Ben was no longer so dizzyingly close. He'd been the one to end their all-too-pleasurable intimacy, not she, she admitted, mortified. Despite her brave words earlier, she wasn't even sure she'd have put up much of a fight if he'd sought to take more from her than he had.

Her brow furrowed with the effort of trying to figure out what in heaven's name had happened to her. She turned to look at him. He'd fallen on his back beside her. Winged with a light mat of curly black hair, the hard, naked breadth of his chest still heaved from exertion. Not surprising that their battle, resulting from his fear of discovery, should have affected him so strongly.

He'd flung one sinewy forearm over his eyes, and his fingers hung tightly curled at a temple. What captured her attention, though, wasn't the large fist or the corded strength of his bent arm, but the pulse throbbing rapidly in the blue vein of his upturned wrist. A curiously intimate exposure. Like when his eyes had briefly eluded his control and flicked open to display his real emotions.

A warm mingling of happiness and pain, confusing and illogical, squeezed her heart. She fought her desire to lay her fingers over his pulsing wrist.

She mustn't let herself care for him.

The caution blossoming quietly at the back of her mind startled her. She hissed in a breath and turned quickly away. Of course she wouldn't let herself care for this man in any personal way. The mere idea was ludicrous. She was a pragmatic, hard-nosed reporter firmly rooted in reality and not given to flights of romantic fancy like her sister. There wasn't a darn thing romantic about Ben Carlyle. A woman would have to be nuts to... to entangle herself in the life of a man who represented nothing but deep, abiding trouble.

She was grateful that he was just lying there in stony silence. She had no strength left to do anything else herself, and certainly no idea what to say about the embarrassing thing that had just happened between them.

Ben continued to battle the raw hunger still clawing at him. He hated himself for wanting to go on exploring the beautiful body of the woman lying beside him. He despised the strength of his longing to let his fingers play again over the silken texture of her skin, and resisted the craving to smooth his hands over soft curves and dip into the warm, intimate valleys to which they had no right. He'd give anything if she'd freely offer him one more taste of the delicious ripeness of her mouth.

No chance whatever of that, he reminded himself ruefully. No chance, after what he'd just done to her, that she could even look at him without repugnance. The soft, lumpy mattress transmitted her continued trembling to his back. He cursed himself again.

He could at least try to do something about her obvious and well-founded fear of him. Very likely what he had to say would be as useless with her as it had been with everyone else. Still, he was responsible for the woman's anxiety and he owed it to her to at least attempt to soothe that worry.

"Kelsey, there's something I want you to know." She made no response, but he didn't have the heart to look at her just to see condemnation written all over her beautiful face. "I haven't killed anyone."

Ben's words so closely echoed the useless wish Kelsey was making that they jerked her gaze back to him. His arm still shielded his eyes.

"You haven't, huh?" She was old enough to know that, as in "Beauty and the Beast," wild wishes came true mainly in fairy tales.

"I haven't. I couldn't kill anyone."

Curious, Kelsey thought, how his usual flat, quiet tone added more conviction to his words than if he'd tried for more convincing passion. At one time her admiration of his selflessness might have led her to accept his claim. Even now, she wanted to believe him. But after what he'd done to her, how could she?

"I'm a reporter, Ben, not some naive teenager. I know that prisons are full of men loudly proclaiming their innocence. The chance that you're the one man telling the truth is not great."

The first time he'd denied the killing, Ben remembered, he'd been astonished that he wasn't taken at his word. After twelve honest citizens had administered that last shattering shock, he looked for nothing but disbelief from everyone. And that's just what he'd gotten from Kelsey. It was foolish to feel so wounded by the answer he'd known would come.

"I didn't imagine you'd believe me. No one else has. I just hoped that telling you the truth might make you less frightened of me."

Better that he think her afraid of him, Kelsey considered, than that he should discover how close she'd come to responding to him in a totally inappropriate way. But since for the last few minutes she'd been experiencing something poles apart from fear, his words served as a strong reminder of her precarious position.

"Less frightened?" she scoffed. "Good grief, man. How could you expect anything else? You brought me with you at the point of a gun, remember?" She yanked furiously on the imprisoning handcuffs. "You've got me chained to the bed."

Ben pulled his arm from his eyes and sat up. His mouth quirked with wry and soundless humor as he looked down at her. "Right. And you're not a woman to forget the bottom line."

He reached into a pocket and brought out the silk scarf she'd packed in her suitcase. Cutting off her protest, he looped the scarf between her teeth and tied it securely at the back of her head.

"Sorry, Kelsey. But I can't take the chance of having you start screaming in the middle of the night."

All the inexplicable tenderness she'd been feeling for Ben Carlyle poured out in a rush. What a dimwit she'd been not to have been screaming blue murder while she had the chance.

She fired off at him a silent barrage of the most colorful curses she'd ever heard in a newsroom. And her eyes shot daggers at his uncaring back as he staggered to the motel room door and fastened the bolt, then headed for the bathroom. Hearing the shower running full force, she threw one more deadly mental curse at him for not allowing her the same privilege.

He came out with a towel wrapped around his hips and his damp trousers folded over his arm. He hung them over a hanger next to his shirt and jacket. Only then she noticed the gun grip sticking out of a jacket pocket. He hadn't even had the weapon close to hand all this time, and she'd been too flummoxed to take advantage of the situation. Lord! She had to get her act together or she'd never get herself out of this mess.

Ben threw back the covers on his side of the bed. As he sat down, the towel slid away from a sinewy thigh. He reached up to rub tension out of the back of his neck. The muscles rippling down the long, hard pillar of his back reminded her that she'd been powerless against him earlier, and she'd be utterly helpless if he . . .

With renewed apprehension she scrambled to the edge of the bed and folded herself into a tight ball.

The questioning glance he threw over his shoulder at her sudden movement transformed more into amusement than threat. "Don't panic, Kelsey." His voice was low, strained. "You're safe enough. I've got to get some sleep, and I suggest you do the same. We've both had one hell of a day."

Sleep? He couldn't be serious. Her eyes would stay wide open and fastened on his every move all night.

"Oh," he continued, "and in case you're wondering what I've done with the key to those cuffs?" He dangled the small key in front of her, then shoved it down the front of the towel. "If you want to go searching for it during the night, that's entirely up to you." He slid between the sheets and reached over to click off the lamp. "But I won't be responsible for the consequences."

Ben waited until the slow, rhythmic rise and fall of his unwilling bedmate's softly rounded chest told him it was safe to move without waking her. If she were anywhere near as tired as he, she wouldn't wake up for a week.

He flipped the ugly green bedspread over her to keep her warm in the cool of the night, then lay on his side and unsuccessfully ordered his eyelids to close. His extreme care not to let any part of him touch her, even through the bedclothes that separated them, proved useless. Unconsciously seeking more warmth in the room's damp chill, she turned and spooned herself against him with a sigh. Her sweet little bottom snugged up into his middle, leaving him racked between delight and torment. Her position left him no place to put his arm except around her and up against her breasts. Welcome, thought-obliterating sleep, he suspected, gritting his teeth, would be one hell of a long time coming.

If only he'd taken the old man with him, instead of the woman who'd been thrown into his path to torment and tease him with her beauty and soft femininity. If only he'd been strong enough to resist the temptation of keeping her near him for just a little while longer.

He'd always set great store in taking responsibility for his actions, for being in control. Events since his father's death had completely torn away that control. In prison he controlled nothing, except his own reactions. Once so in command of his life, having armed guards ordering his every move had been sheer torture. But his worst enemy couldn't have devised a more diabolical test of that stupidly vaunted control of his than forcing him to lie so painfully close to his beautiful captive without making love to her.

He might ache for her—he did ache for her—but no way would he let her ensnare his heart. The thought, so totally off-the-wall under the circumstances, brought him up short. Ridiculous. No chance. He had withstood tougher assaults on his emotions. He wasn't about to crumble just because a woman made him feel like a man again. In the morning he'd set his beautiful prisoner free and complete his escape alone.

Kelsey woke to a gentle touch on her arm that felt so delicious it brought a lazy smile to her lips and a long sighing stretch to cramped muscles. Then the picture of Ben holding a gun on her rushed into her mind. Her body tightened and her eyes flashed open.

Ben knelt by the bed, delicately massaging her wrist. The imprisoning metal ring was gone. So was the scarf she'd chewed on so angrily and for so long.

The drapes that didn't quite close in the middle showed only the beginnings of daylight, but Ben was fully dressed.

"Good morning," he said, as she sat up still groggy from sleep. "I'm sorry I had to cuff and gag you last night, but I had no choice."

She pushed herself up on an elbow and dragged her hair out of her eyes.

"You're sorry," she croaked. "I suppose you think that makes it all right."

"No. It wasn't all right." If she didn't know better, she might think he was genuinely distressed by what he'd done. He handed her a can of orange soda and dropped a package of cheese crackers into her lap. "Have some breakfast. These are all I could get from the vending machine outside."

As satisfying as it was to have the opportunity to berate her conscienceless captor, right now she was much more interested in eating. She gulped down a long swallow of soda, then tore ravenously at the snack's packaging and jammed a couple of the small orange crackers into her mouth. A glance at the man kneeling beside her provoked a double take. She halted in mid-chew.

Ben was smiling as he watched her. Not all that big a smile, but more than one of his usual twitches. The crooked grin didn't quite fit, as if he hadn't practiced enough yet to really get the hang of it. But his eyes actually crinkled at the corners, and much of the harshness had gone from his angular face.

"What's so funny?" she grumbled, after swallowing the crackers and reaching for another. She saw nothing humorous in this situation.

"You just look so damned cute in the morning, with your hair all tousled and those lovely eyes of yours all soft and sleepy. Not to mention the way you're scarfing down those crackers like a kid with a handful of jelly beans."

Being called *damned cute* by a guy who'd kidnapped her sparked her indignation. "My hair is tousled because you didn't let me comb it. And my eyes look like this because I only got a few minutes sleep last night. As for the crackers—you probably scarfed yours down the same way. You had even less to eat yesterday than I did."

Funny. She'd never expect a man as tough as Ben Carlyle to come right out and laugh. But that rasping in his throat sounded suspiciously like a chuckle. She tried not to let the pleasant sound of it soften her any.

"Lady," he said dryly, "you were dead to the world long before I was. But you're right about the crackers. I polished off two packages pretty quick." He knocked back the rest of his drink and straightened to place the empty can on the nightstand.

"I'm leaving, Kelsey."

She blinked. "What do you mean, you're leaving?"

"Just what I said. I have to take your car, but I'll try to leave it somewhere the police will find it. You'll probably get it back sooner or later."

"You're not going to take me with you?" She hadn't considered that possibility, and the fact that her captor was acting contrary to her expectations confused her.

He shook his head and picked up the hand clutching the last cracker to snap the confining bracelet back around it.

"I'll have to leave you cuffed to the bed in order to give myself a head start." When she opened her mouth to protest, he popped in the cracker. "You'll be freed when the maid comes in to make the bed in a couple of hours. She'll find the key to the handcuffs over on the dresser. If you give me your word you won't cause a ruckus for a while, I won't gag you. I know it must be very unpleasant."

She gulped down the cracker. "You've got my word. But I'm surprised you'd take it. How do you know I won't start screaming my head off the minute you leave?"

"I don't. But you strike me as a woman who keeps her word. I hope you don't prove me wrong."

He backed away a couple of steps and looked down at her with no trace left of the half grin that had so charmed her a moment ago.

"All this is just about over for you, Kelsey. Soon you can go on to meet your sister and brother and get back to your normal life. I envy you that normal life. It's not something that has much chance of happening for me."

He plowed his fingers through the rumpled waves of his hair, looking so disarmingly uncertain that she almost forgot he was both a convicted murderer and a kidnapper. "Look..." he said. "Don't let this whole thing give you nightmares or anything." She had the curious feeling that the harshness grating his voice was directed more at himself than at her. "Just try to forget what I've done to you."

It would take her a mighty long time to forget Benton Carlyle, she suspected. And even longer to forget the kiss that had rocked her to her soul.

"As you said," he continued, "you'll have quite a story to write."

"Yeah...sure...a great story." What did she have between her ears? she wondered. Fuzz? This was her chance to escape a dangerous situation. She should be jumping at it. But somehow the thought of Ben's leaving didn't make her as happy as it should.

"I'll be looking for it in the papers," he said. "Just spell my name right. It's *Y-L-E,* not *I-S-L-E.*"

A frown that seemed fashioned of equal parts anger and pain twisted across his face. With what sounded strangely like a groan of surrender, he bent in one swift motion to grasp her shoulders roughly and possess her mouth.

This exciting assault was nothing like his previous delicate, tender exploration of her lips. She should have ignored the searing sweetness that so easily parted them. She should have kept her tongue from so quickly welcoming the urgent intrusion of his. She should have kept herself from noticing that the taste of him carried the same incredible rightness that had marked his first unwitting embrace. Instead, she positively encouraged him to continue his sweet plundering of her mouth by sliding her hand against the rough warmth of his stubbled cheek.

With a sudden quick movement he pulled away. She was still basking in the mind-dulling sweetness of his kiss when he jerked her car keys from his pants pocket and strode toward the door.

A sick, hollow feeling clutched at her heart.

Chapter 5

"Ben. Wait!"

He turned. "Yes?"

"I...uh..." She'd called him back without thought. She just wasn't ready yet to say goodbye to the strangely disturbing man who'd plunked himself down so forcefully in the middle of her life. "Just hold on a minute, will you?"

Without thought, she swung her legs to the floor and made to go after him. The handcuffs quickly jerked her back to sit on the edge of the bed. "I don't... I want to talk to you."

"Really? I expected that you couldn't wait to see the last of me."

"I can't. Believe me...I can't." Since that was true, she was having some difficulty understanding why she was making any effort whatever to delay his leaving. "I just... How's your headache?"

One dark eyebrow lifted in surprise. "I thought I'd managed to hide that from you."

"Is that why you took me with you? Because you were having trouble seeing properly after that head injury?"

"You don't miss much, do you, Kelsey?"

"I'm a reporter. I get paid to notice details. You haven't answered the question, Ben. Did you really take me as a hostage? Did you plan to use me as a protective shield if the cops stopped you? Or did you just need me to drive when you couldn't? Tell me the truth, Ben. Please. It's important to me." Although why any minor gradations of motivation on his part should matter was far from clear in her mind.

He shrugged. "All right. I needed you. That blow on my head affected my eyesight."

"You needed someone. Why me? You hate reporters. You told me so yourself."

He wasn't about to venture into that particular swamp of confusing motive and even more confusing emotion. Especially since her claim was perfectly true. He didn't just share the general irritation of a lot of people at members of the media. His aversion to all of them was scarred soul deep.

"Sorry, Kelsey. I'm not too good at playing twenty questions. The game isn't all that popular in prison. Goodbye, and the best of luck."

He turned to the door.

A feeling close to panic made her call out to him again. "Can you really see well enough to drive, Ben?"

With his hand on the doorknob, he threw her a glance over his shoulder. "Now that it's daylight I can manage well enough on the road."

"It's tough to drive on these twisting mountain roads," she pressed. Why on earth was she trying so hard to keep him from leaving without her, when getting away from an armed kidnapper would be any sensible person's top priority?

"I'll just have to chance it." He turned from the door and stalked back to the foot of the bed to look down at her with a frown. "What is all this, Kelsey? What are you getting at?"

Good question, she thought. This convict, as puzzling as he was fascinating, had hooked with a vengeance onto both her reporter's curiosity and her personal feelings. If he left her behind now, she'd have no further chance of learning the real Benton Carlyle story—of finding out if the jury's verdict really was wrong. And getting that story was her main motivation, she assured herself. Any other would make no sense at all.

During this whole episode, she considered, he'd done nothing to hurt her—other than the fact that he'd dragged her along and kept her overnight against her will—a very big exception. For a con he was remarkably the gentleman. Soft-spoken, reasonably polite, not going out of his way to frighten her. Even his assault on her last night—if it could be called that—had come about only because of his need to protect himself against an unexpected intrusion. She'd seen what it had cost him to pull himself away from her. She'd truly been at his mercy in bed with him all night long—and he hadn't touched her.

"You protected me during the storm, Ben. And you worked hard and unselfishly to help everyone afterward. I like to pay my dues, and I owe you something for that."

"You don't owe me a thing. I only did what had to be done."

Not everyone would have, she knew. Was Benton Carlyle truly the basically decent man that, in spite of everything, she still felt him to be?

"What you said last night, Ben, about being innocent of your father's death . . . was that the truth?"

A dumb question, she knew. A convicted killer could surely lie easily and well. She watched his eyes as he rounded the bed and stood before her, and she tried to see behind that veil he usually succeeded so well in holding firmly lowered over them.

"I did not kill my father."

She could glean nothing concrete from the steady gray gaze. But what if he were telling the truth? The justice system was not infallible. Judges and juries made mistakes. What a horrible situation for Ben Carlyle if he really was innocent. And what a great twist on an already engrossing story. If true, she could hardly blame the man for attempting to escape a penal system that had failed him so miserably.

"But assuming I *had* killed my father, wouldn't it have made more sense for me to claim it was an accident, or self-defense? My lawyer urged me to go that route because dozens of people had seen Dad's prior attack on me. He was sure I'd face no more than a short prison sentence. With luck I might even get off altogether."

As if he knew she was trying to weigh the truth of his words by watching his eyes, his gaze never wavered.

"That attorney, a family friend, turned out not to be as good as I was told he was. Another of my mistakes. And in retrospect, I should have taken his advice. But because I was innocent, I couldn't believe a jury could find me guilty, so I stupidly refused to plea-bargain." He shook his head. "I didn't take into consideration how hard a prosecutor up for reelection would work to prove he'd put a rich and privileged *criminal* behind bars as quickly as any other." He shrugged, and finally flicked his gaze away.

"I can't stick around much longer, Kelsey. If you've got something to tell me, say it. You probably want to chew me out for putting you through this. So go ahead."

"Don't be in such an all-fired hurry," she grumbled, trying to sort out the thoughts buzzing around in her head. "Let me think a minute."

Even if he'd done what they'd convicted him of doing, a man who killed in the heat of passion wasn't like a conscienceless murderer who killed without remorse for some kind of gain. He wasn't likely to kill again. She'd be reasonably safe with him if she went ahead with the plan forming in her mind.

Some would surely call that plan idiotic—and not without some justification, she admitted. Stephen and Cara would warn it was just the kind of impulsive act that had landed her in trouble in the past. But if it panned out, her editor—after justifiably scorching her for violating darn near every journalistic ethic in the book—would be talking page-one material that would be picked up by all the wire services.

On the other hand, Benton Carlyle had held a gun on her. Based on no more than her instincts about him, could she put her life in the hands of a man who'd demonstrated a control over his emotions, even his facial expressions, that most people never achieved?

Why go on? The decision had been made when she'd watched him walking away from her. Admittedly the deep, velvety timbre of a man's voice and the hint of pain in his eyes weren't a whole lot to go on. But something about him—his quiet self-containment, his very real concern for his guard—did inspire trust. She *had* to find out about him. Had to *know*, one way or the other. Instincts weren't all that solid a foundation on which to risk her life. But they were all she had.

"Okay, Ben. Here's the deal. I'm not sure I completely accept your declaration of innocence, but if you are, maybe you're overdue for some kind of break." She was already in over her head, Kelsey thought. And now she was being asked to trust a convicted murderer. Except that he wasn't asking. She was volunteering. "So to prevent your being involved in any kind of automobile accident because of your poor vision, I'll go along with you. At least for a little while, and only if you'll strike a bargain with me."

Ben's eyebrows shot up. That slight parting of his lips, she suspected, was probably the closest a man so uptight would ever come to letting his mouth drop open in shock. She congratulated herself for having been able to shake his control even to that small extent.

"Let me get this straight. You're saying you want to come with me?"

"Let's just say I'm willing to come with you."

"Because you're so worried about me and some potential accident victim, right?" The man could sound a little more grateful, she thought, instead of looking so skeptical. "And exactly what is all this altruism of yours going to cost me?"

"I want an in-depth profile on you," she shot back. "The price of my cooperation will be for you to open up to me."

"If you come with me voluntarily, Kelsey, you could be charged with aiding and abetting an escaped felon."

"I can always argue that I was only trying to prevent anyone from getting hurt, by driving more safely than you could."

"Or that you're just a reporter covering an important story," he added, his voice sharp and dry, "and wanted to be there when they take me in."

"Okay. That, too." Which, of course, was exactly the case. She wasn't about to make a fool of herself by admitting anything else. All sorts of feelings about Ben Carlyle had been bubbling through her since meeting him. It seemed safer not to examine them too closely. "Most authorities aren't keen on locking up reporters. It tends to make them look bad and bring unwanted publicity down on their heads."

She thrust up her chin. "And I'll go with you only if you'll get rid of the gun. That will be the pledge of your innocence, Ben. If you really aren't the killer they say you are, you won't need that weapon."

This last gambit of hers must have totally scrambled his brains, Ben thought. Take her with him? That meant he'd have to continue subjecting himself to her intoxicating nearness, to the sweet, mind-dulling scent of her, to the soft touch of her hand. He wasn't sure he could withstand the provocation. True, it was proving damn hard to leave her. But the emotional pull she held for him that kept him from simply walking out the door was, he assured himself, nothing more than the temptation of the long-forbidden.

"You haven't thought this through, Kelsey."

"I have. You're the one who seems to have the major problem with it. It's simple. Lose the weapon, and I go with you."

Kelsey watched her former captor pacing back and forth by the bed—exactly three long strides forward and three back. The realization that the size of his cell was imprinted deep in his mind and muscle brought her a quick pain.

Ben's prison-ingrained wariness told him it was foolhardy to risk his newfound freedom with a woman he scarcely knew. Not smart to chance letting his unstoppable response to her muddle up what must remain his clear-cut focus on escape. But she held out a powerful lure to him. The lure of his being able to look, finally, into the eyes of someone who believed in him.

In prison he'd had to prove himself to the hard-eyed men who'd looked on him with more than indifference and demonstrate to them that the effort wouldn't be worth it. If only he could prove himself to the woman who'd stirred up feelings he'd long thought were dead in him. She made him feel human again. She reminded him of values he once lived by: honor, kindness, respect for others. He'd always worked primarily on logic, but months in the penitentiary had forced him to rely more on intuition. He'd had to learn to sense which man could pose a serious threat and which man was all bluster. Now Kelsey Merrill was forcing him to bring into play an emotion he'd had no truck with for a long time—trust.

He whipped around to face her and found himself again caught in her challenging blue gaze.

"I learned the hard way never to trust a reporter—or anyone else, for that matter," he said. "Never for a moment do I forget that someone I know, a co-worker, maybe even one of my friends, hung me out to dry on a homicide charge." The sickening possibility that one of his own family might have done so was too painful to dwell on. He tried to hold at bay the bitterness those thoughts provoked so it wouldn't eat him alive. Some days he succeeded better than others. "How can I trust you not to turn me over to the first cop we meet?"

"You were willing to take my word earlier, Ben. Why not trust me again?"

"Trusting you to give me a couple of hours lead time is a lot different from trusting you with my freedom."

This surely wasn't a woman who gave up easily on getting what she wanted, he thought. Actually, she was exactly the kind of gutsy, stand-up individual who could help him with the task he'd set himself—if he could bring himself to trust her. Despite the heavyweight strings attached, he decided, he'd be a fool to refuse the help of the one person who'd offered it.

He'd battled terror, rage and depression. He'd fought off loneliness and self-pity. And he'd worked out his own private survival mechanism, training himself to look no farther ahead than the day, forcing himself to make it through the next hour, then the next. That experience had surely given him the strength to withstand his desire for this woman.

Abruptly he bent to free her. The manacles clattered to the floor.

"Okay, Kelsey, I'll give you a crack at the story you're so bent on pursuing. But I won't get rid of the gun. Someone out there killed my father and allowed me to take the blame for it. I intend to find out who that bastard is. When I finally face him, it'll be with some protection."

He hoped self-protection was the only reason he was holding on to the weapon. He'd assured Kelsey he was no killer, and he prayed that was still true. But there were days—especially those first ghastly days in prison—when he wouldn't have hesitated to blow away the cold-hearted killer who'd let an innocent man suffer for his actions. "That's *my* deal. Take it or leave it."

He hoped she'd leave it. Easier for him if she did.

Put that way, Kelsey thought, maybe she could understand why he'd keep the gun, although his having it still made her nervous. But you'd think she'd just attacked him again, instead of offering to help. That icy armor he'd carried into the diner was once more locked tightly around him. Maybe she *was* making a hazardous mistake, she worried. She'd have to stay alert. And if she ever again felt the slightest personal threat from Ben Carlyle, or caught any hint of a lie in his eyes, she'd take off in a heartbeat.

"I'll take it," she said, the confidence she'd started out with slipping a little. A few minutes to wash up and make herself presentable, and she was ready.

As she reached for her travel case on the bed, Ben slid in front of her, towering over her and blocking her way. The room seemed suddenly stifling, the air too thick and sticky to take into her lungs properly. He didn't touch her, but his narrowed, intimidating gaze triggered an instant rush of apprehension. She steeled herself not to flinch.

"So you've decided you're safe with me, have you?"

Safe? She swallowed. The enigmatic and dangerous smile playing around his lips was making her feel like a doe caught in the paralyzing glare of a hunter's spotlights.

"I've known men who like to live dangerously," he said. "Are you like that?"

"I . . . I don't know what you mean."

He flicked into motion the gold hoop dangling from her right ear. "I haven't noticed any great reluctance on your part to accept my kisses." Her hand flew to her mouth. Oh,

Lord! She couldn't deny it. She'd tried hard not to respond to him, and failed. "Does your consuming interest in writing a story about me extend to a desire to do some intensely personal research on how a man who's been locked in an iron box for a very long time would make love?" His deep, quiet voice hovered midway between threat and equally disturbing caress. "If that's your game, lady, I'd be glad to oblige."

Ben was gratified to see the pink flush rising to color the woman's face. He hoped that pressing his oblique warning would make her keep her distance, because he wasn't entirely sure he could keep his. And he was taking her with him for only one reason, he assured himself: for the help she might give him somewhere down the line—nothing more.

"I want only one thing from you, Benton Carlyle—" Kelsey's soft blue eyes turned stony "—and that's the story of what has happened to you since the day of your father's death."

Ben thrust her from him and turned to shoulder her carryon. "That's *your* primary interest," he said. "But understand this. Mine is in getting out of these mountains. And that's going to come first." Later, after the furor over his escape had died down, he'd return to begin his own investigation of his father's death. "After I get away, you can write anything you damn well please about me." He made no effort to disguise the venom in his voice. "And you will. One more thing. You're coming with me on your own, but I still call all the shots. I want that clearly understood."

Kelsey bristled at his arrogant tone. "I'm not real big on having people order me around, Ben."

"I don't care whether you are or not. You agree that I'm in charge, or you stay behind."

He didn't leave her a heck of a lot of choice. "Okay, you call the shots."

At the car, he opened the door on the passenger side and tossed her bag on the back seat. "Finding an escape hatch from these hills won't be easy," he said. "I can pretty much count on the cops having the main roads and access to the highways covered. We'll have to try to find some way out over back roads. Aside from having the police on my tail, flooding on some of these low-lying valley roads will last for days."

She put out her hand for the keys.

He shook his head. "I'll drive."

"But . . . but you said you needed me to drive."

"No, *you* said I needed you to drive. I'm tired of having other people in charge. From here on I call my own shots, like manning the wheel of this car." Besides, he wasn't certain how far he could trust his self-appointed helpmeet's loyalty. Now that his vision had cleared, though the pain hadn't lessened as much as he'd led her to believe, he intended to keep possession of the vehicle that gave him his only chance of escape. "If I need you to take over, I'll let you know."

He dropped the bag at her feet and strode to the driver's side to fit the key in the door. "I'm not holding a gun on you this time, Kelsey," he said. "Get in, or stay here. It's up to you."

The brittle edge in Ben's voice sent another ripple of unease through Kelsey. She bit down on her lip. He'd demolished the comforting excuse she'd given herself about accompanying him mainly for safety's sake. And apparently he couldn't care less which choice she made because he wasn't even looking at her. He just slid onto the seat and shoved it back to its farthest position to accommodate his long legs. He was twisting the key in the ignition and showing every sign of being ready to drive off without her when she pulled open the door, tossed in her bag and jumped in next to him.

She had no illusions that the quick twitch of his lips meant he was glad she'd stayed with him. He was just happy to be behind the wheel of a car again. She could see with what

satisfaction he spread his hands wide on the steering wheel
and how lovingly he ran his fingers over the leather circle.
He threw the car into reverse and, like a pro driver itching
to leap into a race, burned rubber squealing out of the
parking lot and onto the road.

"Let's get started on that interview you agreed to, Ben,"
she said, after they'd put a few miles between themselves
and the motel. "I have a tape recorder in my handbag."

"Forget it."

His quick refusal left no room for negotiation. She wasn't
too surprised. It had been quite a coup to get the man to
agree to talk to her at all. But a tape of a conversation with
an escaped convict who turned out to be an innocent man
would have been something. Plus, when she listened to the
sound of their voices later, a recording often provided further clues as to how sources really felt about a subject. She
would have liked to have a tape of Ben Carlyle's voice as a
memento of all this, after she'd left him. And that would
have to be soon, she reminded herself, very soon.

"Okay." She gave in quickly to prevent her subject from
getting any more edgy about the interview than he already
seemed to be. "We won't tape it." She flipped open the
notebook she'd taken from her purse. "I need to take notes,
though."

Better to start with easy questions, she decided, and get
him used to talking before delving into emotionally charged
issues like the murder itself, or his prison experiences. She'd
heard of the awful things that could happen to a man—especially a good-looking man—in prison. Ben Carlyle,
though, seemed well able to take care of himself.

"Tell me about your family, Ben. You've already mentioned your sister, how about your brother? As I recall, he's
a little younger than you. How did you two get along?"

Ben's jaw tightened. "This sure isn't something I like doing." He sighed. "But in my book, a deal's a deal."

"In mine, too, Ben."

At that, the look he gave her wasn't quite as fearsome as it had been. "Charles is twenty-nine now, four years younger than I. We weren't awfully close growing up. He resented me because he thought me our father's favorite."

"And were you?"

"My father did pay more attention to me, but that was hardly my fault. And it wasn't necessarily attention I enjoyed. He demanded a lot of me. Actually, my incarceration is turning out to be quite a boon for Charles. Dad took him on at the office, but he made it painfully clear that he didn't expect much from his younger son. And that's just what he got. Charles drew a paycheck, that's all."

Kelsey rolled her eyes. If her subject kept on with these long pauses between sentences, she'd be with him for a week instead of a day. But she knew it would do no good to press him, and so she kept her mouth shut.

"But my brother must have been paying more attention than anyone realized," Ben finally continued. "Because after the heir apparent to the business got locked up, Charles insisted on taking over. With my mother and sister's controlling shares in the company, he was able to do that. I didn't think he could hack it, so I gave my proxy to Walt to vote against Charles. As it turned out, my brother's handling of Carlyle Specialty Tools has proven me wrong. Walt says Charles is doing a good job."

"Walt?"

"Walter Simpson is the factory manager who helped my father set up production. Dad took over a small, failing tool-manufacturing company, modernized and expanded it to turn out quality specialty tools. His business and financial genius put the company on the map, but he had little interest in the manufacturing end of things. Walt is one of the few people who came to visit me in prison. Not that I'm all that interested in the business anymore, but it was sure nice to see a friendly face now and again."

"Didn't Charles visit?"

"Yes. Charles came." Another long silence fell over him. "But I was madder than hell at him for a while there."

"Because you lost the proxy vote?"

"Because I hadn't been in prison a month when he married Helena, my former fiancée."

"I'm sorry. That must have hurt."

"Mostly it hurt my pride," he said, with surprising lightness. "My relationship with Helena was on the rocks before all this happened, anyway. She didn't agree with my decision to strike out on my own. She wanted more security than I'd have been able to provide for a while. I resented them both at first. That's over now. I can certainly understand why Charles wanted Helena. She's a gorgeous woman."

Kelsey clamped down on the urge to ask Ben if he were still carrying a torch for the gorgeous Helena.

"I think now that the main reason I got engaged to Helena was because she seemed quite eager to marry me, and I was ready to start a family of my own." His voice dropped. "Not much chance of that happening now."

Kelsey could offer no contradiction. Ben's bleak assessment of his chances to resume a normal family life anytime soon was unfortunately right on target.

"Why did you want to start your own business, Ben? Didn't you have a good position in the family firm?"

"An excellent position. My father insisted that I take over after he retired on doctor's orders because of serious heart problems. When people said I was very much like Henry Carlyle, I didn't consider it an unqualified compliment. He was intelligent and aggressive, a management and financial genius. He was also obsessive, overbearing, buried in his work and neglectful of any meaningful interacting with his family or anyone else."

The sharpness in Ben's voice didn't entirely hide the hurt beneath. This was exactly the kind of personal observation she'd hoped for, Kelsey thought exultantly, but listening to it was proving unexpectedly difficult.

"I could see myself becoming like my father. That was the main reason I wanted to get out. He paid a high price for his success—a price I wasn't willing to pay."

In the end, Kelsey thought, Ben *had* escaped his father's iron hand. But the price had been enormous.

"My personal financial assets weren't quite enough to start up my business. Walt was willing to back my venture with a loan. Dad was furious."

"What was your venture?"

"I'd found a couple of small companies that offered services to clean up the environment. One outfit produced bacteria that ate oil spills. Another would remove asbestos and lead paint from old buildings. I wanted to buy those and others and eventually expand into a company that could tackle any kind of cleanup challenge."

"Sounds like a great idea, Ben, and ultimately a very profitable one."

"Dad didn't share that view."

"Tell me about Henry Carlyle," she prodded, after another lengthy silence. "Our paper did a story on him at the time of the murder. Said he was the proverbial self-made man who became a millionaire by the age of thirty-five."

"The tool company was his base, but he accumulated most of his wealth through shrewd investments. In business life, my father was smart as a whip. In his personal life, a total failure. He wasn't close to anyone. Certainly not to any of his children. Although he gave us everything in the way of toys or cars any kid could want, none of us ever heard a word of praise or affection from him. And no one crossed my father with impunity. Not even my mother. Her occasional weak attempts to stand up for herself never succeeded. I used to think all families were that way. From what you said about your brother and sister, sounds like yours certainly isn't."

Kelsey laughed. "I can't imagine my mother—or any of us—not arguing with Dad about something we felt strongly about. My parents lavished affection and encouragement on all us kids. Their teaching salaries didn't leave a lot of money left over for luxuries, but they splurged on the country house so we could spend summers together. Now that we're all out on our own, we still spend at least a weekend together there every summer."

"You said you work for a Pittsburgh newspaper. Is that where you make your home?"

"I have an apartment there. I'm not sure you could dignify the place with the term *home*. It's a place to sleep, to stash my few belongings—I'm not a collector or a pack rat like my sister."

"I can understand that, Kelsey. After being forcibly restrained in one small space for a long time, I'm not sure I'll ever want to be tied down to one spot again as long as I live. A place to sleep and eat. That's all I really need from now on."

"I hardly ever even eat a meal at my apartment, except for breakfast and snacks. Cara would have a fit if she knew how often I eat out. But let's get back to *your* story. That's the important one."

That was all he meant to her, Ben reminded himself: the source for an important story. Nothing more. Absolutely no reason why the thought should cause the small, dull ache creeping into his heart.

"Of course," he said dryly. "My story. My father was bent on having his eldest son take over the business, not so much out of any great approval of my abilities, but as a reflection of himself. He wanted a Carlyle to go on heading up Carlyle Specialty Tool Company. He'd have been astounded at how he got that wish. I thought Walt should take over. He knows the production end of the business from the ground up. Walt has always been a good friend to me. He sat through every day of the trial."

"I don't remember seeing any news footage of your mother at the trial."

"She never came. Mother was always delicate. I never expected her to have the strength to sit through the whole trial. She seldom left Dogwood Hill for any reason, but to tell the truth, it hurt that she never even made an appearance in the courtroom. I'm not even certain that she believed me innocent. She never said so. Not even that last time we spoke together before she died."

He'd never confessed that hurt to anyone else. It surprised him that it hadn't been more difficult to make it to his lovely interrogator. In fact, giving Kelsey the interview she'd demanded wasn't nearly as tough as he'd thought it would be. He'd almost forgotten what it was like to share his thoughts, to open himself to another person. A convict never dared do what people on the outside took for granted. To speak his mind in the hell in which he'd existed for so long meant the risk of violence, possibly death. Kelsey didn't realize it, but she was giving him lessons on how to be normal again.

Hold it! He pulled his thoughts up short. It was dangerous to let himself feel too alive, too much a normal man. A mistake to think of himself that way, even for a moment. He had to hold fast to the extreme caution, about everything and everyone, that prison had burned into him. A caution so at odds with his earlier habit of jumping into things with both feet. But that propensity to lead with his emotions instead of his head had already plunged him into a nightmare. He had to keep tighter reign on his feelings for Kelsey Merrill. He'd be a damned fool to give her beauty, her courage, her sheer feminine attraction any further chance to work their way into his heart. Other men might hope to share friendship, dreams, maybe even love with this woman. Not he. That path was barred to him. And he sure as hell shouldn't forget it.

His jaw clenched. Was there one particular man who had the right to enjoy everything about her that he didn't? A woman as lovely as she? Of course there was a man. Probably a gaggle of them. The mere idea of those other men made him livid. But Kelsey's love life wasn't his business. He yanked his mind away from that too-disturbing subject.

"Whoa!" he suddenly shouted. "This car can't handle that. It's practically a river." He brought the automobile to a halt, its front wheels already splashing into the water swirling across the road.

Kelsey had been so engrossed in Ben's story, she hadn't even noticed the water's depth.

"We'll have to go back to a better road," Ben said. "We're getting no place fast on this one."

The road they finally decided on led only to trouble.

"What is it?" she asked, when he jammed on the brakes with no water in sight.

"There's a police cruiser stopped up ahead. I just caught a glimpse of its emergency lights around that bend. We'll have to turn back again."

"We can't, Ben. We already know that those back roads are a trap. If we don't get out of this bag, they'll find us eventually."

"I can't argue with that." He leaned forward over the wheel, frowning in concentration. "So somehow we've got to get past that roadblock." Settling back in the seat, he perused her face for a moment, then reached over and trailed his fingers through her hair. "The time has come for you to fish or cut bait, partner. If you stay with me you could soon find yourself in serious trouble with the police."

"You're going to try to get through the roadblock."

He nodded.

"I'm sticking, Ben." She'd never been one to change her mind just because the going got rough. "What's your plan?

I hope it's a little more sophisticated than just barreling through."

"I figure the cops already have their hands full dealing with the flood emergency. These roadblocks weren't set up primarily to watch out for us, but to assist the local citizenry in a tough situation."

"I'm sure," Kelsey said, "most of the locals are so worried about the continuing effects of the storm that they couldn't care less about some escaped convict. And these county police departments aren't large. Even with state police involved, resources must be stretched thin."

"Right. The cops still might not have much on us yet." The early news broadcast they'd listened to in the motel had focused mainly on the storm. "They have a description of me, of course, but it could take a while to spread my police photos around. They'll have your name. You mentioned it a few times, and they'll probably know about your short blond hair, maybe not much else yet. Witness descriptions are notoriously unreliable. I found that out at my trial. Nobody was sure who'd left the picnic, other than me, around the time of Dad's death. And they may have very little yet on your car. After all, would you notice every vehicle that drives up to a restaurant? It won't be all that easy for them to track down who you are and dig up your car's tags."

Ben turned and reached into the back seat for her tote. He dug out the scarf with which he'd gagged her last night. "Are you game to try my idea, Kelsey?" he asked, holding up the scarf. "The cops up ahead are probably checking for a cowering blond hostage and a gun-waving escapee. You'll have to take over the wheel, so they'll see a woman operating under her own steam."

"It could work," she said, wrapping the length of blue silk around her head to hide the color of her hair. "But we're going to have to do something about you." As Ben loped around to the passenger side, she shifted over to the driver's seat and pondered the problem of disguising a man for whom the police blocking the road ahead might well have a good description.

"Your idea has given me one, Ben. Look at me a minute." When he did, her fingers combed a dark lock down over his forehead to hide the flesh-colored bandage. "That's better. Now drop your head back and close your eyes. Pretend you're asleep. When we get up to the cops, let me do all the talking."

At first she wasn't sure Ben was willing to follow her instructions. It was only after a few seconds of intense study of her face that he angled himself against the door, as if napping. "If this charade of ours doesn't work," he said, "you're to start screaming that you were terrified of me and you had no choice but to cooperate."

She shoved the gear shift into Drive. "Ready, Ben?"

"Let's go."

Following Ben's orders to turn on him, if necessary, wouldn't be all that easy to do, she thought. And she prayed it wouldn't be necessary. She'd ducked his question about feeling safe with him. In truth, she *was* afraid of him. Not afraid any longer that he might do her physical harm. Despite his blatant warning to stay wary of him, that fear was lessening as she listened to him talk. Now she was more afraid that he was starting to mean more to her than it was safe to allow.

She faced another problem. Even as she headed down the road toward the waiting police, she wasn't sure she could flat-out lie to an officer of the law. And that's what it would take to get them through.

Through slitted eyes, Ben saw the roadblock ahead looming closer. He was taking a hell of a chance. He'd just presented his former hostage with the perfect occasion to turn him in, and he couldn't be certain she wasn't about to do just that.

He felt the car slow and stop. He heard Kelsey roll down the window and loudly hail the cop. It took all his effort to keep his eyes closed and his empty hands lying loosely in his lap. What sudden bout of insanity, he wondered grimly, had possessed him to put himself in her hands? He had a gut-wrenching feeling he was about to pay for that mistake with his short-lived freedom.

Chapter 6

"Don't tell me the road up ahead is out, too, officer," Kelsey called. "We're going to the big do at the Hanrahans'. Bill here has had a tough night in surgery. Are we the first ones here?"

"No, miss. A carload of you came through earlier. I'm afraid you'll have to take the next turnoff and go the long way around to the Hanrahan place. Might stop in myself later for some barbecue. Don't expect they'll get the usual crowd this year."

"We're lucky we made it at all." Ben marvelled at the cheery smile he could hear in Kelsey's voice. "Thanks, officer. See you later."

When she told him it was safe to open his eyes, he straightened in the seat and let out a shaky breath.

"Lord, woman. You've got even more nerve than I gave you credit for."

"You're surprised? Aren't you the one who claimed that any reporter would walk over her own mother for a story?

All I did was drive through the police roadblock we had to pass."

She was referring to them as *we* Ben noticed. It gave him the warming feeling he wasn't alone. It had been a long time since he'd felt that anyone was on his side. He was still a long way from being sure of that. But whatever the motivation that had prompted this woman to place herself at his side, he was grateful. She'd certainly proved her worth.

Damn! He'd already forgotten his resolve to keep his personal feelings out of this. His hand had somehow found its way to the delicate fingers resting on the wheel. With brusque irritation at himself, he jerked his hand away.

"What was all that about this Bill fellow having a hard night in surgery?"

"I saw by the markings on the patrol car that the cop was county, not state police, and everyone for miles around knows the Hanrahans. The family has six sons. Two are doctors. Bill went to med school with my sister. We've been to a couple of their famous Memorial Day weekend bashes. Nobody can keep all the guys straight, so I figured you could pass for a Hanrahan. You have their dark hair and tall, lean build, and they're all handsome men—like you."

He'd spent two years handling talk strong enough to peel paint by showing no reaction whatever, but her unexpected compliment almost made him blush. It did make him break out in a flustered grin.

She smiled at his obvious embarrassment. "Well, you are attractive, you know."

He'd never considered himself any more than average-looking. But it was tough to stay distanced when provocations like that made him want to take Kelsey in his arms and show her just how arousingly attractive he found *her.*

She'd only spoken the truth, Kelsey allowed. At least about Ben's good looks. Up until the moment the rain-slickered cop had turned to her, she wasn't sure she could go through with the deception. The only reason she'd been able to do it, she realized, was because every moment spent with Ben was increasing her doubts about the verdict.

Benton Carlyle, she was beginning to believe, may have suffered a great wrong. And if that were true, he deserved the chance to right the life-destroying error, if he could. Even if helping to give him that chance meant putting herself on opposite sides with the police trying to capture him. And since the media had played its part in ruining his life, it was only right that a reporter should help him now.

Publicity had reversed the verdicts of other wrongly convicted people. If Ben were one of them, perhaps a story written by her could do the same for him. But she mustn't let her liking for the man overcome her common sense. All alone and miles from any help, she had to remain wary of him.

"Don't worry, Ben. I'll play fair with you. Frankly, I think the police are bound to find you eventually, but I won't be the one to turn you in. You can trust me."

"Trust you? No way, lady. I've already told you that I don't trust anybody or anything. Only naive people like you, who still see the world as safe, are fool enough to trust. I have no illusions left about the kind of world I live in. At most, I have confidence that your journalistic interest in me will keep you from turning me in. That's about as far as my trusting you goes."

She pulled the car to a halt. Irritation, even anger at his continuing lack of faith in her after she'd just proven herself to him, made some sense. Allowing the cynicism of a man who was no more to her than a story source to bruise her personal feelings did not. "*I'm* trusting *you*," she said, ridiculously wounded by his attitude.

Ben turned in the seat so that he was looking full into her eyes, less than a foot away. A small, enigmatic smile pricked at his lips. He reached over and curled his hand over her leg just above her knee. Not hard. His fingers rested on her lightly, but the skin beneath them on the inside of her thigh burned with their disturbing heat. Her heart started an erratic jumping. Her mouth went dry. She flicked out the tip of her tongue to wet her lips. Deliberately he lowered his gaze to her mouth and held it there.

"Ah!" he said, with the air of a professor who'd just caught a prize pupil in a stupid mistake. "You're forgetting that a judge and a jury found me so little to be trusted that they locked me up."

Lord! This man sure didn't make it easy. One minute he had her liking him—maybe too much—and the next he seemed to be going out of his way to frighten her. She wouldn't let him see that he'd succeeded. Or that his touch had ruffled her nerves, although his quiet chuckle indicated he might already know that. She slapped his hand away.

"I haven't forgotten that. You step out of line and you'll find yourself all alone out here. And may I remind *you* that without me you'd have been stopped back there." She pushed open the car door. "Here. I'm sure you want to take over the wheel again. It's all yours.

"Seems to me, Benton Carlyle," she added when they were once more on their way, "you should realize that you're darn lucky to have me on your side."

He didn't answer.

This woman, Ben thought, had proved that he was damned lucky to have her *on* his side. He wasn't sure, though, that "lucky" was the word he'd choose to describe having her continue close *by* his side.

Her disturbing presence was as much of a problem as it was a help. A more decisive man than he would just drive away and leave her by the side of the road. A smarter man wouldn't let his desire to keep her with him outweigh his knowledge that she was only a professional journalist along for the final payoff. And for sure a stronger man wouldn't have so much trouble holding to his vow to stop wanting her.

Today's wanderings and turnabouts were no more successful than last night's. She was gaining, Kelsey thought ruefully, a deep understanding of how an unfortunate laboratory rat must feel stumbling through a maze that seemed to have no exit.

Sandwiched in between programs of rousing country music and hymn singing, the escaped convict and his supposed hostage made the top of the next local news broadcast. Warning that Benton Carlyle was armed and should be considered dangerous, authorities gave detailed descriptions of both him and Kelsey, including her car's license number.

Kelsey had been concerned about Stephen and Cara's reaction when she hadn't shown up. Now that concern descended in force. "They must have gotten that information from my brother and sister, Ben. My parents are traveling in Europe, but Stephen and Cara will be worried sick about me. I want to call and let them know I'm all right."

Ben refused to let the somber look on his companion's face deter him. "No."

"I'll ask them not to let the police know I'm with you voluntarily. The three of us have always been tight. In the past we've always joined forces to support each other when the chips were down. Like when Stephen's wife died in a car accident, leaving him with three-year-old twin boys to bring up by himself. Or when Cara needed cosigners on a major loan to set up her medical office. They'll keep my secret, Ben. I know they will. I trust them."

The moment the words were out of her mouth, she knew what his answer would be.

Of course her folks would be worried, Ben admitted. If anything similar happened to *his* sister, he'd go nuts. He should never have allowed her to come with him. No matter that she'd been willing, he should have walked out of that motel leaving her chained to the bed, as he'd planned. But when it came to Kelsey Merrill, he mourned, his head was having trouble ruling his strong inclinations. But this time he wouldn't be swayed.

She might trust her family to keep the secret that she was with him voluntarily, but he sure didn't. Whether she wanted him to or not, he intended to protect her as best he could.

"No, Kelsey. If the police come to consider you an accomplice rather than an innocent hostage, I wouldn't put it past them to start shooting if they spot us."

"Not if we don't give them any cause to start shooting," she countered. Then she remembered the gun that lay in the glove compartment only a short reach from Ben's hand, and again hoped that her growing confidence in him wasn't a deadly mistake.

"I said no. And you agreed that what I say goes. If you have a problem with that, just let me know when you want out."

If she had any sense, Kelsey admitted, she'd get out right now. But she wasn't sure anymore if she were running on sense or sheer bullheadedness.

A few miles down the road, Ben slowed the car to a crawl as he studied a house set back among the trees. "Does that place look occupied to you?" he asked.

Kelsey gave the house the once-over. "The doors and windows are all closed, even though the weather is quite warm. I don't see any sign that anyone is around. Looks to me like the owners didn't come up this weekend."

"Which means they probably won't be back until next weekend."

"Why, Ben? Surely you're not planning to break into the place?"

He turned into the driveway and, approaching the house slowly, drove up and parked next to a rusty old pickup painted a bilious green.

"No. I'm planning to...uh...*borrow* that truck. We've got to ditch your car."

Kelsey's eyes flew wide. "We *what?*"

"You heard the APB, Kelsey. Not only are the police in West Virginia looking for us, they'll have brought in the authorities in Virginia, Maryland and Pennsylvania. The cops and anyone else who's interested have a description of this car and its tag number. As long as we stay in it we're sitting ducks. We've got to get rid of it."

"Get rid of it?" she wailed. "I haven't even finished paying for it yet."

"Let's put it this way. I'm taking the truck. You can do what you want. If you decide to take off, I'd appreciate it if you don't tell the cops where I am."

She wished Ben wouldn't keep urging her to leave. It only pointed out the not merely embarrassing, but hurtful, fact that she was a lot more anxious to stay with him than he was to have her along.

"But how can we borrow the pickup? We don't have the keys."

"No problem. A man can get quite an interesting education in the pen. Like how to hot-wire a vehicle. But first I have to get into it. I'd rather not smash a window. Do you by any chance have a wire clothes hanger in your suitcase?"

Kelsey nodded and morosely fetched the hanger. While Ben fiddled at the car window, Kelsey walked around and inspected the vehicle. "I don't know." She kicked dubiously at one of the oversize tires. "This truck looks a beat-up wreck. I doubt if it'll get us very far."

"From where I sit, Kelsey, we don't have a lot of choice."

Ben was right. They didn't have any choice. She gritted her teeth. His earlier observation that she'd do anything for a story sure turned out to have been right on target.

They weren't just *borrowing* the vehicle, she admitted. And she'd eventually face a day of reckoning with her prickly conscience about several things she'd been doing lately. But Ben's survival came first. She'd deal with her scruples later.

He succeeded in breaking into the truck and picked up the tire iron among the tools scattered on the floor behind the seat. She heard the metallic crunch that broke the lock on the steering wheel. He bent under the dash to pull out wires, and a few seconds later the engine choked to life. Ben's dark head speared over the top of the seat, his brows lifted in triumph.

"You're bringing me luck, Kelsey. This thing has a four-wheel drive that'll take us onto some of the worst back roads. Right where I'd like to be."

Without much enthusiasm, she threw him a thumbs-up.

"We don't want to leave your car here, Kelsey. No point in making things easy for the cops. Follow me in the Toyota. I'll look for someplace where we can hide it. You might stand a chance of getting it back sometime."

The possibility cheered her a little. She slid her bags into the back of the pickup and followed Ben down a nearby dirt road. She parked the car in among some trees where she hoped it wouldn't be found for a while. Marking its location, she wrote the directions down in her notebook while trying not to think that the little red car she loved was probably gone for good.

"This old thing can't be worth much," Kelsey said as she hopped into the cab of the truck. "But I'll track down the owners and send them a check right after we get your problems straightened out."

"Stop it, Kelsey. Stop pretending that there's a snowball's chance in hell that my life will be straightened out anytime soon. Even I don't believe that."

"If I'm whistling in the dark, Ben, so what? It can't hurt to have one of us hold to a positive attitude." She was perfectly aware of the formidable obstacles they faced. But if she gave in to her fears about overcoming them, she'd be of no use to either Ben or herself.

Ben shifted into reverse. The truck's gears protested with an ominous scraping sound. They'd be lucky, Kelsey mused worriedly, if the vehicle held up until they made it out of the mountains.

Ben twisted and stretched his arm out along the seat behind her as he took his bearing through the cab's rear window.

"Then you're on your own," he said, carefully guiding the truck back up to the road. "Optimism was ground out of me a long time ago. All I've got left is stubbornness."

"All right, then. Let's cut a deal. You do all the worrying and I'll do all the hoping. Fair enough?"

Her quip brought the hint of a smile to her driver's lips. He shot her a sheepish glance. "Hey, partner. Sorry I snapped at you just then."

"Go ahead if it makes you feel any better."

"It didn't. You did."

"Don't worry about it. This situation we're caught in is enough to make anyone nervous. Even a hard case like you."

She had him pegged right, Ben conceded. He *was* a hard case. Since he'd climbed out of the black pit the jury's verdict had plunged him into, he refused to let anyone or anything ever dent his emotions again. And that went double for Kelsey Merrill. He'd growled at her because it made him angry that he could feel so guilty about making her leave her car behind, even though he had to. He didn't like to be reminded that he was making life tough for an innocent bystander. At least, that's what she'd been when she'd had the misfortune to run into him.

He certainly didn't share her optimism that everything would turn out all right, but he couldn't help but find it touching. She held a hopeful confidence about life that had dropped from him long ago. The five years he had on her felt like a hundred. He was old in a way he hoped she would never understand. He wanted her never to learn that in the blink of an eye life could turn into a nightmare the morning sun wouldn't wipe away.

"We have to stop for gas," he said, as they came up on a country store sporting a single, old-fashioned pump of cheap, off-brand gas. "The tank's almost empty."

"Maybe you should get out here and wait out of sight while I take care of the fill-up."

"You're used to an automatic. I don't think you could stall out the pickup to stop where you want it to stop and then easily start it up again. There's no one at the pump. I'll take care of the gas, you run in and pick us up some food."

"All right. I never thought I'd hear myself say it, but I'm getting tired of candy bars and soda."

It wasn't easy for her to ignore the telephone just inside the store, but she'd given Ben her word that he was in charge.

With the truck gassed up and the supplies loaded, she scooted back onto the passenger seat. "I only have a hundred and eighty-seven dollars left, and I can't use my credit cards. At least, not around here where they might recognize my name. So unless you've got a few hundred bucks of the Carlyle fortune stashed in your pockets, we're going to run out of money fairly soon."

"Two years ago I could have walked into any place of business in the country and bought just about anything I wanted. Right now I have ten dollars to my name. They don't let you bring a fat wallet into prison."

"Well, let's look on the bright side. We have enough supplies to keep us for a few days, and we've passed the police roadblock." She cast her driver a hopeful glance. "Wouldn't you say things are looking reasonably good?"

"Don't let that chronic optimism of yours get out of hand, girl," he said dryly. "We've passed one roadblock. There'll be others. For sure they'll be waiting at highway ramps, so we can't use those. We have to get down to the valley to reach a through road, and along the river we'll probably run into flooding worse than anything we've seen so far. Things will only look good to me when I'm long gone from West Virginia.''

A few minutes later Kelsey's hopefulness washed away in the watery barrier that lay directly ahead of them on a stretch of low-lying road. The wide, muddy torrent cascading across the road was much too strong to chance driving across. It effectively shut down any further escape in this direction.

Ben struck the wheel with his fist. ''Well, that's pulled the plug on us for today.'' He gave a deep sigh of frustration. ''We can't go forward and we sure as hell can't go back. We'll just have to park somewhere and wait it out. If we don't get any more rain, that flooding may subside by morning. Let's hope the road's still there when it does.'' He threw the truck into reverse and swung it around. ''I'll run down that side road back there and try to find a deserted spot to hole up in for the night.''

With very little traffic on the roads and in miles of heavily forested mountains, it wasn't too hard to find an isolated spot to make camp.

''The cops have a description of that suit you're wearing, Ben, and it's in pretty bad shape, so I bought you a pair of jeans and a shirt.'' She handed him the clothes. ''Not exactly designer apparel, I'm afraid.''

''Blue pants, blue shirt.'' Ben shook out the folded shirt. ''Looks just like my prison uniform. I'll feel right at home.''

''Oh, gosh! I'm sorry. I never thought—I should have picked up the plaid shirt instead.''

''Relax, Kelsey. I was just kidding you. It was smart of you to think of new clothes for me. Thanks.''

In the day's heat, he'd already taken off his jacket, soiled and torn across the shoulders. He shrugged out of his shirt, and with complete nonchalance unzipped his pants and stepped out of them.

She couldn't help running her eyes over the hard, well-defined planes of his naked chest and the long, strong columns of his legs. An ill-considered move that unfortunately reminded her of his pulse-pounding hold in the motel room. She hoped he wouldn't notice the tinge of color she could feel warming her cheeks. But she didn't look away. Reaching for the jeans, he happened to glance her way.

"Oh. Sorry," he said. "I've had absolutely no privacy for such a long time I forgot that gentler souls still prefer it." He stepped behind the truck cab, which screened him from the waist down. A little late. She'd already enjoyed a heart-flipping stare at his hard, lean-hipped body.

"Don't worry about it," she said, feigning disinterest. "You're not exactly the first man I've seen without his pants."

"Oh? How many have there been? Just in round figures." Ben tried to tell himself he wasn't seriously interested in the answer. In fact, he wasn't sure whether he wanted to hear that there were plenty, which would tell him one thing about her, or that there were few, which would tell him another.

Kelsey shrugged. "I have a brother, remember? Do the jeans fit?"

"A little big. Not much. Apparently you have a good eye for judging a man's size."

If he meant that comment as anything but a straightforward compliment, she studiously took it as such. "I guessed at your size in relation to Stephen. You're a little taller, a little leaner in the hips."

Deliberately switching her attention to the trees edging the small clearing, she folded her arms and leaned against the side of the pickup. "You're in remarkably good shape for a man long confined in a small space," she observed with studied indifference. "How did you manage that?"

"I exercise as much as I can in my cell, work in the prison metal shop and take on the toughest physical jobs they're willing to give me."

"With your education, I'm surprised they didn't assign you to the prison hospital, or the library."

"I asked for heavy work. Come the night's lockdown there's a lot to be said for a good case of exhaustion." Buttoning up the cheap blue chambray shirt, he walked back into her view.

"We'd better set some guidelines so that my unsavory prison habits won't bring on an attack of the vapors. Ladies to the left. Gents to the right."

"I haven't come down with an attack of the vapors in some time," she assured him. She'd come pretty close, though, once or twice. Like when he'd spread himself on top of her in bed last night.

When she returned from her hike into the woods, she found Ben standing motionless in front of the truck and peering into the trees.

"What is it, Ben? Surely there can't be any cops out there."

"I'm not checking for cops," he said without turning around. "I'm watching the squirrels. Come over here and look." She went to stand beside him. He bent a little and absently fit his arm around her shoulder to draw her into the right position on the same line of sight as his. "In that big oak over there. See?" He pointed. "About halfway up."

Squirrels? The man was practically quivering with excitement over watching a couple of squirrels chase each other around on a tree?

"Cute little devils, huh? I don't usually get to see this kind of thing."

Oh, Lord! He was doing it to her again. Tears stung into her eyes at the reminder of the kind of empty, restricted life he'd been forced to lead for so long. She quickly blinked away the mist so he wouldn't see.

"I figure the big one is ready to set up housekeeping," he added with a chuckle. "But it looks like the little lady squirrel isn't quite convinced yet."

"Yes," Kelsey said around the catch in her throat. "They are cute."

She loved having his arm snug around her in this easy way. She loved seeing his face bright with interest and enjoyment, instead of expressionless control. She loved hearing him talk without strain, without that usual note of cool distance in his voice. The strong personal feelings for him she kept vigorously denying were surging forward at breakneck speed.

One of the squirrels scampered to the tip of the branch and sailed off into another tree. The second dashed after her. The furry little beasts had disappeared, but Ben's arm still rested lightly around her shoulders. She looked up at him as he continued to search for the animals. The soft smile the squirrels had brought to his face so melted her heart, she felt her own mouth lifting into that selfsame curve.

He glanced down at her and seemed startled to find her so close. The surprise didn't move him to release her. If anything, his hold grew tighter, the look in his eyes softer.

The slight increase of the pressure of his fingers at her shoulder was enough to encourage Kelsey to drop her head into the hollow between his shoulder and his chest. The resting place turned out to be every bit as comfortable as it looked. As a bonus, her forehead fell close enough to his mouth that he barely had to move to brush his lips against her brow. The feathery touch of his fingers over the sensitive skin behind her right ear persuaded her to tilt her head to offer him her lips.

He needed no second invitation. His mouth covered hers, dropping a delicious line of kisses from one corner of her lips to the other. It was amazingly easy to ignore the red flags her mind flung up as she moved into his encircling arms and wrapped her own around him.

This time the kisses she unhesitatingly accepted and re
turned were slow and deliberate, and their sweetness buck
led her knees. She had no fear of falling. Ben's arms held he
fast. This time his spellbinding embrace wasn't meant sim
ply to subdue her. But the tender foraging of his heated lips
the seducing comfort of his cradling arms, the excitin
nearness of his solidly muscled body, held a power ever
more invincible than his sheer physical strength.

The warmth of Kelsey's loving response to his kiss jolte
a hot wave of desire through Ben. She felt so damn good i
his arms. With a groan of satisfaction, he nuzzled agains
the side of her neck, his hands smoothing slowly over he
back.

"Holding you like this feels wonderful to me, Kelsey. You
can have no idea what it's like in prison." He spoke so qui
etly, so haltingly, Kelsey wondered if he were trying not t
speak at all. "I hope you never find out—not even for
story. Inside, there's precious little simple human touching
And nothing that comes anywhere close to this." He molde
her softness closer against him. "Behind the walls, each ma
has to protect his space. It's the only thing left him. So, be
sides the big cages they keep us in, we all build our ow
small invisible cages around ourselves. You don't touch
anyone else, and you don't let them touch you."

Kelsey shuddered. She could hardly conceive of such
deadly isolation. She was definitely a toucher, and Stev
claimed she'd hug anything that moved.

This time, Ben thought, the woman in his arms couldn'
be responding to him out of fear. She'd shown no resis
tance to his kisses, had returned them as if she liked them a
much as he.

Unless... A doubt wormed its way into his mind. Un
less, because he'd been away from women so long, he reall
couldn't tell a wanting kiss when he was given one. Unless
his own wanting was leading him to misread what for he
was completely meaningless. She didn't really seem the type

but maybe her aim in responding to him was simply to keep him happy until she'd finished her story. God knew she'd already dared more for that story than simply returning a few kisses.

He'd made a supremely dangerous error in judgment by bringing Kelsey with him, Ben decided. She kept making him forget that he'd escaped not because he needed a woman, but because he had a job to do.

He couldn't deny, though, that even with the major test of self-control she posed for him, he wasn't sorry she was with him. He couldn't regret meeting her. Not even when holding her only left him with a raw ache.

In prison, he'd faced men who could give him a beating, even claim his life, and had handled those situations. But he had the uneasy feeling that this woman would claim his soul if he let her.

He wasn't ready to leave himself open to that. He'd learned how fragile life could be. He knew all too well that she—the sweet respite she offered—could be snatched away from him in a heartbeat. He'd be a fool to take the risk.

Being held in Ben's arms felt blazingly wonderful, Kelsey allowed. How was it, she wondered, that when she was working so hard to maintain her distance, she continually ended up in his arms?

But this exciting embrace, she knew, was pushing dangerously at the borders of a safe relationship between them. Ben must have recognized that, too. His arms loosened. Hers could not.

"Kelsey, you don't have to worry that I'll . . . cause any problems for you." Cause problems? She wasn't sure just what he meant, but she didn't like the chill she now felt between them. "I've been locked up for a long time. It's only natural that I . . . To put it bluntly, I know that any feelings I might have for you can't really mean anything." He unwound her arms from him with a suddenness that left her feeling bereft. "Just as I know that you're only with me because you're on the track of a career-building story. So I guess we're both lucky that you're way too smart a lady to develop any senselessly romantic ideas about me.''

Smart? Her unstoppable feelings for Ben didn't have anything to do with smart or stupid. They were just there, a force beyond her command, like the wind and the rain. She envied him the strong-willed control that could so easily rein in any unwanted feelings.

But her problems in handling her emotions weren't important compared to the life-threatening difficulties he faced. The painfully simple delight he took in watching the squirrels gave her a heart-wrenching glimpse into the horrors of life in prison, and left her aching to do something more for him.

If only he'd let her, she could help give him a future other than the bleak prospect looming ahead for him. She was convinced a positive story about his bravery in the diner would start that process by opening him to public sympathy. The drumbeat of publicity had caused authorities to take another look at other cases of mistaken conviction. Why not his? If nothing else, winning public opinion over to his side might make a lot of difference in how the police treated him after he was caught. She hated to think how they might punish an escaped prisoner.

''Ben.'' She laid her hand on his arm. ''Let me get on the phone to my editor. Let me tell people about the man you really are, the man they don't know yet. It could help. It could—'' Ben's short, harsh curse cut her off.

He grimaced and jerked himself away. The woman's brain-fogging kisses had brought him perilously close to forgetting who she was, who he was. Fortunately he could always count on her to remind him.

''You can never let go of the job, can you?'' he bit out. ''And as I noted once before, you never forget the bottom line. I have a lot of experience with that. My father was the same way.''

"No, Ben, it's not like that at all." It hurt that he could think it was.

"No story about me has ever helped," he reminded her, his voice icy. "And a story from you now would only make my escape tougher. You don't seem to understand that I'd be a lot better off if everyone forgot about me."

"But, Ben—" Kelsey gave up. Ben's face was glacial. His mouth was set hard, as if he'd broken a rule and was determined not to break it again.

A darn good resolution, she thought. One she'd make for herself—again.

Chapter 7

Normally she liked picnics in the woods, Kelsey thought. And the setting was perfect. Clumps of lacy fern sprouted beneath tall oaks lush with bright spring foliage. And high arching branches of white blossoms tumbled like great swaths of bridal veil amid the undergrowth.

But dining on plain sandwiches of salami and cheese washed down with small boxes of juice wasn't a whole lot of fun when you were afraid the idyllic scene might erupt at any moment into hordes of shouting, gun-toting police. Not to mention when you faced an uncomfortable night sleeping in a truck because you had no other choice.

She'd always had choices, so she'd always taken the availability of choice for granted. Since meeting Ben Carlyle, those choices had narrowed considerably. But she couldn't feel too sorry for herself when his options were even more painfully narrow—and had been for some time.

The mossy ground was too damp to sit on. She opened the truck door on the passenger side and angled herself onto the seat to munch her sandwich. Ben prowled around with his sandwich in his hand, frequently darting searching looks over his shoulder like a point man in a military squad sent out to reconnoiter enemy territory. The intimidating stillness he'd worn when she'd first seen him had given way to a non-stop edgy pacing.

That stirring in her heart whenever she looked at him, Kelsey told herself, was no more than eagerness to get to her office computer. It would be foolish for any woman to allow herself to get too close to a man who might have to spend either years in prison or the rest of his life on the run. Not that she stood in any danger of doing that, of course, she added quickly. Benton Carlyle was providing her with a doozy of a story. And that was where her interest in him stopped.

She knew scads of men, most of them pals, a couple a little more than that. One or two would make for a good intimate relationship, should she want one. But none exerted the unwanted yet irresistible pull on heart and mind that Ben had done simply by walking through a door and into her life.

She tossed the last bit of crust on the ground for the family of cardinals swooping through the area, and again reached for her notepad. The copious notes she'd already taken in the form of speed writing she'd devised were easily legible to no one but herself.

"Since we still have a couple of hours of daylight left, Ben, let's continue with the interview."

Ben glanced back at her and nodded, but kept up his antsy pacing. "Sure. Go ahead." He wasn't quite as eager to resume the interview as he sounded. But talking held the advantage of crowding out unsettling thoughts about his beautiful companion.

Kelsey hesitated to bring up what had to be a painful subject for him, but sooner or later they had to talk about it. There was no way to question a man convicted of murder without discussing that killing. "Will it hurt you too much to talk about the day your father was killed?'' she asked gently.

Ben shrugged. ''Don't worry about it. I don't let anything hurt me anymore.''

He probably believed that, Kelsey thought. But from what she'd glimpsed in his eyes, she wouldn't lay odds on it being the truth.

''Look at it this way, Ben. I readily admit that you're doing me a big favor in granting me this interview. But maybe our talking about what happened can do something for you, too. Perhaps my more objective eye can provide a fresh perspective on this whole sad affair.''

She was becoming about as objective with Ben Carlyle as she was about her own family. But she really did believe that her professional training might help them come up with something he may have missed.

''Not likely,'' he said. ''A whole lot of people, including a jury, looked at the case from every angle and saw nothing but my guilt.'' He finished off his sandwich and put the empty juice box down on the truck bed. ''But at this point I'm ready to grasp at any straw.''

They needed a lot more than a straw, Kelsey thought. Overturning a conviction was a tough proposition. Nothing less than a solidly planted tree trunk would hold them up while they attempted it.

''I remember some of the details of the trial, Ben, but I'd like to hear them from you. As I recall, the murder took place at some kind of gathering at the estate, didn't it?''

''Yes. Every July fourth, my father threw a barbecue for all our employees. He brought in a country band, gave away TVs and stereos as game prizes, the works. Usually the outing was a lot of fun for us all.''

Kelsey didn't have any trouble filling in the blank. ''But not this last time.''

''No. Not this last time. My troubles started when Dad stood up in front of the crowd and announced that he was retiring and I would take over as CEO of the company, effective immediately. We'd had a running battle about that, but I made my position perfectly clear. In fact, I'd have been long gone if Dad hadn't gotten so ill that I had to take over more and more of the day-to-day operations. But I warned everyone that my being there was only temporary."

"Your father's illness," Kelsey offered thoughtfully, "must have been very threatening to a man used to running everything and everybody in his life. Maybe he felt that having you, as his chosen successor, take over helped him maintain some semblance of control."

Ben looked dubious. "It's difficult for me to think of my father as a frightened man, Kelsey. But looking back, I suppose some of his more emotional reactions could have been read as fear."

Strange, Ben thought, to think that his father might have shared some of the same kinds of fears that had haunted him during his trial—and still did.

"Anyway, after Dad made his announcement I tried to defuse the embarrassing situation by joking." Ben looked up into the cloudy sky that still threatened rain, and gave his head a little shake. "But, as usual, he refused to let go. I had no choice but to bring the disagreement I'd tried to keep private into the open. Dad wasn't one to take kindly to having someone flatly contradict him at any time, let alone in public. He lost it. Our disagreement turned violent. He always used to carry around a golf club, although he seldom took the time to play the game. And he actually struck me with the shaft of that club."

Kelsey didn't think Ben was even aware that he was rubbing his upper arm, as if he could still feel the blow.

"It was a nasty situation and everyone watching was stunned. It had been a long time since I'd let my father or anyone else hit me. And I'll tell you frankly, Kelsey, it wasn't easy just to stand there and take it. But I simply left and went back to the house to say goodbye to Mother before heading back to my own home in Fairmont."

He stopped for a moment to kick at a small rock in his path.

"A few minutes later I walked downstairs to find Dad lying on the living room floor in a pool of blood. The side of his head was sm-smashed—"

Damn! Ben thought. By now he ought to be used to recounting all this. He'd had to do it often enough. Just get the facts out, he told himself. Don't think about the feelings. Don't let the grief, the rage, the fear come back. Those useless emotions had overwhelmed him once. They'd done him no good then, and they'd only get in the way of what he had to do now. He forced control into his voice.

"There are still gaps in my memory about the death scene," he continued. "It just seems like one minute I was standing at the bottom of the stairs, and the next I'd dropped to my knees beside my father's body. Now, anybody who's ever seen a murder movie," he said dryly, "knows enough not to touch anything at the scene of a crime—least of all the murder weapon. I can't actually recall stupidly picking up that putter, its metal foot smeared thick with blood. I just remember how obscene it looked lying across my father's face."

Ben spoke with an icy dispassion that made Kelsey shiver. Didn't the man feel anything while remembering such a brutal scene? She still got shaky remembering the death of her brother's wife. And that had been in a hospital, and they'd all been prepared for it.

"The coroner said my father had been struck several times. This wasn't the case of a single blow delivered in the heat of an argument. Someone deliberately kept wielding that putter until my father was dead." Behind his back, so his interrogator wouldn't see, Ben clenched his hands.

Just listening to Ben's account was giving her a pain in the stomach. How could he calmly go on describing the scene as if he were reading from a newspaper article?

"That was why," he continued, "I never believed my lawyer's assurances that he could get a plea of self-defense to work, even if I'd been willing to go along with it. I'd like to erase that whole scene from my memory. But I'll never forget looking up to see the county sheriff standing next to me, his hand hovering over his gun and his eyes glued to the bloody golf club in my hand."

He gave a short, raw laugh. "I should have realized right then that the ground had just fallen out from under me. But actually it took me a little while to understand that I was damn near everyone's first choice as my father's killer."

As he strode past her for the umpteenth time in the circular path he was wearing into the ground, he held up a hand and counted off on his fingers. "Means, motive and opportunity. The three requisites for a murder suspect. I had them all. And the sheriff knew it. He'd seen the violent argument between my father and me earlier."

Her subject wasn't even looking at her as he recounted the events that in a way had destroyed his own life as well as his father's. Mostly he just stared off into the distance like a bored student reciting a lesson he'd already learned by rote. She couldn't imagine herself in similar circumstances ever becoming inured to such a terrible scenario.

But then, she didn't possess Ben's emotional toughness. A toughness that kept him fighting for his life long after the battle was lost. It was that toughness that had drawn her to him as much as anything. Whether because she thought that rugged self-sufficiency deserved recognition or just out of plain curiosity to find out if there was some chink in the armor.

"How come the sheriff was there, Ben?"

"He'd come up to the house to report to my father on the background check of Ricky Lee Jackson that Dad had requested."

"Ricky Lee Jackson. I don't remember the name. Did it come up at the trial?"

"No. Ricky Lee is now my sister's husband. At the time he was a company shipping clerk who'd struck up a relationship with Bonnie. Dad and I had always been very protective of her. Perhaps too much so. With the result that my sister was a very naive and somewhat spoiled eighteen-year-old. Everyone but she could see that Ricky Lee—a high school dropout, by the way—was angling for the good life via the boss's daughter."

Ben let out an exasperated sigh. "It only infuriated Bonnie when I told her that, and it didn't change her mind about him one whit. A good-looking young man was telling her what she wanted to hear. She wasn't interested in listening to the cautions of an older brother."

Bonnie, Ben thought, wasn't the only member of his family who had trouble seeing what was right in front of his eyes. The sympathetic blue gaze he could sense on him even when he wasn't looking at Kelsey kept tempting him into fooling himself about what he meant to her. Although why the hell he should be wasting any thought whatever on what he meant to her—since he couldn't let himself feel anything for her, beyond simple gratitude—he didn't understand.

"Eighteen-year-old girls see what they want to see in a man," Kelsey offered, remembering her first year in college. And teenage girls had no monopoly on that position, she dolefully admitted. She kept wishing the softness that swept over Ben's eyes from time to time when he looked at her indicated she meant something to him other than just a helping hand in his escape. But the cool, almost angry way he looked at her most of the time wouldn't let her fool herself that he had any other motivation.

No, she corrected. That wasn't quite true. He'd made no bones about wanting her in his bed. The small, dull ache that had begun creeping into her heart lately started up again. She rubbed at the center of her chest.

"Are you feeling all right, Kelsey?"

She was surprised that a man so engrossed in the sky, the trees, the ground beneath his feet would even notice her small action. "It's nothing. Just a little indigestion. Go on about the relationship between your sister and Ricky Lee."

"You're sure?" Ben asked, and she nodded. "Very well then. Dad did everything he could to break up that relationship, and I seconded his efforts. The boy was so rough I even feared for my sister's safety with him."

"Ricky Lee sounds like a pretty good suspect himself," Kelsey observed.

"That's what I thought, too. But Dad hadn't so much as spoken to him at the barbecue. The kid evidently knew enough to keep out of his way. But the fact that no one could actually place Ricky Lee at the house at the proper time doesn't mean he wasn't there."

"You said that pretty strongly, Ben. Do you believe he *was* there?"

"I can't say that he was or he wasn't. All I know is that someone got away with murder. And it could have been Ricky Lee."

Kelsey hadn't thought about it before: Someone got away with murder. She'd focused more on the fact that Ben may have been locked up in error than that the real killer was still running around free. She shuddered. Free, perhaps, to kill again.

"The sheriff was under a lot of pressure to close the case. Henry Carlyle was one of the area's most prominent citizens. Important people wanted to see his killer locked up quickly, even if that killer was another prominent citizen, like his son. I can understand how it may have been easier for everyone to accept a killing that occurred during a violent family argument. Less frightening, maybe, than the idea that their own community harbored a cold-blooded murderer."

"But didn't the authorities check out any other suspects?"

"They did some investigating, but I was made-to-order as their prime suspect. At first I couldn't figure out what was going on. I was pathetically eager to cooperate with law-enforcement officials. I should have kept my mouth shut. But I kept thinking that if only they knew this next thing about such-and-such, it would convince them they had the wrong man."

Ben halted and hooked his thumbs into the jeans pockets at his hips. "Of course, it never did." He stared off into the deepening shadows among the trees. "They were only interested in facts that fit their own already formed conclusions, and ignored anything that might suggest otherwise. My honesty about the bad blood between my father and me only gave them more ammunition to use against me."

He turned and slowly walked back toward her.

"Back then I made the mistake of relying on others to track down my father's killer. That didn't work. Now my only chance to get out from under this nightmare is to find him myself. That's why I ran when I had the chance."

That wasn't the only reason he'd escaped, though. He used to think of himself as strong. But he wasn't strong enough to spend any more time in a cage without losing everything that made him the Ben Carlyle he wanted to remain. He couldn't take any more of the joyless existence that was destroying his identity and deadening his soul.

If he failed to clear himself, and if fate gave him the chance, he'd live as a fugitive. That idea didn't frighten him nearly as much as the thought of becoming the animal more years behind bars would make of him. At least he'd still be himself in whatever new life he could fashion.

Since he'd been the one to bring up the subject of his escape, Kelsey decided it was time to voice the thought that had been troubling her all day. "You're probably not going to like what I'm about to say, Ben, but I feel obliged to say it."

He stopped abruptly in front of her, his eyes narrowed. "Then go ahead."

"Maybe you should reconsider your escape. That gash on your head is still swollen. I'm worried that it could turn sour on you and put you in serious trouble."

"I'm fine," he said with dangerous composure.

She lifted a delicately arched brow in open skepticism.

"I'm surprised that prison hasn't made you a better liar, Ben. Several times today I noticed you clenching your teeth, and it's not all because you hate talking to me. You're still in pain. You can deny it all you want, but it's obvious to me that you need professional medical care."

"Right now a bump on the head is the least of my concerns. I'm a convicted killer. I can't just walk up to a hospital and ask for help. My vision is perfectly clear, and I'm having no trouble thinking or talking, so If I have a concussion, it probably isn't bad. And as for putting myself in serious trouble, what do you call this?"

She hadn't expected to change his mind. But besides her concern about his wound, what he'd said earlier about the possibility of the police opening up on him with their weapons really had her worried. Turning himself in would be difficult, but it might save his life.

"If you decide to give yourself up, I give you my word I'll continue on with the investigation of your case. I'll work with your family and your lawyer to make the authorities take another look at it."

He shook his head forcefully. "I'm going to handle that job myself. And I'm sure as hell not going to quit under anything short of getting slapped back in solitary. No, Kelsey. The only way they're going to get me back to prison is to drag me there kicking and screaming. I have my freedom and I intend to hang on to it."

"But, Ben," she persisted, "can you really call what you have now freedom?"

"It's a whole lot closer to freedom than what I had back in prison. But you're right, this isn't real freedom. A man with real freedom has no ties, no bonds of any kind to restrict him."

His definition of freedom shocked her. "What do you mean, no ties? Surely you can't mean no personal ties?"

"That's exactly what I mean."

"But...but not even to your family, your friends?"

"We've never been all that close as a family. Not the way you seem to be with yours. And most of the people I considered friends didn't stick around too long after I was indicted for murder."

Kelsey was having trouble getting her brain around the concept of freedom as meaning no love, no caring, no connections to anyone. Surely she didn't understand him correctly.

"But what if you should meet...well...a special woman and fall in love? Wouldn't you want a strong bond with her? Wouldn't you want her to offer you commitment and give her yours?"

"I thought I was in love once," he said in bland dismissal. "The woman married my brother. And as for commitment? As far as I can see, commitment only means you tie yourself to someone else's ideas about who you should be, what you should do. I've got plenty of commitment...to myself...to my goals."

Any woman fool enough to fall in love with this man, Kelsey thought, had better not expect much return on that investment of her emotions.

"If I ever get my real freedom back, I'll never again let anyone else call the shots in my life. I had to take enough orders in prison to last me a lifetime."

Ben sounded as if he'd carved that resolution in stone. He stood with his legs spread, his fisted hands pulled to his hips. Like a challenger daring all comers to take him on. Like a knight sworn to guard a drawbridge. She saw absolutely no give in his stance. And even the gathering dusk didn't soften the sharp, grim lines of a face that signaled, *They shall not pass.*

Up until now she'd been caught up in the adventure of the situation, in the excitement of tracking an important story, of possibly finding some way to change the verdict that trapped an innocent man. A possibly innocent man, she reminded herself. Could a man able to recount such an awful incident as the murder of his father with scarcely a break in his voice really be the man she hoped he was? On the other hand, would a man cold-blooded enough to take his father's life risk his own to save his prison guard? All she had were questions. Solid answers were a lot harder to come by.

A cheerless weariness came over her.

"If you feel that way, Ben, you should have no trouble handling the rootless life of a fugitive. But I couldn't live like that. My ties to those I love are strong. They're the most important things in my life. They always will be. I'm not as self-sufficient as you. Frankly, the idea of being completely alone with no ties to anyone terrifies me."

A life without emotional ties wouldn't be too cheerful a proposition, Ben conceded. But allowing himself to become too close to anyone, only to find his trust again betrayed, was an even more frightening thought. And falling in love with a woman who threatened all his painfully worked-out convictions, a woman who'd taken him on as a kind of professional charity case, a woman to whom he could offer absolutely nothing but danger and trouble—now, there was a thought that made his hair stand on end.

"It seems to me," Kelsey said, unable to look at him anymore, "that a person who equates freedom with emotional isolation carries his own kind of prison around with him.''

"Please,'' he droned. "Spare me the pop psychology. If you'd gone through what I've been through the past two years—and even longer than that—in the added six months between my father's death and my trial, you might feel the same way I do.''

"I didn't say you haven't ample cause for your views. I just say I'd never have the desire or the courage to live by them.''

She didn't want to think about any of it anymore. And she was rapidly losing light enough to write. She slid her notebook back into her bag and stood up to shake out the kinks from spending so much time sitting down. "I'm tired. It's still early, but I think I'll try to get some sleep. Not much else to do, anyway.'' She gazed dubiously at her limited choices for a bed. "I wonder which will be more uncomfortable, sitting up in the cab or lying down on a metal truck bed.''

"Better make it the cab. At least we'll stay dry if it starts to rain again.''

The setting sun had taken with it the day's heat. Kelsey folded her arms in front of her and tried to rub away the chill.

"Here,'' Ben said. "Take my jacket.'' He picked up the suit coat he'd laid over the side of the truck and came over to stand behind her to fit it over her shoulders. His arms lingered as he folded the jacket around her. The firm warmth at her back urged her to relax against him. She refused to give in to the temptation.

Ben pushed the truck seat back as far as it would go to give them as much stretch-out room as possible. Kelsey climbed in and tucked her legs under her in one corner of the cab, about as far away from where Ben would be sitting as she could get in the cramped space.

Ben opened the driver's door as if he were about to get in, then closed it again. "Think I'll stay out here and enjoy the stars for a while."

Kelsey glanced up at the darkened sky through the window. "What with the clouds, there aren't too many stars out tonight."

"I can see a few. And there's a moon." The better part of valor, he thought, was to wait until she was asleep before getting into that tiny space with her. Nerve-racking to think that the armor he'd so painfully encrusted over his personal feelings, she could tear away like paper.

He'd made that grandstand speech about freedom as much to reinforce his views to himself as to explain them to her. He needed to hold fast to his conviction that emotional bonds would obstruct him from carrying out his aims. He couldn't afford to let Kelsey's unnerving presence make him forget it.

Kelsey guessed it was about an hour later when Ben quietly opened the door and got into the truck. She pretended to be asleep when he shoved his legs under the steering wheel and laid his head back on the seat.

She was used to the blackness of night in the country and liked to lie in bed and listen to the natural night sounds of the deep forest. But this time the total darkness surrounding them and the sighing of the wind felt oppressive. And the distant cry of some animal made her feel lonely.

Strange, she thought. She'd felt closer to Ben last night when she'd been his prisoner than she did now when she was with him by choice.

Chapter 8

The loud chirping of birds awakened her, but she was in no hurry to open her eyes. Snuggled in warmth, she burrowed a little deeper into the comfortable pillow she lay on. Beneath the birdsong beat a quiet, repetitive thudding sound, its rhythm lulling and pleasantly familiar.

Awareness of anything but her contentment spread slowly. A slight movement of her firm pillow in the warmth surrounding her made her realize that she was nestled in a man's arms. She was still too fuzzy with sleep to remember how she'd got there, but she felt safe and warm and comfortable. Might as well just stay there and enjoy the rise and fall of his breathing a little while longer.

The man holding her shifted a little.

She murmured a sleepy protest and pressed closer. When he moved again, she pulled open her eyes on blue fabric—the chambray of Ben's shirt, she remembered. The fingers of her left hand had found their way between the buttons of his shirt and made themselves at home against his skin. She left them there.

A vague memory of a dream she'd had of seeking his arms during the night flickered through her mind. No dream at all, but reality. Her hips rested against the solidity of Ben's thigh. His arms held her cradled breast to breast with him, wedged in next to the steering wheel, her legs drawn up close to him on the seat. She was awake enough to recognize that her bed in Ben's arms was off-limits. But a person couldn't be blamed for what they did while asleep.

She felt his eyes on her and lifted her head a little to wish him good morning.

He was wide-awake, staring down at her, his gaze intense. Intimate. And so utterly fascinating it captured all her interest. She forgot to speak. Looking straight into the smoky depths of his eyes made her feel like she was floating dreamily within one of the gray mountain mists that drifted into the hollows at dusk.

She felt as if he were reading her, ferreting out secrets she didn't even know she had. A dangerous intrusion, but one she hadn't the will or the energy to fight. She couldn't move. Didn't want to move. The most important thing in her life at this moment was studying exactly how the gray of his eyes radiated in tiny striations from their dark pupils into a narrow edging of black.

A slow, thick heat seeped into her breasts, her thighs. His eyes still imprisoned hers, but somehow she was most aware of the perfect shape of his mouth. Pulsingly aware of how delicious its firm, sensuous lips had felt on hers last night...yesterday...whenever. She flicked the tip of her tongue over dry lips.

He blinked twice and his gaze released hers only to move slowly around her face. His dark brows were drawn together in puzzlement as if he'd never seen her before and was trying to figure out who she was. His gaze hooked on to her lips. They prickled into warmth, and trembled apart.

The disjointed thought arose that if he didn't kiss her soon, she might just melt away into the warm mist licking

at her skin. She would tell him that, but it would sound silly.
Besides, it took too much effort to talk. But she didn't have
to, after all.

He lowered his head and bonded his mouth to hers. His
lips ranged over hers, nipping and stroking and tugging her
fully awake to the hot, satisfying sweetness of it.

Her fingertips spasmed into the firm, heated flesh of his
chest. A fever of longing blossomed within her. She wanted
his mouth. She craved his tongue. She coveted more, more
of the full, exciting taste of him; more closeness to him;
more of his hand stroking fire down the curve of her hip.

He was giving her everything she desired. And still it
wasn't enough.

He slid his hand between her denim-covered thighs and
trailed it upward to sear against her femininity. She moaned
and involuntarily bent into his frustratingly barriered touch.

He snatched his hand away as if his fingers had just wan-
dered too close to an open flame.

"Kelsey!" His voice cut harshly through the heated, enveloping mist that blotted out perception of anything but
him. "Kelsey. No more of this."

Suddenly totally aware of what she'd come so close to
doing, she froze.

"It's morning," Ben said. "We have to make another try
at that road." His hold on her loosened. "Is there anything
for breakfast?"

Her heart still pounding furiously, Kelsey jerked herself
up. She hit her back against the steering wheel, the dull pain
a welcome jog back to reality.

"Yes." Still breathless, she tucked her blouse back into
the waistband of her jeans. "Yes, I'll get it."

She scooted out of the truck and leaned against the door
to haul in cooling drafts of fresh morning air.

All through a small meal of doughnuts and juice, neither
of them said a word about what had just happened between them. And Kelsey was glad of it. What Ben made of

their embrace, she had no idea. As for herself, she wasn't used to waking up in a man's arms. And she'd certainly had no previous experience with such an embarrassingly intimate gazing into any man's eyes.

She'd have liked to have been able to blame the whole unfortunate incident on Ben. After all, he'd been wide-awake while she'd still been fighting her way up from sleep. Fighting not very hard, she conceded. But he couldn't deny he'd had more of a chance to counter morning arousal than she.

But dumping everything off on him wouldn't work. Truth was, she loved everything he'd done. And she couldn't explain her continuing responses, totally unsuitable in the situation, to herself, let alone to him. So ignoring the whole thing seemed the best move.

"You'd better change into something else," Ben ordered. "A cop saw you in that outfit."

She was more than willing to get out of the grungy jeans and blouse she'd slept in for two nights. The light, flower-printed cotton dress she pulled out of her suitcase was badly wrinkled after being packed away for more than two whole days. But the creases didn't bother her as much as they might have before she'd tumbled into this nest of real problems.

"Are you a praying person, Kelsey?" Ben asked as he swung the truck back toward the flood that had blocked their way yesterday.

"When I need it."

"Then you'd better offer a prayer that the road ahead is now passable. In fact, you'd better pray that the road is still there."

It was. The force of the rushing water, though, had chewed away part of the road on one side and left the rest silted over with mud and rocks. Fortunately there was enough life left in the old four-wheel drive to get them through it.

"We may stand a better chance at escape today than we did yesterday," Kelsey offered, buoyed by their success in pushing through the restriction that looked so formidable yesterday. "By now the police might think you've slipped through their dragnet."

"Maybe. I wouldn't bet on it."

Silence might provide a niche for Ben to bring up the unwanted subject of the early morning's incident. She staved it off with talk. "This bright sunshine will do a lot to sop up the floodwaters."

"Good for the folks who live around here," Ben allowed. "Bad for us. More roads may be clear for us, but the less flooding the police have to deal with, the more they can beef up the search for the vicious murdering criminal on the loose."

Kelsey winced. "Don't talk about yourself like that, Ben."

"It's how they think of me." Weary resignation didn't sit well on such a strong face. It flashed away as quickly as it came.

"Well, I don't like to hear it. And it's not how I think of you." Even if Ben really had done what they said he did, she felt in her bones he wasn't at heart a vicious man.

Ben held his gaze quite deliberately on the road ahead. The less he looked at Kelsey, he'd decided, after she'd held him so damn mesmerized this morning, the better off he'd be. "I know you don't, although I haven't quite figured out why. You have even less to go on than people who'd known me for years and had no problem accepting the verdict."

He was grateful for her willingness to give him the benefit of the doubt, but wished she'd stop being so damn sympathetic. He didn't want any more reason to like the woman. He was having trouble enough just dealing with his desire for her.

Watching her wake up in his arms this morning had been so delightful, so arousing that he'd hardly been able to re-

strain himself from carrying her out of the truck and laying her down on the dewy grass to ravish her. It wasn't gallantry on his part that had prevented it, more like a terrified suspicion that if he gave her the chance, she'd get under his skin so deep he'd never be able to pry her out. The bewilderingly powerful feelings she roused in him warned that making love to her would be playing with fire. And more than just his fingers would get painfully singed.

"Reporters learn not to accept general wisdom at face value, Ben. Sometimes getting at the truth can take a lot of digging. And often what seems obvious turns out not to be truth at all."

That comment hit uncomfortably close to home, Ben was forced to grant. He could handle the idea that he'd brought her with him only as an assistant. If there were deeper truths involved, he didn't intend to dig for them.

"Is that how you see yourself, Kelsey? As a banner-carrying truth teller?" Preferring to keep her irked with him, he'd injected a dash of sarcasm into his voice.

She bristled. "What kind of crack is that?"

He smiled to himself. He'd pushed the right button. "No crack. From what I've seen of you, it wouldn't surprise me if you envisioned yourself as some kind of crusader for truth, justice and the American way. But the way I figure it, you're more open than others to the idea that the jury made a mistake simply because it will suit your purposes."

Her forehead creased in puzzlement. "My purposes?"

He nodded. "Sure. Your story will make a bigger splash—and result in a lot more fame for you—if you can end it with a strong claim of my innocence."

For a moment she looked confused. Then she gave a firm bob of assent. "Exactly," she bit out. That understandable truth she'd eagerly acknowledge, Kelsey thought. There were other less comprehensible verities hovering over her that she was working hard to hold at bay.

Maybe silence was better after all, she decided. When they talked they always seemed to end up on subjects that made her uncomfortable. She didn't have to worry anymore that he'd bring up this morning's kiss. Most likely he'd already forgotten about it. She only wished she could do the same.

But silence, she discovered, posed problems of its own. She tried to keep her eyes on scenic mountain views so beautiful and evocative they inspired song. But her gaze kept traveling back to the strong male hands guiding the wheel. She liked watching the quiet, competent way they moved. She tended to be more active when she drove, shifting her hands around on the wheel, tapping her fingers on it in time to the music, switching stations on the radio.

Something about the shape of the hard knob at Ben's wrist she found curiously appealing. How come she was so taken by such incidentals about a man, she wondered, when most women concentrated on a good-looking face, or well-muscled arms, or a nice tight masculine fanny? Not that she hadn't noticed that Ben possessed all those attractions.

She glanced down at the road twisting down the mountainside below them and grabbed his arm. "Ben, stop!"

He jammed his foot on the brake.

"Look down on the road below us, through those trees." He pulled up the hand brake and leaned over to peer through the window on her side of the truck. "It's hard to see through the thick foliage," she said, "but if you look to the left of that clump of pines you can just make out a couple of state police cars."

Ben muttered a curse. "Another roadblock."

"And this time we can't use the dodge that worked with the cop yesterday."

"No." He sighed. "Getting past this one will be a lot tougher."

Kelsey clasped her hands together tightly to hide their trembling. "I've got a bad feeling about this, Ben."

"Hey, girl," he said, spearing his black brows into arches of feigned surprise. "That's *my* bad feeling you're fooling with. You're the one who's supposed to keep thinking positive."

His limp joke didn't do a whole lot to unwind her tight nerves.

"Okay," he said. "There's just one thing to do." How could he still sound so decisive, she wondered, when it looked to her like they'd reached the end of the line. "I'm the biggest liability to us getting past the roadblock, so I'm going to get out and hike in a wide circle through the forest. I'll meet you farther down, past the cops. I'll have to be careful not to let myself be seen, so it may take me an hour or so to get through the woods."

She became cold all over at the thought of him leaving—at the thought of dealing with the police alone.

"Chances are you'll be okay, Kelsey. The cops shouldn't recognize this truck. Nor do they have any description of that dress you're wearing—very attractive, by the way. You look good in flowers, and I like the way that full skirt swirls around your knees when you walk."

She knew very well that Ben had taken over her job as official optimist because she'd abandoned it. But his light tone wasn't making her worry any less.

"Cover your hair with that big straw hat we found lying on the seat," he suggested. "The sunglasses do a good job of hiding the color of your eyes. If you make it by the cops, park the truck a few miles down the road and wait for me. I'll find you."

He glossed over that big *if* very quickly, she noticed, trying to make her nod of understanding as determined as he sounded.

"Understand, Kelsey—if they so much as ask for your driver's license, that's the end of it. Waste no time in telling them that you just made your escape from me. Then clam up!" He gave her shoulder a little shake. "Hear me? Let what happened to me be a lesson to you. Tell the police absolutely nothing more. Insist on calling your brother and ask him to get you a good lawyer. You'll need one.''

What might happen to her wasn't the main problem. She was a lot more worried about what was about to happen to Ben.

He grabbed his jacket from the seat and pushed open the car door.

"Ben..." He already had one foot on the pavement when she again took hold of his arm. "Ben...I..." She hated to admit her apprehension to a man who never seemed to be afraid of anything. "I'm frightened."

He glanced over his shoulder at her, then slid back onto the seat and leaned close. "Frightened?" The smile he gave her was uncharacteristically tender. "A big-time reporter like you?" He gently drew the backs of his fingers along her cheek. She tilted her face into his hand. "Nah." He dismissed the idea with a firm shake of his head. "A woman as tough as Miz Kelsey Merrill wouldn't let a mere cop or two frighten her. I'd bet my money—if I had any—on you being able to battle a herd of lions to a draw.''

She had to struggle for even a small smile. "Lions don't come in herds," she said, unwilling to show him any more of her anxiety. "They come in prides."

"There you go. A proud member of the fourth estate at work." He curled his fingers around the nape of her neck and pulled her to him. "You can do it, Kelsey. I've no doubt at all about that."

The way he licked across her lips and ground his mouth against hers, the way he caught her lower lip between his teeth, wasn't gentle. It was hard. And sexy. And motivating. Her head fell back against the seat, tipping back her wide-brimmed hat. The pleasure of his kisses blanked out fear. But only for as long as they lasted.

"Don't fail me, girl." He pushed through the door and bolted for the trees.

All the courage his presence gave her dribbled away with his absence. What frightened her most wasn't so much the thought of dealing with the police who waited ahead. As she watched his tall form disappear into the woods, she had a terrible feeling she was seeing Benton Carlyle for the last time.

Maybe she should just wait here for a while, she considered. Maybe a few minutes' delay would build up her courage. Maybe the police would go away.

And maybe they wouldn't.

Ben's last gruff command helped her shake off indecision. Her nervousness wasn't important. Ben's escape was. He needed her. If she didn't put up a front good enough to get by the police, he'd be stranded in the wilderness alone, without food or transportation. She didn't give much for his survival under those circumstances.

She hadn't worked a clutch in a long time and hoped she wouldn't stall the truck. If the motor conked out, she'd have a tough time explaining to the police why she had no ignition key to restart it. The bad condition of the pickup alone, she worried, as it rattled down the road, could be enough for the cops to pull it over. And if she were stopped for any reason, her time with Ben would be finished.

As she drew closer, she could see that the police were involved in dealing with a serious accident. A tow truck was having difficulty winching out an automobile that had tumbled down the bank into the swollen stream. The officer directing traffic around the scene gave the slowly approaching vehicle and its driver the once-over. But evidently the authorities were still on the lookout for a car the same make as the one she'd left behind, and containing a man and a woman. The single woman driving a pickup was just waved on by.

She kept on going, past the area where Ben was to meet her. He'd be gone an hour, he'd said, and police might come by and investigate a truck parked by the side of the road.

After traveling a few miles and parking on different roads for short periods of time, she drove back. Following Ben's instructions, she halted the truck a careful distance from the police presence.

She forced herself not to keep her eyes glued on the hands of her large-faced watch. Still those hands crept around at a snail's pace. One hour. Two. She made several trips away and back again. On one of them she passed without incident the tow truck and the two cruisers heading down into the valley. Worry passed through anxiety and into outright fear for Ben's safety.

Recapture wasn't the only danger he faced. With all the rain, footing in the forest was treacherous. A frightening vision of him lying injured in the woods kept picking at her mind.

Almost as bad was the thought that he'd simply had enough of her and gone on alone. She remembered how angry she'd made him when she'd pressed to be allowed to phone in her story. No. He'd have no trouble leaving her. She gave him nothing but aggravation. Right now he was probably tramping through the woods away from her. Maybe he'd been able to hitch a ride with some passing motorist while she was gone and was speeding away without so much as a goodbye.

She ought to just write him off and drive on, she told herself every five minutes.

But maybe it was her fault that they'd missed each other. What if this were the wrong meeting place? One curve in the road looked a lot like another. She had sited the spot by the rocky gray cliff lunging out of the mountainside. But there were plenty of rock ledges.

It seemed like forever until she caught a glimpse of blue moving through the trees edging the road some distance ahead.

Ben! She jumped out of the truck and raced toward him. She loathed the tears of relief that stung into her eyes, but couldn't hold them back. She ran into his arms and flung hers around him so forcefully she almost knocked him off balance.

"Oh, Ben... I was so worried... you took so long... I thought you were hurt... or that you'd left..."

"Easy, girl. I'm okay. I'm fine. It just took me some time to work my way around a flooded creek. And the underbrush is so thick in there, finding the road—let alone the truck—was a lot more difficult than I thought it would be."

"Oh, Ben." She couldn't help herself. Pulling herself up on tiptoe she pressed her lips to his. Only the first second or two was a kiss of relief. Then Ben radically changed the equation.

His mouth crushed against hers, his tongue demanding entry she was avid to allow. His arms molded her to his body. And she brazenly pressed closer to the enticing firmness she could feel burning against her abdomen. She didn't care if he thought her cowardly for being so fearful earlier, or shameless for the way she was throwing herself at him now. His mouth, his arms, his whole hard body were a dizzying balm to a long period of dread.

The raucous blare of a horn made her jump. A big black pickup, so decrepit its rusted-through fenders were flapping, screeched to a halt opposite them. The two men in the cab and the third sprawled on the truck bed showered them in a spate of lewd noises and filthy remarks.

Ben froze.

"Hey, man!" the driver hollered, pounding on the outside of the door. "We'd sure like to get a piece of that action."

"Yeah!" The man in the back heaved himself over the side of the truck. Lank, dirty blond hair trailed over his shoulders, and his soiled T-shirt could barely contain the heavy roll of flesh that hung over the top of his pants. The baseball-capped man in the passenger seat hoisted himself through the side window and made obscene gestures at them over the top of the truck.

Oh, God! Kelsey thought in panic. She'd left their own pickup twenty or thirty yards up the road. The men would be upon them before they could make it to the safety of the vehicle. And there were three of them.

If Ben were breaking out in a cold sweat like she was, he didn't show it. Evidently the incident, which raised her apprehension, to him seemed totally familiar. With no sign of worry, let alone fear, he calmly moved her an arm's length away from him. Without a word, he took a single step toward the black pickup and stood waiting in tensed stillness. Balanced on the balls of his feet, his legs parted and bent slightly at the knees, his hands not fisted but held loosely by his sides, he appeared totally focused on the movements of his would-be attackers.

Ben's burly opponent, who had at least fifty pounds on him, sauntered across the road toward them. "Hey, lookee here, boys. We got ourselves a hero." He lifted his hands, and his taunting fingers coaxed Ben to approach. "You wanna take me on, hero?"

Ben didn't move a muscle. She'd characterized him as a hard man the first time she saw him, Kelsey remembered. She hadn't known the half of it. The face that confronted his assailant was chiseled in menace and cold self-assurance. And the grungy two-day stubble of beard darkening his jawline made him look tougher and more threatening than ever.

Beer Belly lost some of his jeering confidence. He gave a nervous laugh and dropped his hands. But the man had come too far to back down in front of his friends, who continued to urge him on from a safe distance. He cursed and lunged toward Ben.

Kelsey pressed her hands to her mouth to keep from screaming.

Ben sidestepped and plunged his fist into the bulging midriff. The single blow drove the air out of the man's lungs in a loud *whuff*. Clutching his stomach, his face florid, he sank to his knees beside Ben's mud-caked shoes.

Not even breathing hard, Ben stood over his adversary, waiting for his next move. The man struggled to his feet and glanced back at his friends for assistance. Neither seemed anxious to provide it. And the clearly unexpected outcome of the showdown between their champion and his would-be victim had cut off their flow of crude remarks. Ben's failed attacker turned and stumbled back to the truck. With a last blustering curse, he rolled onto the truck bed.

The fellow in the baseball cap drew back into the cab. Evidently Ben's easy handling of the largest man among them had driven them to the conclusion that even three-to-one odds wouldn't break in their favor. The black pickup lurched forward and sped away.

Kelsey's knees were shaking. Ben slid his arm around her waist. "Let's get out of here."

Ten minutes and several miles later she was still trembling.

Not only because of the threat they'd just escaped, but because of the frightening hardness—beyond anything she'd seen before—that had come over Ben as he'd dealt with the danger. Only that very hardness had saved them both from who knew what horror. She was glad of that. And in all honesty she'd found his tough male competency exciting in a primitive kind of way. Any woman would take a lot of satisfaction from feeling so well-protected. But she was disturbed nonetheless by Ben's frightening display of a toughness she'd never understood until now.

She'd congratulated herself on knowing Ben Carlyle—at least to some extent. But the confrontation had shaken that confidence. Shaken it because she had no doubt that if all three men had dared come after him, he'd have bested them in a no-holds-barred fight that would have been ugly and

brief and very bloody. And while she'd have cheered him on
and rendered what help she could, she also would have been
horrified at what he'd been able to do.

Could the personal and journalistic instincts she so relied
on be playing her false? she wondered nervously. After all,
the police, a judge and other competent authorities in the
justice system, all of whom dealt with criminals for a living, had come to the conclusion that Benton Carlyle was just
such a criminal. Was it sheer arrogance on her part to think
that after only a couple of days' exposure to him she knew
better than the experts?

But if she lost faith in her instincts, she'd lose faith in
herself. And if ever she needed that self-confidence that on
occasion perhaps had degenerated into reckless audacity, it
was now.

She twisted nervously at a fold of her skirt. Ben noticed
and covered her hand with his. "Don't worry, Kelsey. They
haven't followed us. I know when men decide to give up a
fight for good." His mouth tightened. "I'm sorry," he said.
"What happened back there was my fault."

For the first and only time he was grateful for the dangerous man prison had made him. He'd held his own in
boyish scraps, but he'd only learned how to fight for his life
behind bars. And he'd sure needed that skill today to protect Kelsey. He'd seen the police cars drive by, and with the
law gone, the men were taking little chance of interference
on the sparsely traveled road. Anyone passing probably
would have thought twice about getting involved with a
group of louts. He was all she had. Thank God it had been
enough.

"Your fault? It wasn't your fault, Ben. I was thinking it
was mine. But that isn't true, either. The fault lies squarely
with that disgusting, threatening threesome."

"Yes. But I provided them with the opportunity," he said
with an angry tone of self-recrimination. "I need my head
examined. I stood there kissing you out in the middle of the

road in broad daylight." He'd slipped up badly out there. Holding Kelsey, delighting in the taste and feel of her, he'd been completely blind to anything else.

The look in her eyes as she ran to him was so vulnerable, so filled with concern for him, he hadn't been able to barricade himself against it. He wasn't made of steel, for God's sake. Only flesh and blood that became all too weak where Kelsey was concerned. And that weakness had put her in danger. In pure self-defense and for her own sake, he had to teach her not to be so open to him.

"You thought I'd left you, didn't you?" he said with characteristic bluntness.

Kelsey considered denying it. She was sorry now that she'd made the admission while she'd been so upset. But she nodded.

"You don't have to worry about me leaving you before you get the end of your story, Kelsey. I'd be a damn fool to abandon such an effective partner. How could I deal with the police without you?"

She knew that. He didn't have to keep beating her over the head with it. And she had no business letting his reminder cause that quick spike of denial in her mind. It didn't matter that he was using her. She was using him to get a story, wasn't she?

So they were even.

But it didn't feel even. It felt . . . painful.

Chapter 9

Ben had taken the blame for what had happened to them, but she had instigated it. She'd thrown herself into his arms, for heaven's sake. His cool reaction to such a blatant admission that he meant something to her personally was hurtful. But she ought to thank him for the valuable reminder that he kept her with him only to aid in his escape. It would be brainless to forget that.

Evidently that escape remained the sole thing on his mind. So far, to her embarrassment, he'd simply ignored the ample opportunities she'd given him to make love to her. Something she'd never done with any other man. And she shouldn't even want that much from a man who saw trust and commitment only as entangling bonds. But her problem with dealing with her attraction for Ben wasn't the primary thing on the agenda.

She entertained no more illusions that they'd overcome the last hurdle to Ben's escape. As they drove through the mountains, she remained on edge, carefully scanning the road ahead and behind for any further sign of police.

"Looks like we face another night of sleeping in the truck," Ben said.

"If you can handle it, I guess I can."

She could handle it if she had to, but she sure as heck wasn't looking forward to it. And she didn't see how they could keep that up for any length of time. Maybe Ben could keep going indefinitely, but she sure couldn't. She still had a painful crick in her neck from spending much of last night folded up like an accordion.

She'd considered the dangers involved in going along on Ben's run from the law. Fleeing with an escaped prisoner in order to get a story held a certain cachet of glamour and adventure. Bestsellers had been written on less. But she hadn't figured on it being so darned uncomfortable. Besides the rock-hard lump in her stomach left over from the ugly confrontation, she felt grimy and rumpled, and she'd have given her eye teeth for a nice clean bathroom. Maybe she just didn't have the stuff for investigative journalism, she conceded. She'd certainly discovered that she wasn't as brave as she'd like to be.

She happened to glance toward Ben and noticed that his hands had tightened on the wheel. And he seemed mightily concerned with the scene in the rearview mirror. She turned in the seat to look out the back window.

Dear Lord! Not again. She wasn't ready for another emergency.

A highway patrol car was following them at a distance.

"Are they tailing us, Ben?"

"Maybe. Maybe they're just coming up on us by coincidence. I don't intend to wait around to find out."

He wheeled down the first side road they came to—a dirt road full of potholes. Kelsey held on for dear life as they bounced down between the trees, skirting catastrophe with every bump. She hadn't known when they'd been well-off. She found out when the road ahead just petered off into a dead end in front of an old, dilapidated barn. This road boasted only one exit: back the way they came. And if the cruiser was following them down it, they were trapped.

"Well, that's that," Ben said grimly. "If they want us, they've got us." He glanced around at their surroundings. "Maybe if I turn the truck around and edge in behind those trees, they might not spot us for a second or two when they come in after us. Might give me a chance to zoom out ahead of them before they can turn around."

It wasn't easy swinging the pickup around on the narrow space between the road's overgrown embankments. At one point a wheel became stuck in a pothole and Ben had to rock it out in a splattering of mud.

"All we can do now is wait," he said, shifting the engine into idle. He bent forward in his seat at full alert, his eyes glued on what they could see of the road, his head cocked, straining for the sound of a car engine. He gripped the wheel with white-knuckled hands, primed to throw the truck into gear and take whatever evasive action he could.

Ben Carlyle certainly wasn't a man to give up easily. But she already knew that. She, on the other hand, was just about ready to call it quits. Being pursued by the police had lost all its charm. The back of her neck and shoulders were tight and achy, her nerves still shredded from the encounter with the three men. Only two days on the run and already she was a basket case. In her own defense, though, more out of anxiety over what might happen to Ben than for herself.

She could end her own problems anytime she chose. Right now, if she wanted to. She doubted that Ben would try to prevent her from getting out of the car and waiting to be picked up by the police. Come to think of it, forcing the cops to stop and pick her up might give him a bit more of a head start on them. Then by tonight she could sack out comfortably in her own bed. By tomorrow she could pick up the pieces of her normal life.

The idea was tempting.

Ben, though, enjoyed no such options. He could look forward to no normal tomorrows. His tomorrow—assuming he had more than five minutes of freedom left—would be as nerve-racking as today and yesterday had been. Even if he made good his escape, all he faced were long dreary years of running from the authorities. And even with all his demonstrated self-sufficiency, how could he endure such a life?

She looked at him, every line of his face and body carved with determination. She'd never known anyone like him. She'd discovered the greatest strength of character she'd ever come across in a man who supposedly had none. The only person who came close to that level of perseverance was her brother, Stephen, who'd been cited for his tenacity in plowing through acres of diplomatic Gordian knots until he untied every one.

She waited, her heart in her throat, for a police car to come careening down the road after them. Long minutes passed with no sound but the rustling of leaves, the calling of birds.

A sudden clatter made her jump.

Ben laid a calming hand on her knee. "Easy, Kelsey. It's just the wind slamming the barn door shut."

His hand loosened on the wheel, and he relaxed a little against the seat. "They weren't after us, after all. Some guardian angel must be looking out for us. Has to be yours. I don't have one."

Kelsey linked her fingers together and stretched. "Well, whoever the angel belongs to, I hope he sticks around."

Ben shook his head. "This isn't working. The cops and flooded roads between them have pretty much shut us down. We're not going to make it out to a highway right now without getting caught. Later, maybe—if my freedom lasts that long. And I'm not counting on *that* any more."

She made a quick sound of objection.

"I'm a realist, Kelsey," Ben said dryly. "My original plan was to escape the area as quickly as possible and return later in relative safety to begin my investigation into the murder. But that isn't panning out. I've come to the conclusion that if I don't get on with my search for the real killer right now, I'll never get the chance to do it. Let's have that map of yours again."

She retrieved the map from the glove compartment and spread it out on the dashboard. Ben studied it, tracing out various routes with his index finger.

"I wonder..." he said, squinting in concentration.

"You wonder what?"

"I wonder if I may be able to outsmart them." He flicked the map away with his knuckles. "Right. We're going to backtrack."

"Backtrack? You mean, go back the same way we came?" Kelsey refolded the map. "How can we?"

"Not exactly the way we came. We're going to head south for a while, then circle around back to my family's estate."

"Your family's estate!" she repeated, dumbfounded. "You've got to be kidding. Surely the police will have the house covered."

"Probably. But they can't stake out a whole mountain."

"You own a mountain?"

"Since my mother's death, my brother and sister and I own it. I just hope the cops haven't discovered what could be my ace in the hole."

"What's that?"

"There's an isolated old hunter's lodge in the woods on a remote part of the estate. If we can reach it without being seen, we'll find shelter there, at least for a night or two."

Ben gave that pitiful twitch of his lips that always looked as if he were afraid someone would catch him smiling, so he had to get it over with as quickly as possible. "Or would you prefer curling up in the truck again for the next few nights?"

"Let's try for your hunter's lodge." With a whole cabin to roam around in, it wasn't likely she'd end up in his arms again, as she might in the tight confines of the truck cab.

"That's what I thought."

She was seeing more of the West Virginia mountains in two days than she'd seen in twenty years of vacation-home summers. Even their precarious position didn't keep her from enjoying spectacular natural vistas that lifted her spirits and renewed her hopes.

Their beautiful surroundings were having a similar effect on Ben, Kelsey noticed. He often took advantage of the pull-offs in the roads to park for a moment and gaze out over the wilderness at the distant horizon. Distant horizons and panoramas of soft rolling mountains were hard to come by when your world was bounded by high walls topped with razor wire.

"I have to warn you, Kelsey, the place I'm taking you to isn't elegant. It's a small, bare-bones cabin that I discovered years ago on one of my hikes around the mountain. I used it as a private retreat from the pressures of business— or whatever. I fixed it up a little. Pumped in cold water from the nearby lake and hooked up a propane stove so I could make coffee and small meals for the short periods of time I spent there. No one else ever was interested in the place, and I hope they've all forgotten about it."

"Elegance isn't necessary," Kelsey assured him. "I'll settle for a bed." The luxury—or lack of it—of a possible hideout didn't concern her. Its safety did.

"This investigation you want to do, Ben. It's been a long time. How can you expect to find any proof of your innocence now, when no one was able to do that before your trial?"

"I don't know how hard anyone was looking back then. Anyone but me, that is. And I got nowhere. But I wasn't able to devote as much time to my personal investigation as it needed. Actually, I didn't even realize I had to. I was too busy trying to hold the business together after Dad's death. Lots of people depend on the company for their livelihood, and there aren't that many other jobs in the area. I couldn't let it go under.''

It was exactly that kind of selfless attitude, Kelsey thought, that strengthened her belief in him. "Do you have anything at all to go on?"

"Not much. Only the hope that by talking to a few of the people who were present on the grounds the day of my father's death, I can come up with something that might shed some light on what really happened. Something I may have missed first time around. I know that the odds on my being able to puzzle out the identity of the real killer are close to nonexistent, but what else can I do? This is my last shot at getting out from under this nightmare. If it doesn't work..." He shrugged.

If it didn't work, Kelsey finished mentally, Ben still faced a life only a little better than spending further years in prison.

They ran into no more roadblocks, although in lower areas they still came upon flooded roads that sometimes shunted them off in directions that lost them considerable time.

Finally Ben slowed the truck and began to scan the brush on the right side of the road. "The road that runs in front of our house is about half a mile ahead. The cutoff I'm looking for should be right around here. I just hope I can find it. It's an old logging road that used to lead to a small sawmill that closed down years ago. No one's driven over it since they trucked in equipment for the cabin. I always hike to the place.''

"Granted the area is beautiful, Ben, but why is your family home way out here, when the plant is at Fairmont?"

"Mother loved the place, and Dad had a large financial interest in a ski resort not far from here. He also had a place of his own in town, like I did. Mostly he came out here on the weekends."

Ben turned off into what looked to her like no more than a less dense spot between the trees. Calling the overgrown rutted track a road gave it a dignity it didn't deserve. Her car would never have made it. Their borrowed truck barely did. And she wasn't sure it would ever make it out again. The dirt lane halted at a decaying old sawmill, its machinery broken and rusting.

"End of the line, Kelsey. From here on we walk. Let's get everything out of the truck. I'll hide the vehicle in what's left of the mill. Only a few slats left on the roof, but it should provide enough camouflage if a police helicopter flies over."

A helicopter! She made a lousy fugitive from justice. Helicopters. She hadn't even thought of that possibility.

Kelsey lugged her carryon, while Ben handled her other case and a couple of plastic bags full of supplies. He tramped ahead, apparently leading her through the woods by instinct. She could barely see a trail. The trip took no more than fifteen minutes, but she was drenched with perspiration by the time they reached a clearing.

The small cabin built of wood planks probably cut in the heyday of the abandoned sawmill had weathered to a silvery gray that blended into the surrounding forest. A small, curtainless window flanked the door.

They clumped onto the wooden porch jutting out from the tiny dwelling. Ben reached up above the doorframe and found the key to the padlock. The door creaked on its hinges as he pushed it open.

The place smelled musty from long disuse. She dumped her bags on the armless couch near the door and looked around. As Ben had warned, the cabin offered few comforts other than peace and quiet and a roof over their heads. A natural stone fireplace formed one wall. A tiny sink with a single faucet, and a two-burner hot plate beneath a shelf holding a few canned goods, formed the kitchen. Like everything else, the small table and two chairs in the center of the room were grayed by a layer of dust.

"Does that door lead to the bedroom?" she asked.

Ben strode to the door at the back of the cabin and threw it open for her inspection. "The bathroom. The shower's cold water only, I'm afraid. In the summer I usually just bathe in the lake. You can heat water for washing on the stove, if you like, but I don't have any real large pots. The propane level for cooking should be all right. I came up here for a couple of days just before my trial and left practically a full tank. The water pump runs on a gasoline-powered motor. I'll check it. If it doesn't work, we'll have to lug water up from the lake."

Kelsey looked around and saw no other door.

"Then where's the bedroom?"

Ben shoved his fingers into the curved pockets on the front of his jeans and crimped his mouth into a rueful smile. "You're standing in it. I'm afraid that cot is the only bed." He pointed to the couch on which she had dropped her belongings. "This is it, Kelsey," he shrugged. "It was all right for me. But it's a far cry from being suitable for a woman."

"It's fine, Ben. A perfect hideout." Escaping felons—if that's what she now was along with Ben—bent on evading the cops couldn't expect to bed down every night at the Waldorf. And the place was a whole lot better than sleeping in the truck.

She traced a large *B* in the dust on the table, then rubbed the dirt from her index finger. "If I can find a rag, I'll clean things up a bit."

"Try the cupboard under the sink."

She angled her head toward the cot. "What do we do—draw straws?"

"Guests get the bed. There's a sleeping bag around here somewhere. On warm nights, I liked to sleep outside. I can use that."

Guests, huh? A sudden uncomfortable notion sprang into Kelsey's head. "Did you bring your fiancée up here very often?" She detested not being able to prevent the question.

Ben snorted. "Helena? Good Lord, no. You're the only one who's ever been here with me." He unlatched and pulled open one of the only two small windows the house could boast of. She opened the other. "My brother may have come years ago. I don't remember."

Ben wielded an ancient broom while she did what she could with only a damp rag and a spritz of dishwashing detergent. When they were through, the place was still a long way from being what her physician sister would call clean. But at least they could sit on the couch and at the table without stirring up clouds of dust. And the sunlight streaming in through one of the open windows did a lot to brighten up the room.

But her unaccustomed forays into housekeeping had left her covered with dirt. "I need a bath. Where's that lake you mentioned? I didn't notice it when we came up to the cabin."

"It's down the hill to the left. I'd like a swim myself. Come on. I'll show you."

"Let me get my swimsuit on first. I'll meet you there."

Ben rocked back and forth on his feet and arched a suggestive brow. "I don't have a suit, Kelsey. I always go swimming in the buff up here. This is all private property. No one else comes around."

"Oh. Well, then you'd better just get into the water before I show up."

Ben pulled open the doors of a small cabinet that held no more than two towels, one set of sheets and a dish towel. Richly furnished, this hideaway was not. He threw her one of the towels and headed for the door.

A few moments later, Ben tossed his clothes on a low shelf of rock that formed a step at the edge of the lake. There was no dock. He pushed into the water up to his knees, then stretched himself out into the lake, mastering its length in powerful, swift strokes. He was enjoying himself so much he almost broke into laughter for the sheer joy of being free to splash and dive and float indolently on the surface.

From the middle of the small lake he spotted Kelsey picking her way down the narrow path. The sight of her so dazzled him he forgot to tread water, gulped down a large mouthful of lake, slid beneath the surface and damn near drowned himself.

He came up sputtering. Holy Saint Patrick! His prison fantasies had all been pale imitations of the vision that greeted him now. Tiny scraps of pink material beautifully exposed his traveling companion's luscious figure to his entranced gaze.

She dipped a toe into the water, crossed her arms in front of her and shivered. "It's cold," she said, aiming a frown at him that suggested the temperature of the water was somehow his fault.

"It's better if you slide right in all at once," he called.

She didn't take his advice. Instead she waded in a short distance, bent over to wet her hair and started to shampoo it. Every graceful dip and arc of her arms and body as she lathered and rinsed held him spellbound. The afternoon sun bouncing off the lake's wave-rumpled surface threw a watery reflection like a shimmering golden net over her beautiful body.

Something twisted inside his chest.

If he gained nothing else from his escape, he decided, if he were caught tomorrow, seeing Kelsey like this would have been worth it.

Finally she plunged into the lake and expertly cut through the water toward him. She splashed up to him with bubbling squeals of pure delight. "This is great, Ben. Makes up for everything."

The water at the surface was clear, Kelsey discovered, and did nothing to cloak a naked swimmer. As Ben stroked a lazy circle around her, she enjoyed an intriguing head-to-toe view of a taut male line. By anyone's standards, she thought, the man had a body that was just plain beautiful.

Side by side they lapped the length of the lake and back again. It was wonderful, Kelsey thought, to be able to put aside fear and worry about Ben's future for a time and just enjoy the water and the sun and swimming with him.

Suddenly he stopped his smooth forward motion. Holding himself in place with small movements of his hands, he lifted his head from the water and swiveled it from side to side, listening.

"Out of the water, Kelsey," he suddenly ordered. "Helicopter." He pointed to the west, beyond the small expanse of the lake. She saw nothing. Heard nothing.

"Now," he shouted. "Move."

If Ben said there was a helicopter, there was a helicopter.

She cut for shore, furiously kicking her feet and pulling her arms through the resisting water, barely lifting her mouth from the water to breathe. Ben was much the stronger swimmer and he soon outdistanced her by several feet. He looked back and turned, as if he were coming back to help her.

"Keep going," she gasped. "I'm okay." She could hear the drone of the approaching aircraft engine now. He was the one who might alert the people on board, not she.

When they got closer to the shore, Ben helped drag her from the water and rush her toward the safety of sheltering trees. Water ran down her face and into her eyes, blurring her vision. Running with Ben, she couldn't do much to dash it away. Stones and twigs stabbed into her bare feet, but she forced herself to keep going. If Ben could bear the pain without slowing down, so could she. She stumbled. Ben pulled her to her feet and gave her the needed support of his arm. As they rushed past the telltale clothes and towels, he kicked them off the open shale into the underbrush.

The chop of the helicopter blades now echoed loudly from the hills on every side, making it impossible to judge its location. Ben hauled her into the woods and shoved her back against an oak. His dark hair dripping water, his chest heaving against hers, he lifted his head, scanning through the leafy canopy above them for the machine.

"Did they see us, Ben?" She had barely enough breath left to speak. "Are they searching for us?"

"I don't know." Tense with listening and watching, he probably didn't even realize how painfully hard he grasped her upper arms. "I've spotted the chopper. It's the police, all right. I can't see how they'd know to look for me right here already. More likely they're just covering the area, checking the flood situation. But if they saw us in a place that should be deserted—"

Absurdly, she held her breath and closed her eyes when the helicopter droned by directly overhead, and only let it out when the noise faded into the distance.

Ben's warm, slick nakedness pressing against her meant little when imminent discovery loomed above them. That changed when the danger had passed. It sank in on her in a rush that she was standing in the woods clad in a skimpy bikini with a tall, handsome man who was completely and gloriously nude.

Ben's exciting closeness made her pulsingly aware of every part of her body. She'd swear she could feel her fingernails. She could feel the warm wetness on the inside of her mouth, the sweep of her lids over her eyes.

He was still engrossed in following the path of the helicopter with his eyes. When he finally looked down at her, she watched him become as bothersomely aware of their now erotic position as she.

He drew in a deep breath and his chest expanded against hers. His hands slid down a little on her slippery skin.

"We'd better get back to the house," he said, but made no move toward it. His voice had dropped a raspy octave.

His always exciting nearness, the rich, watery scent of him, shivered up a thought, a feeling that had trembled at the edge of her mind, her heart, for days. She fought against letting the thought form itself into words. Clamped down on the strange feeling that teased and frightened—and filled her with aching warmth.

No. It couldn't be. She didn't want it to be. Ben Carlyle was the wrong man. Wrong in every way. He didn't want her. He didn't want anybody. She'd long known the kind of man she'd want in her life. Someday. Not now. She wasn't ready yet. And she'd choose him on her terms. He wouldn't just barge into her emotions and take over. He'd be a man with a normal life. A man she could count on always to be there for her. A husband ready to put down the kinds of roots with her that she already shared with her family. A home of their own. Kids. Ben Carlyle would give her none of those. He wasn't even interested in applying for the job. And an escaped convict was the last person in the world any woman should consider for even a casual acquaintance.

"Yes," she said. "We should go back to the house. I'll walk ahead of you."

He looked at her questioningly, obviously wondering at the tinge of anger she heard in her own voice. There was no way to explain that she was only angry at herself. Angry, and afraid that it was already too late to do anything about emotions that could bring her whole nicely settled life crashing about her ears. Angry because she wasn't sure she'd root out those sweet, tormenting feelings, even if she could.

Chapter 10

Ben allowed her a few minutes alone in the cabin to dress. She slipped into a short denim skirt and a pink top—just about the last of the weekend wardrobe she'd brought with her. When he appeared in the doorway he had pulled on his jeans and rescued her towel, soap and the plastic bottle of shampoo. He was also laden with her sneakers and his own belongings.

"Sit," he said. "Your feet are bleeding."

She looked down and saw that the none-too-clean floor was spotted with smears of blood. She'd been too busy struggling to keep focused on nothing but the mundane process of getting dressed to pay much attention to the pain in her foot. She bent her knee and turned up her right foot to look at it. The small cut on the sole wasn't all that serious, but Ben insisted on taking care of it.

She sat on the couch, and Ben filled a basin from the cold-water tap and brought it and half a box of small adhesive bandages—the extent of the hideaway's first-aid equipment—over to her. He set the dishpan on the floor and went down on one knee beside it to slide his fingers around her ankle and lift her foot into the basin. Handling her foot as carefully as if he were treating an injured child, he sponged off the soil.

Kelsey looked down at his dark head. What an extraordinary blend of gentleness and toughness was Ben Carlyle. One minute he was competently dispatching a bully. The next he was tending to a woman's injured foot.

His hair was still damp and curled over his ears. She had a strong impulse to reach out and touch it, but doubled her fingers into her palm to prevent it. The cool water and gentle warmth of his fingers feathering over her foot soothed its throbbing sole. She winced a little when the sponge found the sore spot.

Gray eyes flashed up at her, full of contrition. "I'm sorry."

Even as her heart gave its usual odd little contraction whenever his eyes met hers, she couldn't help but smile. Ben looked dismayed—as if she were suffering from a gash as serious as the one on his forehead, instead of from a minor cut from a sharp rock. He hadn't yet put on his shirt. The hard, muscular curves of his shoulders and biceps tightened intriguingly with the movements of his arms and hands.

He toweled off her foot and fixed a bandage over the cut. Resting her heel on his thigh, he picked up one of her sneakers, slipped it carefully over her foot and tied the laces.

"Let's see the other foot."

"That one's okay," she protested. "It doesn't hurt." She'd just as soon avoid any further stroking of her foot to ascertain its degree of injury. She liked the feel of it too darn much for her own good.

"Let's see it, anyway."

She let him take her left foot and dip it in the basin. It didn't seem sensible to make too much of a protest. He

might guess how much his completely innocent touches were
affecting her.

With both hands, he began a gentle massage of her foot.
Her whole body tightened and a little squeal escaped her
lips. If Ben were deliberately set on seduction, he couldn't
be doing a better job of teasing her into compliance. These
past few minutes were taking almost as much out of her as
had waiting for the police to show up at the old barn.

"Hurts that much, huh?" He looked up at her in sympathy. "Must be bruised a little. I don't see any cuts."

She was relieved when he finally set her free. "I'll fix us
some dinner," she said, hurrying to the corner of the open
room that served as the kitchen.

She reached nervously for the can of tomato soup on the
shelf. It slipped through her fingers, bounced off the counter
and fell to the floor. Ben, tucking his shirt into the waistband of his jeans, whirled around at the sudden racket.

"I'm getting jumpy," he said, running his fingers through
his hair. "That's not good."

It wasn't entirely the evidence of a police search that kept
him on edge. He expected that, and could handle it. But
anywhere he went in this cramped cabin, Kelsey was not
much more than an arm's length away. Her nearness was
driving him crazy. And he'd already used up his small quota
of saintliness in forcibly holding his hands back from running up her lovely legs while he took care of her injured feet.
He was beginning to think that getting slammed back behind bars was the only way to prevent him from making love
to her at some point. And even being locked up again
wouldn't keep him from wanting her.

"Are you going up to the house to see your family?" she
asked, dumping the soup from the opened can into a pot.
"I'm sure they'll be worried about you."

Ben deliberately looked away and strolled over to sit down
at the table.

"Not today. Charles told me they planned to stay in town after Mother's funeral to deal with some legal business. I'll go tomorrow."

He was in no hurry to face his family. For two years he'd fought the terrible suspicion lurking in the shadows of his mind like a thief. And like a thief, it had robbed him of the confidence in his family that he so needed to support him. He'd hoped he wouldn't have to deal with that painful doubt until sometime in the future. But now it would have to be soon.

He felt Kelsey squeeze his fingers and looked up. She'd left off her cooking to come and sit opposite him.

"I'm sorry, Ben. I'm afraid I forgot that you'd just lost your mother."

"Not surprising. You've had a lot of other things to occupy your mind since we met."

So did he, Kelsey thought. But his mother's death wasn't something he could just forget, as she had done. Another reminder of how much more difficult his life was compared to hers. He wasn't even allowed time for normal grief.

He tightened his hand around hers for a moment, then drew it away and tipped his chair to rock back on its legs. A bad habit—according to her mother—that he shared with her father.

"That soup ready yet?" he asked, lifting his arms and locking his fingers together behind his head.

Kelsey got up to dish out two bowls of hot soup and set one down in front of him. "I'm not sure how long food stays good in a can, but two years should be okay. It smells fine."

Ben thumped his chair to the floor and reached for a slice of bread. "Before I see my family, I have to talk to Walt Simpson, the plant manager. When it gets dark, I'm going to drive to his house."

Kelsey dropped her spoon back into the soup and looked at him in dismay. "Oh, gosh, Ben. Isn't that taking a big risk?"

"Maybe. But Walt and I have been friends for a long time. He's been a sort of mentor to me. Every step of the way he encouraged my plans to set up my own business. I'm hoping our friendship will keep him from hollering for the cops when he sees me. You'll stay here."

"No way," she bridled, amazed that he'd think she was just going to sit around and wait while he tried to pick up the trail of his father's killer.

"No need to be frightened of staying alone. You'll be quite safe. And I'll be back as soon as I can."

"It's not a question of being frightened to stay alone. We've come this far together. I'm going with you to Mr. Simpson's."

He'd learned better than to argue with her when that obstinacy showed up in her voice. It irked him, but at the same time he had to admire her dogged determination to get everything she wanted for her story.

And though he knew intellectually that she would be safer without him, he felt more comfortable being able to see that she was all right. Whenever she was out of his sight, he kept imagining that something bad was happening to her. But then, something bad had already happened to her. Him.

Kelsey found it no easy task hiking back to the truck in the dark. Ben walked a little ahead, searching out the way with the flashlight. He walked slowly because he knew she was favoring her right foot. She followed, holding tight to his free hand, afraid he'd disappear into the black without her.

It was a miracle Ben was able to guide the truck over the dirt road, barely visible in the dark, at all. She decided to up the amount of the check she'd eventually send its owner, if she could ever track him down. The pickup had already proven to be a lifesaver. Fortunately, once they'd driven away from the estate, they encountered no further problems.

They weren't able to take what Ben said passed for the direct route over the road that led in front of Dogwood Hill, the Carlyle house, so it was over an hour's drive west to the Simpson place. Ben drove up to a beautiful French-provincial-style home set on a hilltop and parked the truck a little way down from the house.

"No point in letting anyone get a good look at the truck or the license plates," he said. "I'll be glad to see Walt again. I'm not sure, though, how happy he'll be to see me."

Dumbfounded was more the operative word for the large, jovial-looking man with an attractively full head of white hair who stood in the doorway of his home staring at Ben.

"Well, Walt," Ben offered hesitantly, "are you going to ask me in?"

"Of course, m'boy. Of course." Walt shook Ben's hand vigorously, then pulled him inside. "Come in, both of you. Quickly."

Simpson led them into a large, beautifully furnished family room. Ben didn't introduce Kelsey. She guessed he thought it better for both Walt's sake and hers not to have her name on the record. The older man seemed almost as surprised at seeing her as he had on opening his door to his former employer's son. Simpson must have guessed who she was, and if he wondered why she didn't act in the least like the hostage she was supposed to be, he asked no questions.

Walt waved them toward a deep, comfortable sofa.

"Can I get you a drink, Ben? Or one for you, young lady?"

"I'll join you in a beer, if you have one," Ben answered. Kelsey murmured her refusal.

"Don't mind telling you I need a drink, Ben, after that surprise you just gave me." Simpson poured himself a bourbon from a bottle in the room's well-stocked bar. Then filled a heavy frosted glass mug for Ben.

"You were at the funeral this morning, Walt?" Ben asked.

The old man nodded and settled his girth into an overstuffed chair opposite them. "They wouldn't even let us bury your poor mother in peace, boy. The church was jammed with police and reporters, all hoping you'd show up." He shook his head sadly. "Even had the TV cameras there."

Kelsey saw Ben clench his hands around the mug. She was both shamed and angered by colleagues who'd go so far as to invade the sanctity of a church—and a funeral—for a story. Had they really expected a man hunted by the police to be stupid enough to appear at a place they were sure to be watching? Over the last couple of days, she'd come to understand very well the reasons for Ben's contempt of both the media and police authorities.

"You're always welcome in my home, Ben. But I have to admit I'm pretty surprised that you'd come here—what with the police after you. They've spoken to us all. Warned us to let them know if we heard from you."

Ben faced his old friend squarely. "Are you going to do that?"

"Hell, boy. I've known you since you were knee-high to a grasshopper. I'm not about to turn you in." The man, Kelsey thought, seemed genuinely pained by the suggestion that he might. "I'm glad you came to me. Since Emma died, I'm here all alone, so you'll be safe in this house. You can stay as long as you need to. You and the lady." Walt nodded firmly. "You'll both stay here with me."

The man's generosity toward Ben warmed Kelsey's heart. After all he'd been through, he certainly needed a friend like Walter Simpson.

"Thanks, Walt." She caught the slight crack of emotion in Ben's voice. "I really appreciate the offer, but I'm not looking for a place to stay."

"You're not? Where are you holed up, then?"

"Sorry, Walt. Better for you if I don't tell you that."

"Huh? Oh, yes. See what you mean, m'boy. If I don't know, I can't get in trouble with the cops for not telling them."

Ben nodded.

"Then at least let me give you some money. Got enough right here in the house to help you get away. I can stop in at the bank for more tomorrow."

Ben shook his head. "No, Walt. I can't take your money, either. But thanks."

Kelsey wished Ben hadn't been so quick to refuse the liberal offer. They weren't exactly rolling in getaway money. Maybe he was too proud to accept a gift of cash from a friend. But it seemed to her that a man in Ben's position could ill afford any overly large doses of prickly masculine pride.

"Then what can I do for you? Don't expect you've stopped in just to pass the time of day."

Ben sipped at his beer, then put the mug down on the coffee table in front of him. "I came back to make one last try at discovering who really killed Dad."

Walt took a long pull on his drink. "Well, now. Don't want to discourage you, Ben. But seems to me that's going to be a pretty tall order."

"I can't disagree with you there, but I have to try. I've played the day of the murder over and over again in my mind, but I hoped that kicking it around with you might lead to some clue, anything at all that will give me some thread to follow."

Ben and Walt started talking about the company workers who were on the grounds that day. Kelsey kept one ear tuned to the conversation and looked around.

Ben had told her that Mr. Simpson had been widowed within the year. That beautiful collection of expensive dolls in the glass display case must have belonged to his wife. Mounted on the opposite wall was an impressive display of antique guns and swords that her historian father would have loved to inspect.

Ben had mentioned his brother's name several times, she realized with a start. Where he was going with that strange line of inquiry was beyond her.

"Hell, Ben," Walt said, in answer to Ben's question. "Sure, Henry and young Charles had their run-ins. Lots of 'em. Some of 'em pretty serious. Henry always was too hard on the boy. But you know your father—the man would argue with a chicken over the color of an egg. Never did take the kid seriously. I don't think any of us did. But that was our mistake. Your brother will never be the expert businessmen you and Henry were, Ben, but he's doing a surprisingly decent job as president of the company."

"I'm glad to hear that. I was afraid the Carlyle Specialty Tool Company might go under when you didn't get in as its head." Ben seemed to hesitate for a moment, as if he were considering his next words. He bent forward on his elbows and laced his fingers together over his knees. "I'm not saying here, Walt, that Charles, or anyone else, could have predicted that I'd be convicted of the killing." His voice was flat, expressionless. "But my brother didn't hesitate to take advantage of the situation, did he?"

"Whoa, now, boy." Walt slowly put down his empty glass on the table in front of him, puzzlement written in the affable lines of his ruddy face. "You're not saying... You can't think that Charles..." Walt shook his head in flat denial. "Not his own father, Ben. I'll never believe that. Now, Ricky Lee—that's another matter."

Ben nodded. "And with Dad out of the way, Ricky Lee proceeded to marry my sister. At the time he died, my father was moving heaven and earth to prevent that."

"He sure tried. Henry was set to offer Ricky Lee a sizable sum to get lost."

"I didn't know that."

"Yep. Don't know whether he ever did or not, but he was thinking on it." Walt got up to pour himself another drink. "Now, maybe this don't mean anything at all, Ben," he said, staring down into the amber liquid swirling around in the glass, "and maybe I've got no call to bring it up, but you've set me to thinking, and..." He trailed off, looking very uncomfortable.

Ben went over to the bar to stand by his friend. "And what, Walt?"

"Well, remember that softball game I started up right after... well, after..."

"You suggested they begin the softball game to cover up everyone's embarrassment after Dad and I had that ugly public argument."

"Thought it might be a good idea to get things settled down a bit after all that. Henry sure did let himself get out of hand that day." He shook his head, as if he still couldn't make sense of the incident. "Did for a fact. But it hit me as you were talking, boy. Most folks came over to watch the game. 'Course, it didn't last but an inning because of what happened up at the house, but I don't recall seeing Ricky Lee there." The old man rubbed thoughtfully at his ample chin. "Now that I think of it, can't say I remember Charles being there, either." He immediately dismissed his observation with a shrug. "But there was a big crowd. Couldn't see everybody. And my memory's not as good as it once was. Both of 'em could have been there. And if they weren't, they could have been in the pool."

"No." Ben's face hardened into the impassivity it had let drop more and more over these past three days. "I passed the swimming pool on my way back to the house. There were only a few people in it. Not Charles or Ricky Lee. I remember, because a couple of the guys hollered over to me and waved."

His brother and his brother-in-law? Kelsey thought, horrified. Ben actually suspected that a member of his own family had wielded the lethal golf club and then let him go to prison for the crime? No wonder the man had given up on trust. Who could blame him when he feared that someone so close to him might have betrayed him. She couldn't conceive of any such horror happening in her own tightly knit family.

Ben again fell into the uneasy pacing that had become such a habit with him. Walt followed more slowly.

"It's sure a lot easier for me to accept that Ricky Lee did it, too," Ben said. "The kid always was too hot-tempered. Has he had any more run-ins with the law since he married Bonnie?"

"Just minor stuff. Speeding. Getting tossed out of the local bars occasionally. That kind of thing. Can't say I ever liked Ricky Lee much. Used to work in the shipping department. Witless as dirt. Sent a shipment to Topeka once that was supposed to go to Richmond. I wanted to fire him. But Henry kept him on because your sister threatened to run off with him if her dad let him go."

Walt halted and grasped Ben's arm to stop his back-and-forth stridings. "Look here, Ben. Granted you could make a case that either Charles or Ricky Lee might have wanted to get rid of your old man. To tell the truth, a couple of times I saw them damn near go for each other's throats. And Ricky Lee is one sneaky son-of-a—" Walt glanced back at Kelsey and cleared his throat. "But the fact is, there's not a lick of evidence against either one of 'em."

"I know that."

"It's hard for me to say this, boy, but maybe you'd best put the whole thing behind you. You're out of that prison. It's a big country. Why not just keep on going and get lost somewhere. Go make a new life for yourself someplace far from here. California, maybe. You always liked California. Remember that trip you made out there to develop new markets for us? We had the devil of a time getting you to come back." Walt patted Ben's back in fatherly fashion.

"Think about it, boy. Might be better all around. Both you and the rest of the family have already been through...well, you know that as well as I do."

A sudden tiredness seemed to come over Ben. He rubbed at the back of his neck. "You could be right, Walt. I'll think about it." He stopped at the coffee table for a few more swallows from his mug, then held out his hand to Kelsey to help her up from the deeply cushioned sofa. "Thanks for the beer, Walt, but we've been here long enough. Better get going."

"If you need my help," Walt said at the door, "for money—for anything at all—come to me." Ben again refused the man's offers of both sanctuary and escape money.

Back at the cabin, Kelsey told Ben she'd take care of lighting the oil lamp sitting on the table in the middle of the room. She agreed with him that the old-fashioned lamp that threw soft shadows on the rough old planks of the walls was a lot more atmospheric than the sharp, unwavering beam of a battery light.

Ben sat down heavily on the couch and leaned back against a cushion, his eyes closed. The weight of his silence hung heavily in the little room.

Kelsey adjusted the flame and replaced the lamp's glass chimney, then stood by the table watching him. A breeze blew through the windows, open to the natural sounds of the soft summer night, and stirred the black lock falling over the bandage on his forehead. A piercing wish to feel his arms about her again slashed through her. But he'd told her in so many words that he didn't want the only kind of caring that meant anything to her. The caring that came with tight strings of commitment attached. *No strings* had never been her credo. And there was no point in fooling herself that it could be now.

She'd be all right, she decided, if she could only stay away from him. But how to stay away when the farthest she could get from him was no more than twelve feet?

The restless pacing Ben had resumed didn't result from nervousness. She understood now that it served more as a safety valve to work off emotion he could barely contain. Raw emotion of rage and heartache that would have laid her low long before this.

Ben's conversation with Walt had to have been painful. Kelsey wasn't sure if it would be better for him to let the subject drop, or to bring it up again. But whether he spoke of it or not, the pain was still there. She opted for openness.

"You could be wrong, Ben. As Walt said, there's no evidence that points to your brother, or to your sister's husband as the killer."

Ben stopped dead and snapped his head around. "For God's sake, Kelsey," he lashed out. "Do you think the probability that Charles murdered our father is something I *want* to think about?"

Let Ben vent his anger on her, Kelsey thought. She knew his rage wasn't really aimed at her, and he'd kept it bottled up long enough.

"I was hoping that talking to Walt would somehow convince me my suspicions were all wrong. It didn't. I can understand a man's being provoked to the breaking point by Henry Carlyle. I can even forgive that. It almost happened to me that last day. But that my own brother might have allowed me to take the blame for it, might have just sat back enjoying his lucky break while I spent years in prison—" He choked off, the twist of pain and fury in his face even more affecting because it was so unusual. "God! That's— that's—"

He turned away and stood looking up at the ceiling, rubbing the back of his neck as if it pained him. When he dropped his hand and walked back to her, he had regained his usual distanced composure.

"Never mind all that. I want to discuss something else." He stopped and clamped his hands over the back of the wooden chair next to her. "Do you think I should do what Walt suggested? Should I just settle for what I've got now? After all, it *is* freedom, of a sort. Maybe he was right. Maybe I *should* just go out there and lose myself somewhere, instead of continuing to beat my head against a stone wall."

She'd been considering the question all the way home from Simpson's house and wished she'd come to a different conclusion. "Losing yourself somewhere might be the safest thing for you to do, Ben. And frankly, I'd like to see you do that. You might stand less chance of getting caught."

His gray eyes remained intent on her face as she spoke. She crossed her arms in front of her. "But I've learned a lot about the kind of man you are. You're a fighter, Benton Carlyle. After what happened to you, most men would have given up. But you're still trying to claw your way out of that terrible incident. I don't think you can stop. I don't think you can just forget about your father's death and what someone did to you, and just go off and lose yourself somewhere. You're an innocent man, Ben. You've got to keep trying to prove that."

Ben's heart lurched. He couldn't breathe. Not sure he'd understood the words Kelsey had just spoken. Afraid she meant something entirely different from what he'd thought he'd heard. The same stunned, utterly defenseless feeling he'd had while listening to the jury's verdict came over him. His mouth worked. "Did you say..."

"I said, you didn't kill your father and you've got to keep on trying to track down the man who did."

"You...you believe me, Kelsey?" He couldn't keep the tremor from his voice. "You truly believe the jury was wrong?"

"I believe you, Ben. Remember when you said you couldn't understand how I was willing to give you the benefit of the doubt when I had nothing to go on? I have plenty to go on. You talked a lot of threat to me at first. But you haven't done a thing to hurt me. In fact, you've looked after me. I saw you risk your life for a man to whom you owed nothing at all. You faced down three bullies—mainly to protect me.'' Holding his gaze, she shook her head. "You're no coward, Ben Carlyle. And you're not vicious. You only hit that man on the road after he'd attacked you. If you *had* killed your father, it could only have been an accident. And if it had happened that way, you'd have owned up to it immediately and dealt with the consequences.''

He hadn't consciously let go of the chair and curled his hands over her shoulders. "To hear you say that, Kelsey...to know that after everything that happened someone can still believe in me...'' He trailed into a low moan.

The heat from her body curled sensuously through his hands and up his arms.

He couldn't do it anymore, Ben thought. He'd reached his limits. He'd been so long empty. So long hungry. So bitterly long alone. It was beyond him to keep trying to close himself off to his desire for Kelsey. She'd penetrated the last of his defenses with her belief in him. She'd called all his savagely repressed emotions to life with the tenderness of her touch.

His need for her was overwhelming, almost frightening in its intensity. He wanted so much to feel safe enough, just for a few moments, to let down the protective cage that took so much energy, so much of his will, to maintain. Safe enough, just for a little while, to open himself to another person. To trust someone completely—just for tonight. He hadn't been able to do that in so long.

He was starved for a loving connection with another human being. If he didn't take this chance to fill his mind with something other than fear and despair, he couldn't go on.

There was no way on earth he could keep himself from cupping his hands around her lovely face. Her skin was soft as mist, but warm. She unlocked her arms and slid her outstretched fingers across his chest. He loved the feel of the electric awareness of her the action crackled through him.

"I want you, Kelsey," he said simply. He wasn't interested in seduction, in games he'd sometimes played long ago in another life. He wanted—needed—to give and to receive, openly, honestly. "God knows I want you. But it's more than that. Prison is the loneliest place in the world. You can't imagine how lonely. Surrounded by hundreds of men, each prisoner is still terribly, achingly alone. To be alone like that is hard... so hard. I *need* to be with you tonight."

This was the man she'd once thought cold and heartless? Kelsey thought. The man who only yesterday had sworn he needed no one in his life? The same man who intended to cut all close ties to everyone if ever he regained his freedom? Maybe he really was aiming for that kind of isolation. But his wrenching admission proved he remained a long way from it.

A tentative ray of hope flickered to life within her heart.

"You're not alone, Ben. You're with a friend who..." She couldn't speak the word that first sprang to mind. "A friend who cares about you."

The softness of her smile reached in and folded a sweet warm pain around his heart. A pain that frightened him, because it hinted that much more than sexual need was involved here. And it was safe to allow no more than that. He had no *right* to allow more than that. Had no right whatever to ask anything of her. But the guilt that thought provoked wasn't enough to hold him back from making love to her.

"You deserve it all, Kelsey. Everything the best of men can give you, and I'm far from being the best of men. You know my situation. I can't stay with you. I can make you no promises. I have nothing to give you but myself. And even that can't be for long." His reminder of their uncompromising reality was aimed at himself. She wasn't likely to need it.

"I understand, Ben." She well knew that for them tomorrow might never come. That an hour, a night of lovemaking, might be all they could ever share. That he wanted no more than that. None of it mattered. All that counted now was the magic of Ben's arms. The sweet pulsing heat he'd already kindled inside her. The impossibly strong longing to feel him as close as he could get. "And I want you, too."

He bent and touched his lips to hers. Instantly she responded, tilting back her head and sliding her arms around him.

A kaleidoscope of sensation—the intoxicating taste of her, the arousing softness of her body, the dizzying perfume of her skin—burst over him. A miracle to be able to *feel* again—to experience sensation—after such a long time of forcing himself *not* to feel anything.

He could hold on to careful gentleness with her no longer. His hunger for her wouldn't let him. He searched the blue eyes looking at him in that straight-on way of hers. Her eyes had darkened to indigo and were clouded with some emotion he couldn't identify.

He stiffened. If she were offering him compassion, he'd have none of it. He wanted the fire her responses had already told him was there. Needed the sense of vibrant life—of hope—she always brought him.

He wound his arms around her, pulling her closer to him, crushing her soft breasts into his chest. "If you're thinking of bestowing yourself on me as on some kind of charity case, Kelsey," he said tightly, "forget it. You've admitted you want this. I don't think you know how much."

He crushed his mouth down on hers and took the warm, moist intimacy he knew she would make no effort to deny him. His tongue plunged deep inside her, he swept her up in his arms and strode with her to the couch.

The narrow cot gave space to no more than one body. He laid her down and stretched himself over her. For days he'd ached to fill his hands with the soft, enticing rounds of her breasts. To find out if the reality of the tiny nubs whose outlines beneath her shirt had so teased at him was as delightful as his mental picture of them. He waited no longer. He tugged the pink top out of her skirt and slid it up, revealing a sight so lovely it stopped his breath in his throat. To his satisfaction, she showed no reluctance whatever. When he began to pull the material above her head, she arched her breasts toward him in a movement he thought the most beautiful he'd ever seen.

She reached for the buttons on his shirt, fumbling at them in her eagerness. He took over, tearing off his shirt and tossing it to the floor. He'd never get enough of stroking the delicate skin of her breasts, he thought. Never enough of the sweet taste of their dark crests, or of the whimpers of pleasure his laving of them with his tongue called from her.

Every touch, every kiss fired him to ever more sweetly intimate invasion. Anxious to search out her hidden warmth, he slipped a hand beneath the edge of her short skirt and stroked up the tender skin on the inside of a bare thigh.

She pulled down the zipper of his jeans and released his fullness into her hand. He groaned. Her gentle touch seared into him a craving to lie the length of her, mouth to mouth, heart to pounding heart, skin to burning skin. Their clothing was a hindrance he could tolerate no longer. He tore away the last of the barriers between them and began again to touch and taste and love her naked body.

Kelsey opened herself to his sweet invasion. Soon she was trembling, ready to beg for him to bond himself to her. But she could feel him shaking, as well. He was expertly carrying out his sensual threat to show her the depths of her desire for him. But she could revel in a victory of her own. Scarcely a trace remained of the iron control that had bound him so tightly the first time she'd seen him. His breathing rasped as rapid as hers. His hands and mouth were as famished as hers. His impatience to claim her as wild as hers to give herself to him.

Ravenous for all of it, all of him, she threw open all her senses to feed on every new, exciting sensation. The piercing cry of a night bird cut through the silence, but it was Ben's ragged gasps she strained to hear. She filled her lungs with moist night air and caught the rich, earthy smell of fertile loam and forest, the musky odor of some feral animal. But it was Ben's scent that arced directly to her brain, triggering a small fierce flame that raced along every nerve like a trail of gunpowder and exploded a furious longing deep within her.

The stubble of his beard chafed her cheek. He locked his hands palm to palm through her fingers so tightly it hurt. She didn't care.

Coherent thought was burning away. Only the incredible rightness of his naked body stretched over hers filled her mind. Yes, she exulted. This was exactly how his body—excitingly new, achingly familiar—should feel against hers. His body called hers into an erotic dance to the mad rhythm of her heartbeat, the frantic drumming of her blood.

Ben surrendered himself, a willing prisoner in the soft, sweet cage of her arms, her legs. Every nerve, every muscle, every cell of his body strung tight with pleasure. He felt like a man, dying of thirst, who was suddenly showered in life-giving rain. Like a man who'd lived in a desert of the senses, suddenly transported to a lush tropical paradise of sensation. Seductive. Captivating.

Terrifying. As if she heard his singing soul, she poured into him everything he'd ever dreamed, filling his emptiness, tempting him to give more and more of himself. He struggled to hold back, not to lose himself entirely in her. What would happen to him if he abandoned all the control, the self-discipline that had defined him for so long? Would there be anything left of him?

Risk a little more, the haze of pleasure enveloping him urged. Just a little more.

He felt her tighten around him. She gasped his name and strained toward him. He gloried in her ecstasy, in knowing that he was its source.

Pleasure expanded into joy. He thrust himself deeper into the caressing velvet of her body. Again. Again. His lungs were bursting. His heart thudding into a crazy tattoo. The frenzy built and built and shattered the last of his control.

A soft-eyed doe, edging into the water to drink, leaped away, startled by the loud, mindless cry echoing over the lake.

Chapter 11

Kelsey woke and knew immediately that she was alone. They'd slept overlapping on the narrow couch, Ben's weight comforting even in sleep. She heard a faint splashing from the direction of the lake. Evidently he had gone in for a morning swim. Her immediate instinct was to jump out of bed and run down to join him. She resisted that urge. Last night her life had changed forever. She needed time away from Ben to figure out how to deal with that change.

Ben had defeated all her efforts to wall him out of her heart. Day by day he'd pulled away bits of the handy camouflage that she was staying with him only because of a story. She was no longer sure that pursuing the story had ever been the real reason she'd come with him. And while she yearned to help him prove his innocence, even that wasn't the primary reason she stayed.

Last night in Ben's arms, the truth she'd worked so hard to keep safely dammed up in a small corner of her mind flooded out. She was in love with Ben Carlyle. She looked toward the window, toward the lake and Ben, and gave a rueful smile. A dingy diner in the mountains. Not the place she'd expected to meet her heart's desire. And surely not the kind of man she'd expected to fall in love with.

But then, she hadn't known a darn thing about love. She thought she did. She thought her smarts would guide her to the right man—the man who'd fit neatly into the niche she would provide for him in her life. But smarts didn't have anything to do with it. Love, she knew now, was the hot melting feeling in her chest whenever she looked at Ben Carlyle. Love was the commanding need to touch him, to hear his voice, to have him near. Always. Always. He gave her the new and wonderful—and terrifying—feeling that he was part of her and always would be, even if she never saw him again.

But it was all very different for him, she reminded herself. For a man fresh out of incarceration, any woman would have served the purpose. She could hardly blame him for that. Even so, his lovemaking hadn't been rough and selfish. He'd been mindful of her. She'd felt his caring.

Last night he'd whispered soft, exciting words to her, called her soft, exciting names. But a man couldn't be held to secrets gasped out into the darkness in the heat of passion. In broad daylight, in full possession of his senses, he'd spoken aloud his cynical views of trust and freedom. Those were the words she had to go on. And they weren't words calculated to encourage a woman to tell a man she loved him. She'd always expected that when love happened to her, she'd shout it happily from the rooftops. In that, too, she'd been mistaken.

She got up from the cot and showered with cold water in the tiny stall, dressed and sat at the table with pen and notepad to pull her story notes into some kind of order.

She was standing at the stove, pouring boiling water over the tea bag in her mug, when Ben came in. His jeans rode low on his hips and were plastered to his wet body. He slid an arm about her and drew her close. She automatically relaxed against him. His skin was cool and droplets of water sparkled amid the dark, curly hair on his chest. If there was a man in this world more heart-stoppingly beautiful than Benton Carlyle, she thought, she hadn't seen him yet.

"Are you all right?" he asked, nuzzling her temple. "You didn't get a whole lot of sleep last night."

She was grateful for the tenderness, even if she could expect no greater commitment from him.

"Neither did you," she reminded him.

"I'm not complaining, love." Just a friendly name for a woman who'd shared his bed, she quickly reminded herself, in the wake of a spurt of hope. "You can keep me up all night anytime."

Not *anytime*. Not for the years she wished for. Not for the rest of their lives. Just for another night or two.

"By the way," he said, fingering the lobe of her ear. "Where are those earrings of yours?"

"I took them off to go swimming yesterday and forgot to put them on."

"I like the way they swing when you move. They look . . . cheerful."

"All right, Ben. I'll put them on again." She dug the gold hoops out of her bag and slipped them into her ears.

Ben walked around her to inspect the dangly jewelry from every angle and grinned his approval.

"Are you up for a hike to the house, Kelsey?" he asked, over a lunch of the last of the sandwiches. "It's a fairly long walk, but there's less of a chance of us being seen under cover of the forest than there is driving on a supposedly deserted road."

"I can handle it, Ben. I'd enjoy a good walk after spending so long cooped up in one vehicle or another."

Ben didn't rush their trek to the house, which was just as well because Kelsey found it pretty tough going. Patches of wet, slippery leaves skidded them precariously down hills. And soon her sneakers were as crusted with mud as were

Ben's shoes. Still, she enjoyed the exercise and the sense of freedom rambling through the forest gave her.

Almost an hour into the hike, they came upon the heart-tugging sight of a family of deer lunching on fresh green shoots in a small clearing. With Ben's hand at her elbow, they stood watching so silently, so motionless that the animals moved off into the forest without even noticing their rapt observers.

When she started to drag a little, Ben called a time-out. She sat resting on a large rock, while he picked a small nosegay of tiny blue flowers and presented it to her with a brief kiss. Apparently thinking better of the lightness of the kiss, he came back for a second, not quite so brief. And a third that left her dizzy.

"Have you ever made love outside in a forest?" he murmured against her ear. He was already working at her belt buckle.

She shook her head. Apart from Ben, she'd hardly made love at all. And never had her few experiments come close to the magic he brought her.

"Neither have I." His chuckle was soft and sexy and let her know exactly what he was thinking. "I think it's time we did, don't you?"

In answer, she just pressed her lips to the fascinating pulse point on the side of his corded throat and started in on the buttons of his shirt.

Together they dropped to the mossy bank. The soft groundcover was cool and damp against her back. Ben's body was as warm as the sun and excitingly heavy on her breast and belly. A raccoon, his pointy nose twitching, waddled out to investigate the intruders. Kelsey's soft, delighted laugh sent the little bandit skittering away. Ben, too, had seen the curious little animal and joined in her laughter. Their mutual burbles of delight in the green leafy world around them, in each other, trailed off into sighs and whispers. The miraculous feel of his heat inside her spun her up into the whirling blue sky.

Whatever happened, she thought, shoving her arms through the short sleeves of her top, she'd never again see a forest—even a picture of one—without thinking of Ben and the ecstatic half hour they'd spent in this woodsy clearing together.

It was another hour before the imposing white-stuccoed house came into view.

"Have you ever talked to Charles and Ricky Lee about your suspicions, Ben?" Kelsey asked as he helped her climb over a fallen tree lying across the trail.

She was sorry she asked the question when Ben's beard-darkened jaw turned hard again. "No. Ricky Lee never came to see me. And it was impossible to talk to my brother freely through the glass barrier and telephone of the prison's visiting room. To tell the truth, I wish I could put off that confrontation forever. The idea that Charles might have done all this enrages me. But at the same time, I can't bear the thought of seeing my brother's guilt in his eyes."

For Ben's sake, she hoped he never would.

They were approaching the house Ben called Dogwood Hill from the rear. Henry Carlyle had good taste. The house—oddly, more of a family home than the showplace she'd expected—had two full stories and a wide sloping dormer in the green roof. It was built, according to Ben, in the 1920s as a summer dwelling for a Wheeling coal magnate. Beyond the well-tended back garden, there was a large, screened-in porch.

"Wait here in the trees," Ben ordered. "I'm going to take a look around. Don't worry. I can keep from being seen. I know every tree and rock on the estate."

That didn't keep Kelsey from worrying until he returned.

"There's a police car parked out front in the driveway, but we can skirt around to the back door."

The porch door squeaked a little. Ben was careful to hold his fingers on its edge to keep it from slamming shut behind them. They tiptoed over the deck to the back door and Ben quietly pushed it open.

A young, dark-haired woman in a black-and-white print dress was in the kitchen arranging a vase of flowers. From what Ben had told her, Kelsey recognized Bonnie. Ben's sister must have sensed the movement at the door in back of her, because she spun around. Her enormous brown eyes grew wide and she dropped the red roses she was holding. With a sobbing cry she rushed into her brother's arms.

"Oh, Ben. I'm so glad you came. I was so worried. Are you all right? They said you were in a building that collapsed in the storm." The words tumbled out in a rush as she hugged her brother.

"I'm fine, honey. Pull down that blind, will you please, Kelsey?" Kelsey moved to drop the poufed Austrian curtain at the kitchen's large window. Ben nodded toward the arch leading from the kitchen into the rest of the house. "Bring them in, Bonnie. But do it quietly."

Looking back over her shoulder at Ben, as if afraid he might disappear, Bonnie left the room. She returned almost immediately, a small group of people following her in obvious puzzlement. Seeing Ben, their confusion changed to astonishment. Astonishment, Kelsey noted, that seemed none too happy.

One of the two men was a younger version of Ben, but with much less strongly defined features. Charles, Kelsey decided. The strikingly beautiful red-haired woman by his side, who seemed in no great hurry to greet the man to whom she'd once been engaged, had to be Helena. Elegant in a blouse and slacks of ivory silk, she made Kelsey distressingly conscious of her own none-too-clean tan slacks and simple pink cotton camp shirt.

Ricky Lee was easy to recognize. She'd never cared much for pretty men, but she could understand how a woman might be dazzled by his curly blond hair and angelic features. The man possessed a soft, rounded handsomeness that wouldn't last beyond his thirties without a lot of hard work. And Ricky Lee, she judged, wasn't the type to work at his looks or anything else. She wondered if Bonnie had yet recognized the childish pout of her husband's admittedly sexy mouth. Or the indolence reflected in his heavy-lidded, but beautifully long-lashed brown eyes.

Ricky Lee's surprise turned to a glower. He tried to tug his wife away from her brother's side. "Don't be stupid, Bonnie. The guy's an escaped convict. I'm going for the cops."

Bonnie turned on her husband, her dark eyes flashing. "No you won't, Ricky Lee." Her voice rang with warning, and she clenched small, delicate fists. "You do, and you'll find yourself out on the street so fast it'll make your head spin. Ben is family. And he'll stay here—safe—as long as he wants to."

Ben's quickly lifted eyebrow indicated surprise—pleasant surprise—at seeing Bonnie stand up to her husband.

The greeting Ben received from his brother was a lot less welcoming than his sister's.

"You brought the woman here, Ben? Are you out of your mind?"

"They said you had a gun, Ben," Bonnie added nervously. "They said you took her hostage."

"I'm afraid that's true, honey. But Kelsey isn't my hostage now. She's my friend. And she's not here under duress."

"You shouldn't have come." Kelsey couldn't tell if Charles's protest sprang from anger with or fear for his brother. "You're only making more trouble for yourself. For all of us. What's the point of escaping like this? That place you were in is awful, but we're doing everything we can to get you out of there, legally and for good."

Helena allied herself to her husband's objections by placing a hand on his arm and adding a small nod of assent.

"You're just putting your life in danger by doing this crazy thing," Charles persisted. "You can't run forever. You can't hope for any kind of decent life as a fugitive from justice."

"Everything you say is true, Charles," Ben returned quietly. "I can't argue with you over any of it."

"Then turn yourself in, Ben. That's the best thing. Let me call the lawyers. They'll see that you get back to prison safely and make sure that the reprisals don't get out of line. And they can take Ms. Merrill home."

"No, Charles. I'm out, and I'm going to stay out. As for Kelsey, she's free to leave at any time."

Bonnie thrust herself between her warring brothers. "Stop it, Charles. I can't stand to see you two arguing. Ben's home. We can be a family again for a little while. Stop talking—both of you—about all these hurtful things we can't do anything about." She turned tearful eyes up at the elder of her brothers. "Please, Ben. I can't take anymore. With Mother just gone..."

Ben folded an arm around his sister. "Bonnie's right, Charles. We're all under a lot of stress, but let's not argue. I won't be here long. For our sister's sake, if for no other reason, let's try to make this reunion as pleasant as it can be under the circumstances."

It took Charles a long moment to accept his brother's outstretched hand. Ben gave Ricky Lee only a cool nod.

A short respite with his family—at least with his sister—would be good for Ben, Kelsey thought. But she wasn't sure that Bonnie understood that ignoring hard reality wouldn't make it go away.

She could see nothing but politeness in Ben's handshake with his former fiancée. Plenty of barriers between herself and Ben already existed, but she was glad that he apparently carried no torch for an ex-lover.

"Let's go to the upstairs sitting room," Bonnie urged. "If the police are watching the house, we won't be seen from the windows up there."

They used the narrow service stairs at the back of the house and grouped themselves at the far end of the large room, away from the windows.

"Wait a minute, Ben." Charles was still standing. Everyone else had taken seats on sofas or upholstered chairs. He frowned at Kelsey. "The news reports said the woman is a reporter."

"That's right."

"I don't want any reporter sitting in on this illegal reunion. And I don't think any of us should talk to you in front of an outsider, let alone a reporter."

"Kelsey is no outsider. As I said, she's my proven friend."

She wanted to be much more than friend to Ben Carlyle, Kelsey thought. But she'd take what she could get.

"No problem," she interjected hastily, rising to her feet. "I'm willing to bow out. I can see your brother's point, Ben. Your family would like to have some time with you alone. I can understand that. I noticed a full coffeepot in the kitchen. I'll just pour myself a cup and sit down somewhere and wait."

"Are you sure, Kelsey?" She could see that Ben was ready to overrule his brother's objections. But those objections cleared the way for her to do something more important than join in a family discussion."

"I'd prefer it."

"Very well then. If you don't mind waiting. Just be careful to stay away from the windows."

Pouring herself a cup of coffee wasn't what she had in mind. And she knew exactly the "somewhere" she wanted to sit. On the way upstairs, she'd caught a quick look into a room that seemed to be a home office. She sneaked into it and found it well-equipped with both computer and fax machine.

She sat down at the computer and snapped it on.

If she could wave a magic wand and make Ben's life right again, she'd do it. But she had no magic wand. All she had was the ability to reach readers and hopefully move them with her words. She had to make people see Ben as she saw him. Had to make them aware that his conviction was a terrible miscarriage of justice.

She was risking Ben's wrath, she acknowledged. She hadn't been able to convince him yet that the good publicity her story would provide might be his only hope. She'd confess what she'd done later, when they were alone. When he read the story, she was sure he'd understand what she'd done and why she'd done it.

Unleashing Ben's anger, though, was far from her greatest risk. The article she hoped would enhance her career could also destroy it entirely. The published story would put her in legal jeopardy. After reading it, the police were bound to question whether she was still a hostage, or whether she'd become an accomplice in a convict's escape. But she ached to do something that might help to lift the terrible verdict from him, and she was ready to accept the consequences.

She placed her notebook by the keyboard and began to tap in words.

A small, isolated diner in the mountains of West Virginia isn't the place you'd expect to meet a convicted murderer. Nor is it a place you'd expect to run into an old-fashioned, real-life hero. Benton Carlyle is both. And despite the findings of a jury, he makes a strong, unblinking claim of innocence.

When she finished, she reprogrammed the fax machine to display only her own name, not its original sender's name and address. Then she dialed the number of her paper and, holding her voice low, so as not to be heard by the group upstairs, asked for her editor.

Mike Parsons erupted into the expected rush of questions, which she hastened to cut off.

"I'm all right, Mr. Parsons. You don't have to worry about me. Carlyle hasn't hurt me, and he won't. There's no time to explain, and I can't tell you where I am. I've got the whole story of what happened in the restaurant—pretty dramatic stuff—and why he's running from the law, and I'm ready to fax it in."

The squawk of Parsons's voice grew so loud she had to pull the receiver away from her ear. "I'm sorry, Mr. Parsons," she said, politely but firmly. "I can't talk any longer. My story's coming through on the fax now."

By the time Ben and the others came down, Kelsey was sitting in the windowless library with an empty cup of coffee, well into the first chapter of a noted author's latest techno-thriller.

"But you must stay for dinner, Ben," Bonnie insisted. "I want you with us just a little longer. I'll start fixing it right now. We can eat in a few minutes."

"No, hon. We can't stay."

"Please, Ben. It's safe enough. The police just sit out in the driveway in their car. They never come up to the house. I want to show off a little for my big brother. I've become a good cook since you...since you went away. Took a course in gourmet cooking, didn't I, Charles? I had to find some way to tempt Mother into eating as she got sicker. You know I looked after her this last year."

Taking care of a cancer patient was no joke, Kelsey thought. Bonnie had to be a lot tougher than Ben gave her credit for. Maybe all older brothers were the same way with younger sisters. Stephen still thought of her as the baby of the family and persisted in giving her advice on what to do. Sometimes she listened. Sometimes she didn't.

"Please stay, both of you," Bonnie pleaded, enlisting Kelsey in her campaign to get her brother to linger. Apparently Bonnie viewed her status as Ben's friend as overriding the family's aversion to having a reporter in their midst.

"Thank you for the invitation, Bonnie, but it's up to Ben."

Kelsey wasn't greatly surprised that Ben couldn't hold out against his sister's pleas, although none of the others, not even Charles, rushed to second them.

"I guess both Kelsey and I could use a decent meal, hon. But make it fast, will you?"

They had to get back to the cabin before dark. A long walk through the woods at night posed considerably more peril than following a mile-long trail from the cabin to the truck in the dark.

They ate in the breakfast room off the kitchen instead of the large formal dining room at the front of the house. Ben seated himself at the head of the table as if it were automatically his rightful place. Kelsey didn't think he noticed that Charles started for the same position, then made for the chair at the opposite end of the table.

Bonnie hadn't exaggerated her skill in the kitchen. They sat down to a meal of fork-tender chicken breast sauced with a mouth-watering blend of white wine, shallots and mushrooms.

Ben's sister definitely was no slouch when it came to getting her way, Kelsey noted. Not only had Bonnie coaxed him into staying, when his good judgment must be prodding him to leave a place uniquely hazardous for him, but her whole family was sharing the meal with Kelsey, politely if not too amicably, despite the fact that most of them would have preferred not to have her there.

"Walt says you're doing very well at the plant, Charles," Ben reported.

"He's just being kind. Frankly, I'm having a tough time managing the firm. And I wouldn't be doing half as well without Walt's help. But considering that you didn't think I could handle the job at all, I think I'm doing reasonably well." Kelsey read outright belligerency in the hoist of the man's chin. "When I learn a little more, I'm going to be a good president of Carlyle Specialty Tools, Ben. And I am going to make it."

"I'm sure you will." The ring of sincerity in Ben's voice had to be evident even to his brother. "Dad would be proud of you."

Charles looked as if he hadn't expected Ben's approval. And as if he didn't quite know how to respond to that unlooked-for support, he displayed a sudden keen interest in his food.

Kelsey could sympathize with Charles. It wasn't easy trying to compete with accomplished older siblings. Not even in her own family, where their parents took great pride in all their children and never played one against the other.

"Why you want to take on the job at all is beyond me," Ricky Lee chimed in, reaching for a third helping of chicken. "Don't see the point in it when you can afford not to. Me, I'm glad I saw the last of that loading dock. Bad enough that the work was boring as hell and the pay lousy. But the old man was always griping about how we were all ripping off the company."

Kelsey saw Bonnie's lips tighten, and suspected that if her handsome but boorish husband didn't smarten up soon, Ricky Lee might not be around to enjoy the fruits of Henry Carlyle's labor too much longer.

The loud knock on the front door startled all of them. Kelsey jumped. Ben went perfectly still.

"Pick up everything in front of you, Kelsey, and put it under the table," he ordered with a calmness she couldn't match. "Charles, take your time in answering the door."

Kelsey quickly followed Ben's lead and piled her telltale coffee cup and eating utensils onto her plate and hid them under the floor-length tablecloth. Ben shoved his chair in at the table as if no one was sitting at that spot. Kelsey did the same before Ben caught her hand and rushed her out of the room. The insistent knock came again. Charles was moving slowly toward the foyer when Kelsey rounded the corner to the kitchen. Bonnie, too, had gotten up from the table and was following him.

"You have no right to barge in here without a search warrant," Bonnie shouted loudly enough from the front hall to warn her brother that police were inside the house.

"We have a warrant for Benton Carlyle's arrest, miss. And we've reason to believe he's been in touch with you. You there, Jackson. Do you know anything about this?"

Backed against the wall next to Ben just inside the archway, Kelsey clutched his hand. Her heart pounded. Not by accident, she suspected, had the police questioner homed in on the Carlyle family's weakest link.

"He doesn't know anything, and neither do the rest of us." Kelsey thanked God that Charles was coming through for his brother when it counted. And apparently Bonnie's earlier warning was enough to keep Ricky Lee's mouth shut. "This family has had trouble enough. We don't need any more. You can see that my brother is not here. Now please leave us alone."

"Sorry, Mr. Carlyle. We've got to take a look around."

Kelsey held fast to Ben's hand as they stole toward the back door. She didn't even breathe as he slowly turned the knob and held it motionless while she crept out. He released it very slowly after closing the door behind him. The squeak in the porch door sounded to her like a screech. She hoped Bonnie's continued hollering at the cops would cover the betraying noise.

Bent double and keeping away from the side of the house where the police were, they ran to the cover of a large woodpile. Then to a garden shed and from there to the woods.

Ben didn't speak until they'd pushed well into the forest.

"You rest, Kelsey," he said, eyeing a tall, thick-trunked oak. "I'm going to climb up and and try to find out if anyone's on our trail." He crawled onto the low bottom branch of the tree and hoisted himself higher and higher until he almost disappeared into the foliage.

"No sign of activity," he said when he'd clambered down again. "I don't think they saw us make it into the woods. Let's keep going."

"It sounded to me," she said, out of breath again within minutes, "that the police didn't come to the house by accident."

"No. They expected to find me there. The question is why? And the answer is obvious. We didn't all stay together every minute. It wouldn't have been difficult for Ricky Lee or Charles to make a quick phone call."

She hated to think that a man couldn't even depend on his own family to give him safe shelter.

"Now that I've met Ricky Lee, I can't say that I like him any more than you do. I wouldn't put anything past him. And the cops went right for him, didn't they?" Climbing down a series of rocks, she slipped. Ben caught her before she fell.

"But I don't know, Ben," she said when they'd reached an area that offered slightly easier passage. "I wonder if your brother-in-law would risk losing everything by going against Bonnie. I have the impression that your sister's marriage might not be the strongest in the world."

"No. I guess Ricky Lee himself is doing what neither Dad nor I could do—convincing Bonnie that he's no Prince Charming. If Ricky Lee did blow the whistle on me, and Bonnie finds out about it, I'm pretty sure they'd be through. But I can't forget that Charles didn't pull any punches in letting me know he didn't want me there."

"But he stood up to the police, Ben. He didn't give you away."

"What else could he do? He knew I was listening. So was everyone else. Maybe he doesn't mind betraying me in secret, but he hasn't the guts to do it in front of others."

Ben stopped and looked worriedly up at the sky, which wasn't nearly as bright as when they'd left the house. "It's getting dark. We'll have to hurry to make it back to the cabin before we can't see well enough to keep walking. I don't want you to have to spend the night out here in the forest, so I'm going to take a tougher but more direct route."

The route they already were on was tough enough. It got worse. She hoped Ben knew where he was going, because she'd lost all sense of direction.

She'd never get used to this sort of thing, Kelsey thought, tearing free of brambles that caught at her legs. She didn't know how anyone could. Including Ben—for all his toughness.

Chapter 12

They made the last of the hike home in pitch darkness, orienting themselves by the reflection of the line of moonlight on the lake. Home. Kelsey smiled wryly to herself. That's what the little hidden cabin had come to mean to her. Home. Because she shared it with Ben. Would he laugh if she confessed that?

He fumbled for the oil lamp in the dark and lit it. The lamp's pale glow etched into life the stark, disciplined profile of his face, the straight, powerful lines of his bare forearms.

He'd come perilously close to being captured tonight. Kelsey shuddered at the narrowness of his escape. She didn't think she could stand seeing him dragged off by the police. If that happened, she was afraid she might lose it completely. Might degenerate into the kind of hysterical woman she loathed.

She folded her arms in front of her and shivered.

"You're cold," Ben said. "I'll build a fire."

Kelsey sat on the couch while Ben knelt on one knee and put a match to the logs in the fireplace. The dry wood caught immediately and blazed up, setting shadows to dancing on the walls.

"You didn't confront Charles and Ricky Lee with your suspicions about them, did you?" Kelsey guessed. If he had, he'd have mentioned it during the long trek back.

Ben shook his head. "I didn't want to upset Bonnie again. She's been through so much these last few days." Bracing himself with both hands on the stone mantel above the fireplace, he stared down into the leaping flames. "And when it came right down to the wire, when I finally found myself face-to-face with my brother, I found it terribly hard to flat out accuse him of betraying me." The fire spit and crackled. "I guess you could say I chickened out."

"I don't call it that," Kelsey objected softly from the cot. "You didn't want to hurt the people you love. I call that sensitive."

"Sensitive, huh?" Ben glanced back at her with a mirthless chuckle. "The men I knew in prison would laugh out loud at anyone calling me sensitive."

Kelsey didn't laugh. "Maybe you hesitated because you don't have a heck of a lot to go on. It's true that each of them did benefit in some way by your father's death. But the fact that neither was seen with the rest of the crowd at the ball game doesn't mean one of them went so far as to kill him to achieve that benefit."

"I'm aware of that, Kelsey. And seeing my brother and sister again, being in that house where we all grew up, I was just about ready to put aside my suspicions—at least about Charles. Not about Ricky Lee. But when the cops showed up so deliberately like that..." He sighed and rubbed at his eyes.

Kelsey uncurled herself from the couch and walked over to him. "Has your headache returned?" she asked, stroking along the frown line on his forehead.

"No. I'm just tired."

She pulled out a kitchen chair for him. "Sit down here anyway, Ben, and let me take a look at the wound." She moved the lamp closer to the end of the table. The cut looked clean, and the skin around it healthy. If Ben did have a headache, she thought, it probably stemmed more from problems on the inside than from the external injury. "You're lucky. I think the cut's healing like it should."

"Yeah. Lucky Carlyle, that's me."

Kelsey gently pulled away the old dressing that had gotten wet a couple of times and replaced it with a smaller stick-on bandage.

"With the police on the prowl," Ben said, "I can't count on this cabin to provide a safe hideout much longer. I'll have to start running again. Soon. Maybe tomorrow. We'll just have to play it minute by minute."

"Bonnie had the right idea, Ben. Let's not talk anymore about problems. For now—for tonight—we're safe." She was getting a lot better than she ever thought she would be at holding her attention on the *now* and not jumping ahead to some iffy future.

She went over to the corner of the room and picked up the rolled-up sleeping bag.

"What are you going to do with that?" Ben asked. "You're not thinking of sleeping outside, are you?"

She placed the bulky bag on the table and stood behind Ben's chair. "No." She leaned over and circled her arms around him. "I'm not thinking of sleeping outside." She dropped a kiss on top of his wind-mussed hair. "I'm thinking of sleeping with you. On a bed that's more than two feet wide." A thrill of anticipation raced through her. Already it felt so natural, so right to spend her nights in Ben's arms. "The opened-out sleeping bag won't be as soft as the couch, but we'll have a lot more room to...uh..."

Ben sidled her a glance and twitched a smile. "A lot more room to...uh..." he repeated. "Yes. I like that idea."

"Then help me flip this thing out on the floor."

They stretched the puffy square out on the floor and added a couple of toss pillows from the cot, and a blanket.

Kelsey slipped off her sneakers and started to undo the top button of her blouse.

"Hold it," Ben said, his voice low and vibrant. He caught her hands and lifted her fingers to his lips. "We did things in somewhat of a hurry last night. Tonight we're going to take it slow."

He curved a hand around her bottom. It took no more persuasion to let her body go slack against him. She dropped her head back so he could slide his lips enticingly across her throat. Slowly he freed each button and pushed the shirt from her shoulders. When she was clothed only in the flickering golden glow of lamp and firelight, he stepped back and gazed at her, his eyes dangerously dark and focused.

He stretched out his hand and drew a finger from the top of her shoulder down the outside of her arm to her wrist. Slowly. Attentively, as if he were embedding the line in the synapses of his brain.

"You're so beautiful," he whispered, hooking his fingers around her wrist. He brought her hand to his mouth and pressed his lips into her palm.

God forgive him, Ben thought, for not having the strength to hold himself away from her when he knew that was what he should have done from the beginning. A mighty sense of guilt washed over him. Contrition, though, couldn't compete with the hot, irresistible passion to possess her again that had him throbbing just from the exquisite sight of her.

He'd almost been able to convince himself that his first lovemaking with her had been no more than the result of sexual need. And considering how long he'd been imprisoned, that might have been true. But he could no longer blame his yearning for her simply on physical desire. Need of a different, deeper kind compelled him to take her in his arms.

The way she instantly eased her naked softness into him made him want to gush out a torrent of thanks for accepting him without reserve. But he couldn't think of words that wouldn't sound like senseless adolescent babble. Instead, he lightly kissed the tip of her elegantly shaped nose.

She laughed deep in her throat and went for his mouth. To his delight, she prodded at his lips with her tongue and took from him what she wanted.

Tonight, he vowed, lowering her gently to the sleeping bag, he'd hold back nothing. He'd give to the limits of his giving, to make up—at least a little—for what he'd done to her. For what he had yet to do.

Her skin was soft as water and as cool against his burning lips. Her breasts were firm and heated in his hands. *Maybe* was his last thought before his dazzled senses took over—maybe the ancients who worshiped their life-giving goddesses this loving way were onto something.

Long after she'd offered him her last abandoned cry of fulfillment and had fallen asleep in his arms, he lay staring at the red sparks of the dying fire.

He'd been afraid that Kelsey Merrill might take away his soul. But he'd had that backward. He'd already lost his soul in prison. She had returned it to him. She hadn't just given him back his self-respect, she'd given him hope.

With luck he might eventually elude the police. But he'd never escape the feelings for her that lodged deep in his heart and mind. He was in love with her. Desperately in love. Just the way the books said and that he'd always thought was drivel, fit only for weepy love songs.

If only he could tell her of his love, of how he wanted nothing in the world so much as to spend the rest of his life with her. The rest of his life. A life that held no options but years in prison, or a fearful game of hide-and-seek that would leave him no rest. What could he, a marked man, offer a woman who deserved the very best of everything?

He moaned and tightened his arms about her.

Kelsey woke. Her heart swelled with happiness. Ben. She sighed his name and elbowed herself up on one arm to gaze down at his sleeping face, already so familiar, so loved.

This was how she loved him best, she decided, stroking his bristled cheek. When his gray eyes first opened, soft and vulnerable from sleep. Before he could curtain them with distance and control.

Never would she have shared herself so completely with a man she didn't love. And she didn't believe it possible that Ben could have taken such care of her, cherished her so tenderly, if she wasn't important to him.

She wasn't comfortable with secrets. Especially not with the wonderful secret that rained joy into her heart. That discovery was too important, too life-changing not to let Ben in on it. Who would not want to know that he was loved? She cast about for words to make her declaration poetic, romantic, to convey all the elation and fulfillment her love of him gave her.

"I love you, Ben," she murmured.

The fascinating dilation of his eyes, the quick, startled parting of his lips, encouraged her to continue. "I want to stay with you always. Whatever comes your way tomorrow or ten years from now, I want to be there with you to share it. I love you."

The slight shift of his eyes away from hers told her as plainly as shouted words that she'd made a terrible mistake.

"I love you," she repeated shakily, the courage she'd garnered to speak what was in her heart dribbling away. She'd been so full of the happiness of her love, she'd forgotten its pain.

Ben felt as if he'd just been punched in the stomach. The first words he'd heard on waking from the stupor of exhausted sleep brought him a burst of jubilation. They loved each other. Somehow, someway, they could be together. The fantasy scraped away as quickly as it had come. Love was a luxury and a bond a fugitive couldn't afford.

The glint of tears in Kelsey's eyes almost unmanned him. But this was what he'd bring her always. Heartache. Tears.

It was torture to keep from folding her in his arms. Torture not to confess that he returned her love. But he'd learned of her strength and perseverance. She wasn't the kind to refuse a future just because it would be difficult. If she knew that he loved her, she'd see it through with him, whatever the cost. And at best the cost would mean her sharing the demeaning, isolated life a hunted man must lead.

He wouldn't allow it. Imprisonment had planted a rage for freedom deep in his bones. Like most people—like Kelsey—he hadn't really understood the value of freedom until it was taken away from him. Whether she wanted it or not, he would gift her with the real freedom he couldn't have.

Kelsey wondered if Ben had actually heard her. She tried to read his face. Nothing. Lengthening seconds—an agony of silence—closed in on her. A sick flutter started up in her stomach. Anything—even a *No way, José* or a *Get outta my life, woman*—would be better than no reaction at all. He sat up abruptly, a movement of his shoulder warding her off.

"When I leave here, Kelsey, I leave alone."

Without thought, she pulled up the blanket to cover her naked breasts. "But... but you said I was a help."

"So you were. And I want you to know how much I appreciate it."

Oh God! she thought. He was being kind. *Shut up!* she told herself. Not another word. He obviously didn't feel as she did. Let it go at that.

"But, Ben...I love you. I want to stay with you always."

The knife already stabbing through Ben's gut twisted deeper. She wasn't going to let him do it the easy way. Wasn't going to let him keep his dignity, or save her pride. She left him no choice but to cut it off between them quick and sharp. He had to set her free to get on with her life after he left or was caught.

He forced a smile and flicked at one of her earrings. "I wish I *could* take you with me, Kelsey. But frankly, the pleasure of having you in my bed like this on the road wouldn't be worth the bother. From here on, it'll be trouble enough just having to look out for my own skin."

Kelsey froze, her emotions in tatters, her mind in shreds.

Sex? He was talking about sex, when she was bleeding love in front of him. Where had the man she'd called "sensitive" gone? This wasn't the Ben Carlyle she'd come to love in a few short days.

But it was, she realized. Precisely so had he looked at her in taunting warning just before they'd left the motel. Exactly so had he set her earring to swinging then.

She was the one who'd taken a wrong turn in their relationship, not Ben. He'd always been honest with her. More than once he'd told her in no uncertain terms what he wanted from her. So how could she blame him for taking what she so freely offered? It was her own delusion that gave her the hope that he didn't really mean what he said about wanting no ties of any kind.

She turned from him. Hurt. Embarrassed. She grabbed at her clothes, ready to fling them on and run away. Flee from him in tears like a child when her words of love weren't even cold on her lips? She wouldn't do that. She loved him. That hadn't changed. It never would.

He'd made it perfectly clear that she meant little more to him than a helpmate in his escape. If that was all he wanted of her, her love demanded that she continue to provide it until he chose to leave it behind.

She gathered the blanket around her and, forcing herself to hold her head high, she got up and walked—she didn't run—to the tiny bathroom.

When Kelsey had disappeared into the bathroom, Ben fell back against the floor and covered his face with his hands. If he lived to be a hundred, he'd never forget her stricken look when he'd spoken those lying words. Slowly and methodically he began to blast himself with every single one of the terrible curses he'd learned in prison.

He'd expected her to walk out the door after she'd dressed. He'd even told her he'd accompany her to the pickup and start it up for her. But she'd politely declined the out and fixed them both a meager breakfast with the last of their food.

What an incredible woman, he thought. She'd just offered him the most treasured possession she could give any man—her love. And he'd just let it lie there, without so much as a thank-you. But she was just going about her business as if he hadn't kicked her in the teeth. He well knew how much that kind of toughness cost. And it convinced him that he'd done the right thing by speaking to her so coldly. Anything less and she'd follow him to the ends of the earth. He'd done nothing to inspire such loyalty. That he had to reject a prize he so wanted was just one more ordeal he had to combat in the long war that his life had become.

He picked up her empty teacup and rinsed it out along with his at the sink.

"I'm going back to the house," he told her. "We need more supplies. And I need a change of clothes. I can't wear these for the rest of my life. I won't stay long."

Kelsey didn't bother reminding Ben of the danger involved. He knew that as well as she did.

"Besides," he continued, "I've got to face that blunt talk with Charles and Ricky Lee. I'm not sure how far confronting them will get me. The guilty person will just deny it, of course. But I can't leave here without giving it a shot."

They slowed for no sweet encounters on this trip to Dogwood Hill. Bonnie was sitting at the kitchen table, ostensibly just having a cup of coffee. But Kelsey thought Ben's sister was purposefully waiting for him. She rose quickly when she saw him.

"I hoped you'd come back, Ben, but you can't stay long. The police may return." She took a step toward Ben as if she were about to greet him with a hug as she'd done yesterday, but stopped in midstride and hung her head. "It was my fault that they almost caught you yesterday. I should never have made you stay."

Ben closed the distance between them and draped his arm around his sister's shoulders. "It wasn't your fault, hon. And this will be a quick visit. We need food. Will you put together a box or a bag for us? Lightweight items—packets of soup, crackers, tea bags. That sort of thing. Make it enough for two or three days."

Bonnie nodded and started toward the pantry. Halfway there she stopped and looked back at her brother hesitantly. "Ben? I don't think Ricky Lee informed on you yesterday. At least—" She bit her lip. "At least, he said he didn't."

Kelsey didn't envy Bonnie. The poor woman had considerably less faith in her own husband than she herself had in Ben.

Ben gestured toward the stairs. "I left some things in my room when I stayed here those few weeks after Dad's heart attack. Are they still here?"

"I think so."

"I'll run up and see what I can use."

Kelsey went to the pantry with Bonnie to load a cardboard box with supplies.

Bonnie handed Kelsey a small jar of instant coffee and regarded her thoughtfully. "You're in love with my brother, aren't you?"

Bonnie wasn't nearly as naive as some thought her, Kelsey decided. She added a couple of small pull-top cans of salmon to the box.

"Yes," she answered. What was the point of denying it?

"I'm glad. Ben needs something good to happen to him after all the awful stuff that's come down on him the past few years."

Ben didn't share his sister's belief that Kelsey Merrill's loving him was all that good, she thought. But that was between the two of them, not Bonnie.

Ben came down wearing an expensive nubby-knit cotton sweater in shades of blue that topped a pair of gray slacks and clean black walking shoes. A better outfit for a man seeking to pass as an honest citizen than filthy shoes and clothes not that far removed from his prison uniform. A shave, too, had made him look less like a rough character. But she kind of liked that former grungy look better. He was carrying a small travel bag she guessed held a change of clothing and some toiletries.

She heard Charles's angry voice while he was still out of sight on the stairway. "You're saying I killed Dad, aren't you?" He followed Ben into the kitchen, Ricky Lee hard on his heels, scowling. "You're actually accusing me of his murder."

Bonnie rushed toward her brothers, shocked. "What are you talking about, Charles?" Both her brothers ignored her.

"No, I'm not," Ben said, setting the small nylon duffel bag on the floor. "I'm just saying you *could* have done it. I didn't know it before, but you had the opportunity. Neither you nor Ricky Lee were seen with everyone else around the time of the murder. You weren't in on the start of that ball game, Charles. Where were you?"

"I sure as hell wasn't off killing our father."

Kelsey saw that Ben, too, had caught the nervous glance Charles darted at his wife. Helena looked down and began to play with the gold buttons fastening the bodice of her fashionable green silk dress.

"You know something, Helena," Ben charged. "Let's have it."

Kelsey rather liked the way Charles moved to place himself between his brother and his wife. "All right, Ben. I'll tell you. Right after that big blowup between you and Dad, I was with Helena. We . . . well . . . we . . ."

"You don't have to explain, Charles. I get the picture. You were having a romantic moment with my fiancée."

"You and I were already having problems, Ben," Helena interjected. "We'd just about decided to break off our engagement."

"I don't care anymore if you and Charles were having an affair, Helena. I'm just trying to figure out who at the picnic could have murdered Henry. I know I didn't. Although I've never been certain that any of you really believe that."

"Of course we believe it, Ben." No one else joined in Bonnie's quick endorsement. Kelsey rose to swift anger that those closest to Ben didn't rally round him with quick and staunch support. But she knew he wouldn't thank her for leaping to his defense, so she kept her mouth shut.

"Helena and I were together for no more than a half hour," Charles continued.

"But I didn't follow you back to the picnic right away, Charles," Helena added. "We didn't want anyone to see us together like that, remember?" The abashed looked on her face showed her belated realization that her comment hadn't exactly helped her husband's case.

Charles gave his wife a cool nod. "Thank you for backing me up so strongly." Kelsey thought his sarcastic tone was justified. "You've just stoked my brother's belief that I set him up."

"Not belief, Charles," Ben returned sharply. "Only suspicion. It could have been Ricky Lee."

"Get off my case, Carlyle," Ricky Lee raged. "Whether you like it or not, Bonnie and I are married, and there's not a damn thing you can do about it. I don't remember where the hell I was at whatever time. I was probably someplace making out with your sister. I didn't kill anybody. And if you go around saying I did, I'll . . . I'll sue."

Kelsey didn't like the look of that threatening stillness that had come over Ben at Ricky Lee's crude reference to Bonnie. It wasn't that she minded Ricky Lee receiving a well-deserved punching-out, but she didn't want Ben to do something she was sure he'd feel sorry for later. She placed a gentle warning hand on his back. "Come away," she urged. "This isn't doing anyone any good. We need to get out of here."

She wasn't sure she'd saved Ricky Lee's hide until she felt Ben release the tight muscles of his back. He looked down at her and nodded.

Just in case Ricky Lee persisted in running off at the mouth, Kelsey dashed into the pantry, picked up the box of groceries and thrust it into Ben's hands. Holding it, he couldn't flatten anybody. "Will you handle this, please, Ben. I can take care of your bag."

Bonnie followed them to the door. "Where are you going, Ben? How did you get here? You haven't told us anything."

"We've a car parked nearby, out of sight of the cops. But after what happened here last night, I'm not about to say anything more." He turned a flat gaze on his brother. "None of you have to worry about seeing me again."

Tears flooded into Bonnie's eyes. "Oh, Ben."

He bent to kiss his sister on the cheek. "I'm sorry, hon."

In the woods, Ben stopped to look back at the house through the trees.

"Thanks for keeping me from doing something stupid back there, Kelsey. We didn't need that. I can take the bag for you if it's too heavy."

"No problem. It's not heavy at all."

A mild curse evidenced Ben's frustration. "Laying out my suspicions to Charles and Ricky Lee was a complete waste of time. All it did was make relations between my brother and me more difficult. I was naive to think that instinct alone would tell me whether either of those two was the killer. The truth is, Kelsey, I'm no more able to sense their guilt than a jury was able to sense my innocence."

She hadn't really expected Ben's investigations to produce much result, but it was painful to watch his efforts continually come up empty. "I've been wondering, Ben," she said. "You're all assuming that the attack on your father was instigated by a personal argument. Isn't that the reason why you fastened on both Charles and Ricky Lee as suspects?"

"Yes. And it's a pretty good reason. If you'd known my father, you'd agree that personal argument with him could provide grounds for murder."

"Unfortunately for your family, it seems so. But couldn't the killing have resulted from something other than a personal argument that got out of hand? Might it not have had some tie-in with the business?"

Ben shifted the box from his left arm to his right. "I looked into that possibility. So did the cops to some extent. But I found no business-related problems serious enough to kill over. Of course, I wasn't exactly on top of things at the office those last few weeks before Dad's death. I was pretty much up to my ears in setting up my own venture."

"How about what Ricky Lee mentioned yesterday. It doesn't seem very serious, I admit, but..."

"What? I don't remember what he said. Maybe I try not to listen to him."

"He mentioned something about your father chewing out shipping-room personnel for stealing company merchandise."

"You're right, Kelsey. He did. I missed that. If Ricky Lee were involved in any large-scale thievery that I didn't uncover—" He put down the box. "Wait here. I'm going to run back to the house to make a phone call. I have to talk to Walt about this. There's a telephone in the basement. They won't even know I'm there. Better stay right here. We don't want to take a chance on you getting lost in the woods."

Kelsey only breathed easy when she saw Ben making his way back to her through the trees a short while later.

"Walt confirms that there were some unexplained losses back then. Henry had him perform an investigation, but he found no more than minor pilfering of company property, and none was traced to Charles or Ricky Lee. Still, it just reinforces my suspicions that something was going on between my father and one of them, maybe over the shipping department. But I can't for the life of me figure out what, and unless I can find out very soon..." He didn't need to finish the sentence.

He was making such an effort to lead her through more easily navigated parts of the forest, she suspected, in order to make the walk easier for her after yesterday's forced march.

They were both ravenous after the walk to the house and back. She fixed them a late-afternoon dinner, which they shared holding to an excess of painful politeness. Afterward, she rinsed out some of her clothes in the lake and draped them over some bushes to dry.

She aimed another worried glance at Ben, who was stretched out on the porch on his stomach, his head pillowed on his arms. Shirtless and in jeans, he looked like he was doing no more than soaking up unaccustomed sun. But the rigid line of his mouth told her his burdensome situation wasn't far from his mind.

He suddenly sprang to his feet, startling her.

"Careful, Kelsey," he said quietly, his sharp gaze scanning the woods. "Someone's coming."

Chapter 13

She heard it, too, now: the soft whicker of a horse, the thud
of hooves approaching along the trail from the sawmill. The
sound confused her. Would the police be coming for Ben on
horseback?

He stepped quickly inside the cabin. When he returned a
moment later, he was pulling his hand from the back of his
waist. She went cold. Though she couldn't see the gun Ben
had stuck in his pants, she was sure it was there.

"Get inside, Kelsey," he said.

She didn't argue with him. She simply placed herself at his
side. If it was the authorities, maybe her presence would
cool the situation.

A chestnut horse pushed through the trees. When she saw
the rider, she breathed a sigh of relief.

"Charles?" Ben strode from the porch and approached
his brother. "Charles. How did you find me?"

Charles brought his animal to a halt and dismounted. "I
knew you had to be somewhere in the vicinity. You couldn't
come and go from the house if you weren't. At first I

thought you might be at Walt's place. I drove over to his house, but found no sign of you. Then I remembered this old hideaway of yours. I'm surprised it's still standing."

Charles walked over and planted a booted foot on the porch. "Good thinking, Ben." He nodded. "Perfect place to hide from the cops."

Ben's reaction to his brother's unexpected appearance was about as cordial as Charles's had been yesterday. "What am I supposed to do?" he asked coolly. "Invite you in for tea?"

Smiles—even if they were filled more with irony than pleasure—came a lot easier to Charles's face than to his brother's. "We can skip the tea. I've come to do you a favor."

Ben looked as if he believed that any favor from Charles must be booby-trapped. "Like what?"

Charles pulled a folded-up page of a newspaper from the breast pocket of his silk broadcloth riding shirt.

Her story, Kelsey thought excitedly. Her hand flew to her mouth. Oh, Lordy! What with all the emotional upheaval since she'd sent it in, she'd forgotten to warn Ben of its appearance. Charles unfurled the sheet and held it up for Ben to see. She stared in horror at the heavy black print splashed across the top of the page: Interview With A Killer.

Ben glanced at the page and snatched it from his brother's hands. Without pausing to read the story, he rounded on Kelsey in fury. "You had to do it, didn't you? You couldn't wait. My freedom—my life—is at stake here, but your all-important story is what counts, isn't it?"

"I'm not responsible for that lurid headline," she protested. "It's meant to sell papers."

"Hey, Ben, calm down," Charles threw in. "That story is very favorable. You didn't tell us that you'd saved a guy's life in the diner. It's the best story I ever read about you, and I think it's likely to build you a lot of public support."

Kelsey didn't think Ben was even listening to his brother. His face was still thunderous. "I thought I could trust you. I thought you were different from everyone else."

The rage in his voice cut like a whip, but she didn't back away from it. "You *can* trust—"

He balled up the page and tossed it away as if it dirtied his hands. "You just proved that my unflattering opinion of reporters is justified. You're no different from that pack of hyenas who hounded me during the trial. Except you went a whole lot farther, didn't you? All that playacting about—" He broke off, but she knew he was referring to her profession of love. "All you ever wanted was a story. Period."

"That's not true, Ben." How could he even think that after what they'd shared the last few days? "I'm trying to help you. You'd see that for yourself if you'll just read what I wrote."

Ben had turned his back on his brother. Charles's eyes finally lit on the weapon shoved into the waistband of Ben's jeans. He stiffened with apprehension.

"That gun, Ben," he interjected. "Did you plan to use it on me?"

"I'll use it to protect myself." Ben held his gaze on Kelsey, his answer to his brother clipped and inattentive. "After all that's happened to me, I need the protection."

"Maybe so. But if the police so much as see it in your hand, they'll gun you down."

"That's just one of my problems. I'll deal with it when the time comes."

Ben wasn't looking at his brother, but Kelsey could see that Ben's curt answer inflamed Charles. Angry crimson flushed into his face. His mouth worked. He looked about to cry.

"That's you, isn't it, Ben?" Charles flared. "Always in charge. Always the one who knows best. *Ben'll deal with it.*

Let Ben handle it. With Dad—with everyone—it was always Ben. Always you."

Charles's outburst broke through Ben's angry focus on Kelsey. Evidently startled by his brother's impassioned reaction to remarks so offhandedly delivered, Ben turned to him.

"Not always in charge, Charles. Certainly not now. You're in charge of the family. You're in charge of the plant. Isn't it about time you got over that childishness about me being the favorite? I long ago stopped being anybody's fairhaired boy."

"Yes, you did." Charles's reply was as blunt as his brother's question. "And you're right. It's time I stopped comparing myself to you. So forget it. Let's stick to the reason I came. I know how you loathe stories about you. We all do, and with good reason, but you ought to be thanking Kelsey for this one."

She didn't care if Ben thanked her or not. All she hoped was that he wouldn't hate her.

"You don't have to worry that she gave away your whereabouts in the article. She never mentioned any specific place but the restaurant, and the cops already knew that." Charles flicked his gaze from Ben to her and back again, as if he couldn't quite figure out the reason for his brother's continuing hostility toward her.

"But I still think you'd better hit the road soon. Whether you acknowledge it or not, Kelsey's story has given you a big break. As a result of it, the cops have been inundated with tips that you've been spotted everywhere from Charleston to Pittsburgh. Checking out all those reported sightings is taking so much manpower they've pulled the stakeout car away from the estate. So while it's a little safer around here for you right now, you'd better not push your luck. It won't take the police long to decide you're not in any of those other places, and when they do, they'll come back here in force."

Charles nodded a brusque farewell to Kelsey and walked back to his horse.

"Goodbye, Charles," Ben said to his brother's retreating back. "You'll be glad to hear that I'll be gone by tomorrow."

"Good luck, Ben," Charles called, turning his mount back the way he came. "And whether you believe it or not, I mean that."

Charles's leaving threw all emotional tension back on the two of them. "So you're leaving," Kelsey said. An inane remark. But everything that came to her mind right now seemed as pointless. Ben was going away. And she wasn't going with him.

Ben nodded briskly. "At first light tomorrow I'll head out over the mountains on foot. You can take the truck." Absently kneading the back of his neck as he usually did when trying to puzzle things out, he walked to the edge of the slope and gazed out over the lake to the darkening miles of wilderness beyond. "I'm an experienced hiker and camper. I have a fighting chance of making it out of these hills."

Kelsey wondered who he was trying to convince: her or himself.

"Won't you even listen, Ben, to what I think my stories can do for you? Readers often root for the underdog against authority, especially when it looks like officialdom could be wrong. You could become a *cause célèbre*. At the very least, I can keep you in the public eye so that the police will have to be careful how they treat you, should you be caught. This is the kind of story the rest of the media will pick up, but we have to do it now, while you're still out. Interest will fade when—" she caught herself. "I mean, *if* they hide you away in prison again. Don't you see, Ben? Widespread publicity might spur the governor to order a review of your case."

Ben dropped his hand from his neck. "I don't believe that," he said flatly. "I've already had plenty of publicity and it didn't do me a lick of good. I used to think that the justice system would work for me. Now I know it won't. It's over, Kelsey—your tagging along after a source, your stories direct from the horse's mouth. From here on out what you do about them is your affair. I won't be involved.''

Ben looked back at Kelsey. She hadn't moved from the spot where she'd stood while he'd lashed her with his anger, taking out on her the frustrations of days—of years. She was wearing the flowery dress he liked. The wind blew the diaphanous skirt against her body, outlining the lovely shape of her legs, her hips. The angled rays of the setting sun picked out no trace of tears in her eyes, but her lips trembled. Those soft, full lips, he was sure, would haunt him forever. Twenty feet separated them, but his lips felt as if they were pressing on hers. That he couldn't prevent the reaction inflamed him.

It was all falling apart. His hope of clearing himself. His fantasy that she could truly love him. How could he believe that when he couldn't even trust her? Anger at Kelsey, anger at himself for having been fool enough to put his faith in her, stirred his emotions into a tangled snarl. Good Lord! Hadn't he already learned enough about betrayal not to be surprised that she, too, had turned on him?

She'd done a lot for him, risked a lot. But the bottom line remained that she'd done it all primarily for a story. And this time tomorrow he'd be miles away from her, never to see her again. Never to see her again.

So what difference did it make whether she'd given herself to him because she truly felt something for him or because she hadn't balked at using any means she could to get that story?

None at all, he told himself, locking his jaw in a hard line. "I don't mind anymore that you'll do anything for a story," he said coolly. "In fact, right now I'm all in favor of it."

His head had begun to ache again. Still, he had every intention of striding over and taking her, right now, on the ground where she stood. But the clouded look in her eyes stayed him. And her defensive stance, with her arms clamped in front of her, triggered a sharp, painful memory of the way he'd felt standing in the courtroom the day that awful judgment had come down on him.

His stomach churned. Time seemed to curl in on itself. The confused and frightened anger he'd felt then—the sickening sense of his utter helplessness to stop the juggernaut rolling over him—swirled out at him again. He felt wobbly on his feet and pressed his hand to the side of his head to stop its spinning. The world around him was losing its sharp edges, was taking on the disorienting heat waves of a highway undulating in the broiling sun.

A sudden vivid picture of the stifling courtroom—packed with people—stabbed into his mind. He recalled exactly the murmur of the spectators, one man's irritating cough. The jury was filing in. He heard the shuffle of their feet as they took their places in the double bank of black leather armchairs on one side of the room. He felt the eyes of the courtroom artist fixed on him, as always. *All rise.* He broke out in a cold sweat. The judge's voice echoed through his mind: *The jury finds you, Benton Robert Carlyle, guilty of murder in the second degree.*

He was afraid he'd cried out. A glance at his attorney, who was still looking impassively at the judge, told him he hadn't. He wouldn't.

No, he told himself, trying to grab on to solid reality. He couldn't be in the courtroom. But he could still hear those condemning words.

The shaking started in his legs and spread throughout his body. He wasn't able to stop it. Wherever he was, he was going to be sick, he thought with curious dispassion. Dimly he heard someone call his name. Through the chill in his blood he felt the warmth of a steadying hand on his chest. Kelsey. Her face wavered into view. The delicate scent of her cut through the haze of anguishing memories.

"Ben. Are you all right?"

He blinked away the past and shook his head hard. The ground solidified under his feet. Another damn flashback. Triggered by stress, they'd told him. They'd come on him a couple of times before, especially in the first few weeks after his father's murder. Again right after the trial. Frightening to feel so helplessly out of control.

"Ben. Answer me."

"I'm fine."

"You don't look fine. Your head injury, it could be—"

"I said I'm fine." That she could do that to him—call up memories that left him weak and indecisive—that he could allow her that kind of power over him, turned his fury inward.

To rid himself of the frightening jumble of emotion—to prove to himself that he was in control—he grasped her arms and jerked her to him. "This will be our last night together," he said, glad he'd achieved the harshness in his voice. "So let's provide you with a little more background color for your story."

When she stiffened and tried to pull away, he trapped her in his arms and ground his mouth over hers in a punishing kiss. She deserved being treated so, he told himself. She'd made him love her and then she'd deceived him. Whether the story helped him or not, he'd asked—demanded—that she not print it.

"No, Ben," she gasped when he allowed her room to breathe.

"It's a little late for *no,* isn't it? But I have no problem with your dropping the *I love you* act. After all, I let you know from the first that sex was all I wanted," he rasped into her silky hair. "It's all I want now."

A black and rotten lie. It had never been just sex with him. Even now, when he was trying to make it so, he was aching to lose himself one last time within her sweetness. This final soul-searing union with her—a joining that always gave him so much, whatever it did for her—would have to last him the rest of his life.

The knowing twist that slanted Ben's lips brought a bitter taste to Kelsey's throat. But his arms were about her, as she wanted so much for them to be, and she could do nothing but cling to him, driving herself into every harsh kiss. No assault of his mouth could be hard enough, no hold tight enough for what she needed. Never again would she know his raging desire for her. Never again lie in his arms. To be united in pleasure with him was better than no last union with him at all. She wanted to devour him, to fill her senses with him so that some faint trace of him would remain in her when he was gone.

When she was alone.

A hot whirlwind tore away her breath. She moaned and tangled her fingers through his hair to hold him to her. He gathered up her skirt and slipped his hand between her thighs. He was making no effort at delicacy, at seduction. Nor could she. She wanted him too much, too desperately for gentleness. She fumbled at his jeans to free him.

They dropped heavily to the ground. He whipped her panties off over her sneakers and fell on her, as voracious as she for their merging. His lips were drawn wide in a grimace of pain, of ecstasy, she couldn't tell which. He thrust himself into her. She felt him pulsing inside her like a heartbeat. She locked her arms and legs around him to hold him there forever.

Forever didn't last. The same darkness cooling her fever carried forever away. With a strangled moan, he rolled off her and threw himself facedown onto the ground beside her. At least he hadn't tried to make believe his lovemaking was anything but sex. She'd have recognized the lie and would have hated it.

Ben, his lungs still heaving, lay prone on the cold damp ground. Loving her had been so good. He slammed his clenched fist into the turf. And all wrong. He heard a sob and raised himself on his elbows. Kelsey was lying on her side, her back to him.

"I'm sorry," he said, through gritted teeth, not entirely sure just what he was apologizing for. "I'm sorry."

He folded himself back on his knees to straighten her skirt and stood to arrange his own clothing. Hauling in a deep sigh of regret, of guilt, he knelt to slide his arms under her slender form and picked her up to carry her inside. He knew the small room so well he needed no light to find the cot and lay her on it. He covered her with the blanket and she turned to the wall.

He filled a glass of tepid water at the sink and gulped it down, then sat at the table in darkness. At dawn he had to be on his way, but there was no point in trying to sleep. Would he ever again know a good night's sleep with thoughts of Kelsey pounding at his brain? he wondered.

The storm of discouragement and rage provoked by his brother's arrival with Kelsey's story was over. How could the actions of one woman make him so crazy when he had so much else on his mind? He'd weathered other disappointments, other disloyalties, without flying off the handle as he'd just done with her.

No doubt about it, being with her had changed him. In making him human again after years of functioning more like a robot than a man, she'd also robbed him of his ability to shut himself off from hurtful circumstances. Even so, he couldn't regret it. He didn't like the hard, closed-off man prison had made of him and didn't want to be that man ever again.

Was it true her story could help him? he wondered. He'd been stupid and unfair to throw it away. He could at least have read it. Now he had a strong desire to read it. If he could glean from the article that she didn't really love him as she'd claimed, he ought to be glad. A generous, truly selfless lover prevented from returning a woman's love would be grateful if his loved one didn't feel for him too

deeply. But he could make absolutely no claim to selflessness where Kelsey was concerned. There was no hope for a
life with her, but he still stupidly wanted her to care for him.

He lit the lamp and carried it over to the cot. She was
sleeping, her tear-stained cheek curved into her hand. It was
good that she'd soon be free of him, he told himself, hating
to admit that truth. She didn't need him to drag her any
farther into his mucked-up life.

Holding the lamp high, he went outside. His light fell on
a ripple of pink fabric that brought him another wave of
guilt. He picked up the panties he'd torn from her and
shoved them in his pocket. No wonder she'd started to cry
after their lovemaking. He'd fallen on her like a hungry animal. He found the crumpled newspaper page fluttering
against the base of a tree where the wind had blown it. He
brought it inside and smoothed the page out on the table.

Charles was right about the story presenting him in a
positive way. Although Kelsey had gone overboard a little
in describing what he'd done for Whittaker and the others,
she hadn't flavored the article with personal opinion. She'd
presented his case factually, mainly in his own words. He
was glad to read in the sidebar that his guard was expected
to make a full recovery.

Her story was nothing like the appalling trial by media
he'd endured before his real trial ever started. Countless articles that twisted every word he'd uttered—every aspect of
his life—into something ugly, had provoked his futile rage.
He owed Kelsey an apology for assuming she'd produce only
more of the same.

He doused the lamp and sat in the dark and silent cabin,
his head propped in his hands. Had he flared up at her so
quickly, he wondered, because subconsciously he'd been
looking for a way to wrench her out of his heart? That theory made more sense than his actions had. If so, it hadn't
worked. His love for her still filled every nook and cranny
of his being. And he'd hold fast to it, whatever the future

might bring. She'd given him something he'd never expected to have—a soul bond that nothing—not even returning to prison—could ever break. The magical union they'd shared in this place would always be there, locked into his heart forever.

The habit of pacing out the same restricted pattern his prison cell had imposed was so ingrained, he scarcely noticed when he rose from the chair and fell into it. He always seemed to end up at the small cot, looking down at Kelsey. The moon spilled silver over her hair and lovely face from the window above her.

Gasoline, he recognized with a start. How could he smell gasoline when the truck was parked almost a mile away? A small light gleamed for an instant at the edge of the trees. A flashlight? He leaned closer to the window to try to make out the cause. There it was again. A man carrying a flashlight and running toward the path to the sawmill. A man whose identity he intended to learn.

He turned to rush toward the door and realized he could no longer clearly make out its position. His eyes were itching and his throat hurt. Smoke. The cabin was filling with smoke.

"Kelsey!" he shouted. "Kelsey, wake up!"

Almost blinded in the smoky darkness, he felt for the door. A thin tongue of flame licked upward from beneath it. Between one second and the next, it seemed, a narrow glowing line traced out the shape of the door.

He called to Kelsey again and reached for the metal handle. Pain seared his palm and fingers. He jerked his hand away.

He whirled to check the small window above the cot as a possible escape route. Flame leaped behind the glass, closed at night to keep out flying insects. No other way out. He had to open that door.

Pulling out the panty he'd shoved into his pocket, he padded his hand with the flimsy piece of cotton and wrested the door open. He reared back from a door made of fire that leaped into the wooden ceiling joists. Intense heat scorched his skin and seared his throat. He looked back. Kelsey was stumbling toward him. In two long, quick strides he covered the distance between them.

The walls around them burst into flames.

Mindless of his burnt hand, he swept her into his arms and dashed toward the blazing rectangle that spelled safety. Even the porch was aflame. His foot twisted on its edge. He dropped his precious burden and fell. Kelsey was up in an instant, pulling him away from the inferno. Coughing and gasping for cooling air, they staggered away from the blazing cabin.

The propane tank exploded, the force of it throwing them both to the ground. They picked themselves up and scrambled to the edge of the clearing a safe distance from the fire.

Kelsey clung to him. She was shaking so hard her teeth were chattering. Her eyes were wide and staring as she watched the flames now totally engulfing the cabin. The fire tossed glowing cinders into the night sky, most of them drifting, fortunately, toward the lake.

"My purse," she gasped, her voice thin and reedy. "It's still in there. My credit cards...my driver's license..."

Ben understood her fastening on minor details during an emergency. He'd done something of the same when he'd positively agonized over the choice of a tie to wear at his trial. Let her concentrate on lost belongings for the moment. She needed a little time to recover from the immediate terror of barely escaping with their lives before he told her that someone had deliberately tried to incinerate them.

The place had gone up so quickly because their would-be killer had drenched every wall in gasoline before tossing a match to it. Only the fact that the cabin's old wood hadn't completely dried out from soaking rains had given them the seconds they needed to survive. If the little house had been tinder-dry, as it often was deeper into the summer—if they'd both been asleep...

He tightened his arms around her.

"Sorry, Kelsey. There's nothing we can do. Everything's gone."

"Oh, Ben," she mourned. "That old place meant so much to you. I'm so sorry you lost it. What happened? We didn't use the fireplace tonight. Did the lamp somehow...?"

"Not the lamp. You might as well know that the fire was no accident. Someone came out here and set it."

"You mean, someone wanted to..." She shuddered and dropped her forehead onto his chest. "Oh, my God, Ben. Oh, my God."

He squinted over Kelsey's head as if night, distance and a mountain didn't bar his view of Dogwood Hill. His fear for their lives was slackening. Taking its place was grim, white-hot rage.

Not only had someone tried to get rid of him, he hadn't balked at taking Kelsey's life, too. And he knew who that murdering bastard was. He'd caught only a fleeting glimpse of the man skulking about the cabin just before the fire, but for that instant the moonlight had played on light-colored hair. Ricky Lee.

Chapter 14

Ben, Kelsey thought, must have used some kind of sixth sense to lead them to the truck with only moonlight to guide him.

"You'll have to start 'er up and drive, Kelsey. I burned my right hand."

"Oh, Ben. How bad is it? Let me see."

"Never mind. Nothing we can do about it now. I'll take care of it later. The wires under the steering mechanism will be hard to see in the dark. I'll tell you exactly what to do."

She felt quite a sense of accomplishment when she touched the third wire to the other two and the engine started. She was learning all kinds of new skills with Ben.

As Charles had told them, the long driveway was free of a police car. Kelsey wheeled the truck up to the house and parked next to a silver Mercedes. With no necessity for stealth, Ben ran up the steps and pounded on the front door. After several seconds a light flicked on upstairs, then the porch light came on. Charles's astonished face appeared at one of the narrow windows flanking the door. A lock scraped back. Charles had barely cracked open the door when Ben pushed through.

"Ricky Lee!" he shouted. "Where are you, you S.O.B.?"

Bonnie's husband was padding sleepily down the stairs in slippers and a pair of blue silk pajamas. Ben took the steps two at a time and grabbed Ricky Lee's pajama top to yank him threateningly close. Ben cursed as a stab of pain reminded him of his injured hand, but he didn't let go.

"What the hell's the matter with you?" Ricky Lee shrieked, struggling helplessly in his brother-in-law's grip. "Have you gone crazy?"

"You know exactly what's the matter. You just tried to kill me—kill both of us."

"Kill you? You've lost it, man."

If Bonnie's husband had set the fire, Kelsey thought, he was putting on one heck of a good act. She'd swear his air of frightened befuddlement was for real. Ben apparently had no such doubts. "Don't bother to deny it. I saw you. I was getting too close, wasn't I? You were afraid I might finally figure things out. Well, I have."

Bonnie was having no luck tugging away her brother's hands. "What are you talking about, Ben? Ricky Lee hasn't done anything. Let him go. Let him go."

"He hasn't done anything? This poor excuse for a man just tried to eliminate me, just as he did Dad." Ben contemptuously shoved his sister's husband away from him. Ricky Lee fell back against the steps, his face pasty white.

Charles and Helena were standing at the bottom of the stairs, looking up at Ben as if they could make no more sense out of the stunning scene than the trembling, sobbing Ricky Lee.

"Call the police, Charles," Ben ordered, running back down the steps. "I intend to accuse Jackson of attempting to murder both Kelsey and me and of Dad's murder, and give myself up.''

''You're crazy, man,'' Ricky Lee yelled and ducked back behind his wife for protection. ''You're totally crazy.''

''Attempted murder?'' Charles sounded baffled. ''You and Kelsey? When? How? You're not making any sense, Ben.''

''Less than an hour ago Ricky Lee came out to the cabin, doused the whole place with gasoline and burned it down. Unfortunately for him, we managed to escape.''

''The cabin, Ben?'' Bonnie walked slowly down the stairs. ''You've been staying out at that old place of yours?''

''Cabin? What cabin?'' Ricky Lee was gaining some measure of bravery now that his tormentor was farther away, though he apparently thought it safer to stay where he was. ''I didn't burn down any cabin. How could I? I've been right here all night. Ask your sister. Tell him, Bonnie.''

''It's true, Ben. Ricky Lee and I went to bed about eleven o'clock. He never left the room. I know, because I haven't been sleeping well lately and I never even dozed off.''

''I tell you I saw him, sis.''

''You couldn't have. He's been in this house all night. I'm certain of that. Do you think I'd lie about this, Ben?''

Kelsey didn't think Bonnie was lying. And she didn't see how Ben could think so, either. Of all of them in this house, his sister was clearly on his side.

For the first time since storming into the place, Ben looked unsure. His uninjured hand went up to knead his neck. Growing ambivalence showed in the gaze that traveled uncertainly from Charles back to Ricky Lee on the stairs.

If Ben was wrong about Ricky Lee, Kelsey realized, that left only his brother. What a horrible thing for any man to have to face.

"I was sure I'd seen a man with blond hair," Ben said, with a hesitant shake of his head. "But it was dark. I may have been mistaken." His voice hardened. "But I'm certain that someone in this house wants me completely out of the picture one way or another. And that *someone* obviously knew where Kelsey and I were staying."

Ben's face was impassive as he stood before his brother, but Kelsey could guess what the confrontation was costing him.

"You knew, Charles. You were there only this afternoon. Did you tell Ricky Lee where I was?"

"I told no one. So I guess now you're going to accuse *me* of trying to kill you tonight. Don't bother. Helena will tell you that I never left her side until we heard you pounding on the door."

"Helena?" Ben looked to his former fiancée for corroboration.

"I don't think he did, Ben."

The usual ringing endorsement from good old Helena, Kelsey thought. With a wife like that, Charles didn't need enemies. Right now Ben had precious little to be thankful for, but he had to be grateful that Helena had chosen his brother over him.

"Would you be able to swear to that on a witness stand, Helena?" Ben pressed. "It could come to that."

"Umm..." Helena looked nervously at her husband. "You know what a sound sleeper I am, Charles. You've said yourself that they could set off a bomb next to my bed and I'd never hear it."

Charles gave Ben a bitter smile. "So, brother. Looks like I don't have an alibi after all. In your eyes, that probably makes me guilty."

"Someone tried to kill us tonight. That's a fact. Someone who had to be close, had to know where I was. Bonnie swears it wasn't her husband, and I have to believe her. So *you* tell *me*, Charles. Who else in this house fills that bill?''

Charles, Kelsey thought, faced his accuser with rare composure.

''I do. And all I can say is I didn't leave this house tonight. I don't expect you to believe me. This is how it was for you, too, isn't it, Ben? No one would listen to you. No one would believe. Consider this, my brother.'' The word was freighted with obvious irony. ''You're now doing to me exactly what others did to you. You're judging me guilty by circumstantial evidence a lot more flimsy than what convicted you. You at least had a trial. I don't even get that. You're setting yourself up as both my judge and jury.''

''I'm not, Charles. I'm just trying to find out what really happened tonight, and when Dad died.''

''Don't you think I want to know that as much as you do? Yes, I could have killed Dad. Lord knows he often made me mad enough to want to do it. But I didn't. And I had nothing to do with burning down the cabin. At worst, I'm guilty of wanting to get out from under your shadow. I admit that. But I would never have wished all this on you. You're my brother.'' Charles turned away, raking his hand through his dark hair. ''My God, Ben.'' Anger and distress filled his voice. ''I know we've never been close, but do you really believe that I'd do something so horrible to you?''

He no longer knew what to think, Ben conceded. The certainty that had come easy behind bars—born of festering rage and anguish—was slipping away as he stood here face-to-face with his brother. He well knew what it was like not to be believed. If any man should accept another's plea of innocence without backup proof, it was he.

Amid the little group of family anxiously clustered around him, Kelsey was holding her steady blue gaze on him. Kelsey, who'd accepted his innocence solely on the basis of his word and some strange insight she had into him right from the first. She'd go on believing in him, he sensed, no matter what.

Everything Charles had just said was true, Ben realized. He had condemned his own brother without proof of any kind. And ties of blood, years of living with his brother, were convincing him his verdict was as wrong as the one that had sent him to prison. He took a step forward.

"No, Charles," he said firmly. "I don't believe you did that to me." He thrust out his hand. "And I'm very sorry I accused you of it."

Not quite sure how to express his feelings, Ben delivered a gentle punch with the side of a loose fist to his brother's shoulder and ended up with a squeeze. "Yesterday when you were trying to tell me how you felt, I should have been listening harder. That bit about getting out of my shadow? Forget it. You don't stand in anyone's shadow."

The brotherly embrace he and Charles attempted was tentative and a little awkward, Ben admitted, but it lifted an emotional burden that had weighted his heart for too long. And it brought relieved smiles to everyone, including Kelsey.

But he was no closer now to learning the identity of his father's killer—of the man who'd tried to up his victim count to three—than he'd been back in prison. When he'd started his useless quest, at least he had some suspects. Now he had none.

Ricky Lee yawned and announced he was going back to bed. Helena seemed to be having trouble holding her eyes open, but she gamely followed the others into the living room and plopped onto a sofa next to her husband.

Kelsey and Bonnie fussed over his blistered hand. They treated it with soothing burn ointment and wrapped it gently in sterile gauze.

He had to be missing something. Motivation. That's what he still didn't get. An army of people strongly disliked

Henry Carlyle. But someone who hated him enough to kill
That was a lot more difficult to pinpoint.

"I don't have much more time to come up with an
swers," he told them all. "The burning cabin is in a remot
area, and with all the rain we just had I don't think it wil
spread to the forest, but the authorities are bound to hear o
it by morning and show up here. If any of you have sugges
tions on what I should do now, I'd like to hear them."

"The fact that someone tried to kill you," Charles said
"should convince the police that the real murderer consid
ers you a threat."

"I wouldn't bet on it. Maybe I just burned down the cabin
myself to make them think that. We both survived, didn'
we?"

"I know you've already gone over everything a hundred
times, Ben," Kelsey offered. "But the only thing I can think
of to do is to start over again, right from the beginning, and
try to examine every moment of that crucial time."

Ben nodded tiredly. "All right, everyone. Once more
from the top. Let's reconstruct the scene immediately after
I was discovered with Dad's body."

Charles leaned back against the sofa. "Very well, I'll lead
off. Mother's scream brought several of us running to the
house. Besides myself and Helena, there was Bonnie—" He
shifted his gaze from the ceiling to his sister. "Ricky Lee was
with you, wasn't he?" Bonnie nodded. "There were also
two or three people from the plant who came running in the
front door immediately behind us and followed us into the
living room."

Ben rubbed at his forehead. "Two or three people from
the plant? Who were they?"

"I can't remember exactly. A couple of women who still
work on the line. One or two others. Walt was with them."

"Wait a minute, Charles," Bonnie threw in. "Mr. Simpson was in the room with the rest of us, but didn't he come in from the patio?"

"Did he?" Charles thought for a moment. "You're right, sis. I remember now. He did. Not that it matters much."

"The patio." Ben didn't halt his slow, restricted pacing. Kelsey wondered if he might hold to the habit for the rest of his life. "I don't remember either of you saying anything about that before."

"I guess I just forgot about it," Bonnie said.

"No one ever asked about it before," Charles added.

"The patio isn't easily accessible from outside the house," Ben mused. "That's why we didn't set up anything there for the barbecue. To reach the living room from that direction, Walt would have had to walk halfway around the outside of the house and come in through the garden gate."

"But people were wandering everywhere that day, Ben," Charles countered. "And the patio isn't completely cut off from the rest of the grounds. It's not so strange that someone might come into the shade to sit and relax for a few minutes. Especially Walt, who's been in and out of this house for years. He even dined with the family out there a few times."

"I know. I'm just trying to cover all the bases." If the motive for the killing had been personal hatred, that had to leave out Walt. The man had been able to put up with his employer for almost thirty years and was facing retirement. It didn't make sense that he'd blow his top after all this time. Besides, Walt was a good friend.

But it hadn't been a stranger who'd let him take the blame for a murder.

What if the killing had nothing to do with hatred? What if Kelsey's suggestion that it could have been business-related was correct? Both he and the police had investigated that possibility, but not in any great detail.

"Tell me something, Charles." Ben looked down at his brother. "Ricky Lee complained that Dad often accused the shipping clerks of diverting inventory. Walt says there was nothing to that. What do you think?"

"There wasn't, Ben. I was in charge of shipping and receiving for several months before Dad's death. I made sure that every shipment that went out had its proper invoice, and every incoming shipment accepted was covered with a purchase order."

Well, Ben conceded, that shot down that theory.

"On the other hand," Charles continued thoughtfully, "Dad may not have agreed with Walt's assessment of the situation. I remember seeing them in heated argument a couple of days before the murder. I couldn't hear details of the conversation, though. Frankly, Ben, I didn't think a whole lot about it at the time. Dad was always on someone's case. Most often mine."

Ben hated even to consider the disheartening possibility forcing itself upon him. Walt, too, knew about his cabin. He'd even given him some suggestions about refurbishing the place years ago.

He stopped and stared into the darkness beyond his reflection in the window, trying to recall precise details of the man he'd glimpsed running into the trees. No good. He'd seen nothing but shadowed movement, and just for an instant the glint of moonlight on light-colored hair. Painful realization burst into his mind. Pale hair. Not blond like Ricky Lee's. White... like Walt's.

But how in the world could he prove anything against the plant manager? Walt would just deny everything. It would be the word of an honest citizen against that of a convicted killer.

The company's computer records. A small ray of hope began to flicker through his growing depression. Answers—if there were any—had to lie there. He'd looked at them before, when he was readying his defense, but that had been a general overview of all financial records. This time he could focus in on one department. If only the police gave him time to carry out his search.

"Give me the keys to the plant, Charles." The brusqueness of Ben's order snapped Helena awake. "And the keys to your car."

"The keys to—? Yes, Ben. I'll get them." Charles left the room to run upstairs. He was back in a few moments to pitch two sets of keys into his brother's hands.

"What are you going to do?"

"All of you might as well go back to bed. Bonnie, please find a room for Kelsey. I don't expect to be coming back here. One way or another, I'll try to keep in touch." He strode from the room to a chorus of cries for him to wait.

Kelsey dashed after him. "Ben, wait," she called as he ran down the steps to the Mercedes. "I'll drive you."

"I can handle it with this bandage on." He pulled open the door on the driver's side. She got in next to him.

"Walt?" she asked, as the engine purred to life.

"Maybe. I don't know yet. I'm going to the plant to check out some of the computer records on shipping and receiving. No serious losses could stay hidden for long without someone tampering with those records. And there aren't a whole lot of people who could do that. Only myself, Dad, of course—"

"And the plant manager," Kelsey finished for him.

"And the plant manager."

"You're taking a big chance, Ben. Someone might see you."

"I'd be taking a bigger chance if I didn't check this out. We don't have a night shift. At two o'clock in the morning there shouldn't be anyone around."

The Carlyle Specialty Tool Company overlooked the Monongahela and was one of the very few manufacturing plants in the area. The building was dark, and they had no trouble getting in. Ben headed into the main office that had once been his and was now his brother's. He flicked on the light and tossed the heavy ring of plant keys on the desk.

"What can I do to help?" Kelsey asked as he booted up the computer.

"Just keep a lookout through that window. I'm hoping that any passerby seeing the car will just think Charles is working late. I used to do it a lot myself."

Following Ben's request, Kelsey stationed herself at the window and cracked the venetian blind to scan the parking lot in front of the building. After half an hour, she dragged over a chair to sit on. After nearly two hours, she could barely keep her eyes open.

Ben's sharp exclamation jerked her head up. She went over to him.

"You found something."

He leaned back in the chair and stretched the cramped muscles of his shoulders and arms.

"The person who did this was good. Damn good. If I hadn't specifically been looking for that carefully concealed discrepancy in the inventory, I'd never have found it. And only the fact that I'd met most of our customers personally allowed me to pick out this record." He touched a key. Kelsey bent to look over his shoulder. The file that flashed onto the screen didn't mean anything to her.

"This seems to be the purchase record of one of our large customers. I've never heard of them."

"But you haven't worked here for a while, Ben. Maybe they're new."

"No. Look." His index finger marked the place on the screen. "The first entry goes back to more than a year before Dad's murder." He clicked a couple more keys. "Here's another. And this entry lists a supposed supplier from whom I know we never bought anything before I left. Notice?

Same address as the other two. There probably are others. Unless I'm dead wrong, and I don't think I am, someone has set up phony accounts for dummy vendors and customers."

"What does that mean, Ben?"

"It means that the company has been paying for supplies it never received and shipping merchandise to nonexistent customers. My guess is that address will turn out to be a warehouse from which merchandise can be resold." Ben typed in a command and the printer started to produce hard copy.

"As plant manager, Walt was in the perfect position to do all this. And he's done it so cleverly that it must have been difficult even for my father to track down the deception. If he ever did, he didn't tell me about it. Maybe he didn't have time. Maybe he forced the issue of my taking over because he guessed something of the sort was happening. In any case, this level of theft and embezzlement is surely motive for murder."

Kelsey took Ben's hand in both of hers. "You've done it, Ben." Her eyes began to fill above her broad and happy smile. "You've cleared yourself. Your long nightmare is over. When the authorities read all this, you'll be free."

Oddly enough, Ben thought, he felt no exhilaration. Instead, a cold, deep weariness was settling over him. "I see now why my so-called friend was eager for me to leave the company and start my own business. Why he wanted us to stay in his house where he could keep his eye on me. Why he offered me money to disappear."

Ben heard a sound which he instantly recognized as the sharp cock of a pistol.

He quickly swiveled around to face the door.

"You should have taken that offer, boy."

No longer the affable, generous host, Walt stood in the doorway, pointing his weapon at them. Ben cursed himself silently. He'd been so engrossed in his find, he hadn't heard the plant manager enter the office. And the gun he'd counted on to protect himself in any dangerous confrontation with his father's killer was lost in the cabin's smoldering ruins.

"As for that—" Walt nodded toward the print-out "—the authorities aren't going to read it. Just came by to make sure those records were buried as deep as could be. Good thing I did. Don't mind telling you it gave me quite a shock to see you here, Ben."

"You should have stuck around a while to make sure the fire got us," Ben said, with a coolness Kelsey could hardly believe.

Walt nodded in agreement. "I slipped up there. Don't slip up often, though. Believe me, boy, I hated to do that. I like you. You always treated me decent. But you're just too damned smart for your own good. After that last phone call from you asking about the shipping department, I had to do something, didn't I? I figured all your nosing around would lead you to the records sooner or later."

"How long has this been going on?"

"Don't see as how that matters much." Holding his pistol steady on the two of them, Walt walked into the office and stood in front of the desk. Ben began to get out of his chair.

"Stay where you are!" Walt's threatening order shot out quickly. "And just keep your hands on the desk where I can see 'em. You, young lady, move away from your boyfriend. Stand there at the side."

Kelsey did as she was directed. Walt's weapon carefully tracked her movement.

"You see where this is aimed, Ben. Any wrong move from you and she'll pay the price."

"Like Dad did."

Ben faced his former friend with the same cold stillness he'd shown the louts on the road. But how did he hold his voice so steady, when she was afraid she wouldn't be able to speak at all? He was succeeding in keeping their would-be murderer talking. For that she was glad. But in the end, she was all too terrifyingly sure, Walt intended to use that gun.

"That was Henry's own fault. I didn't want to kill him, but he left me no choice. I could tell by the kinds of questions he asked that he was getting too close."

"Think, Walt," Ben pressed. "A good lawyer could make a jury see that Dad provoked you to the breaking point. But this is different. This would be cold-blooded murder. You don't want to use that thing. Put the gun down, Walt."

"Sorry, son. I'd like to. Really. But I'm afraid I can't. So you just sit tight."

"I will, Walt. That gun puts you in charge." True enough, Kelsey thought, trying to control her shaking. But she had no doubt that Ben was stalling for time while seeking any opportunity whatever to change that situation.

"The least you can do is tell me how it happened," Ben said. "Dad's murder, I mean. Did you come to the picnic that day meaning to kill him?"

"Yep. Had to. He wasn't spending as much time at the plant as he used to, and wasn't working late alone, where I could get at him, at all. I was real careful not to let anyone see me slipping into the house. I was going to use this—" the gun he was holding on Kelsey moved only slightly "—but Henry made it easy for me. He left that damn golf club of his right where I could reach it. He never saw me coming. A few good whacks—"

Kelsey winced. Ben didn't even blink.

"I hoped only that using the golf club they'd all seen Henry hit you with earlier might slow the cops down some. I never thought I'd be lucky enough to have them put you away for the killing. I was kind of sorry about that, boy, but

it did solve all my problems. I didn't have to worry abou
Charles. The kid's not smart enough to figure out what
was doing."

"That's where you're wrong, Walt. If you get rid of us
I'm sure my brother will be able to put two and two to
gether. You can't keep on killing people to protect you
self."

Walt shrugged. "I've got Charles covered. He won't fin
out anything." The boastful grin snapped off the plan
manager's face. "Enough of this chewin' the fat, Ber
Think I don't know what you're up to? This one won't cau:
me any more problems than the last. You're an escape
criminal, and the lady's no hostage. After that story, th
cops know she's your willing accomplice. I came to do som
work and shot me a couple of burglars in the dark."

Walt took a couple of steps backward to better cover ther
both. He gripped the pistol with both hands.

Kelsey's heart pounded. Desperately she sought Ben
eyes. It would be easier if it happened while she was lool
ing at him. But his gaze was spearing into Walt's as if shee
willpower alone could stay the man's trigger finger.

"Nobody'll be around to say any different," Walt sai
with grim finality.

"Yes, there will."

Charles was standing in the doorway.

Walt whipped his gun toward him. Ben snatched th
heavy ring of keys from the desk and threw them at the plan
manager's head. The jagged bits of metal struck Walt's face
As fast as lightning, Ben vaulted to the top of the desk an
hurled himself on Walt. The gun went off with a shatterin
blast. Plaster spewed from the ceiling. Kelsey dashed ove
to help, but Ben and Charles already had Walt pinned to th
floor. Ben twisted the gun out of Walt's outstretched han
and stood up, breathing hard.

"Okay, Charles. I've got him covered." Charles let go of the arm he was kneeling on and got to his feet.

"Over on your stomach on the floor, Walt," Ben ordered. All his former bluster gone, Walt's curses mixed with sobs as he turned himself facedown.

"Are you all right?" Ben asked his brother.

"I'm fine."

"You, Kelsey?"

"I'm okay, too, Ben."

"Thanks, brother." Ben's voice filled with emotion. "If it weren't for you—"

"You bet." Charles, too, had to clear his throat. The brothers, Kelsey suspected, had connected more closely in the last few hours than they ever had before in their lives.

"Took me a while to figure out what was going on," Charles continued. "Bonnie was sure you were heading for the hills again. I thought you needed the keys because you wanted to help yourself to the petty-cash drawer, and I had no problem with that. When I came here the front door was unlocked."

"How much did you hear?"

"Enough to give you some solid backup this time, Ben."

"Computer files will give us everything we need. Take the gun, Charles. I have to make a phone call."

Ben shifted the weapon from his left hand to his brother's right. He stopped on his way to the telephone and pressed Kelsey's arm. "You sure you're all right?"

"I'm sure. Just a bit shaky is all."

"You got a lot more than you bargained for when you decided to come along for a story, didn't you?"

She wished he hadn't dropped his hand. It separated them when she longed to feel his arms safely around her. He turned from her briskly and picked up the receiver of the desk phone.

"This is Benton Carlyle. I want to give myself up. You'll find me at the Carlyle plant."

With no further conversation, Ben hung up the phone. As if the lateness of the hour and the stress of the last few days were finally getting to him, he sank to a seat on the edge of the desk. Fatigue and stress had long since gotten to her. She could hardly hold herself upright.

"When the police get here," he said, "I want you two to keep quiet. I don't expect them to be gentle with me. I've given them a lot of trouble, and from their point of view I'm just a dangerous escaped con. So let them go about their business and both of you stay out of it, understand?"

She understood, all right. He thought the cops might be ready to slap him around, and he didn't want her or Charles to get into any trouble by trying to intervene. But how could she stay out of it when her heart was so entangled in him?

Already they could hear sirens in the distance. Charles grimaced. "Sounds like they're sending an army."

"I hope they beat the hell out of you," Walt spat out from the floor.

She went to the window to peer out. Several police cars, both local and state, shrieked into the parking lot. A horde of officers stamped into the office, guns drawn.

"Drop that weapon," one ordered. Charles laid the pistol on the floor and backed away, hands in the air. A group of uniforms converged on Ben. Two grabbed him by the arms and whirled him around to slam him facedown on the desk. He grunted in pain.

"Don't do that," Kelsey cried. A cop kicked Ben's legs apart. She tried to push herself between him and one of the policemen. He easily shoved her back.

"Get away, lady. This guy's a killer."

"He's not. Listen to me. He's an innocent man. There's Henry Carlyle's real murderer." She pointed at Simpson. "We found the proof. It's all there in the computer."

They ignored her.

"Don't treat my brother like that," Charles protested loudly. "He's giving himself up. Walt Simpson here killed my father and was ready to kill these two. That's why I was holding the gun on him."

"And who are you?" demanded the officer who'd relieved Charles of the gun.

"That's Charles Carlyle," one of the locals informed them. "He owns this place."

"He's clean," said one of the officers holding Ben spread-eagled over the desk. They yanked his hands behind his back and slapped the cuffs on him. He gasped with pain.

"Stop!" Kelsey's anxiety over Ben fueled her anger at the police. "You're hurting him. His hand—"

"Quiet, lady. This man is a prison escapee. And he's going back there."

"I'm a reporter. You treat him decently or you'll find charges of police brutality spread all over tomorrow's papers."

"Hey. She's that reporter they want to talk to. We'd better take her in, too."

"Take 'em all in. We'll sort it out later."

The two burly policemen hauled Ben to his feet. His hands chained behind his back, they propelled him toward the door. His eyes, his face, were locked into total blankness.

Anguished, hating what was happening to him, helpless to stop it, she stepped in front of him. His gray metal gaze flicked to a point just to the side of her head.

"Congratulations, Kelsey. You got what you wanted. You're in on my capture. All this should give you a colorful climax to your next story."

Sharp pain corkscrewed through her chest.

"Please stand aside, ma'am." One of the officers brushed her aside and the two men hurried their prisoner off.

"Ben," she called after him. "We'll get you out soon. Ben?"

He never looked back.

Chapter 15

Kelsey sat in her rental car and watched the media crowd gathering at the high iron gates set in the prison walls of grim gray stone. A reporter spotted her and rushed over. She quickly rolled up the car windows.

That didn't discourage the woman who pounded on the window next to her. "Do you have a romantic relationship with Ben Carlyle, Ms. Merrill?" she shouted.

"No comment," Kelsey mouthed.

"What happened during those nights you spent with him in the mountains?"

She controlled her impulse to shout back, *None of your bleeping business.* She'd become a media target herself since Ben's recapture. Maybe it was only fair that she was getting back some of her own. A hard lesson that made her vow to treat subjects of her reportage a little more gently from now on.

Failing to elicit a response from her target, the reporter returned to the flock of waiting journalists.

Ten days since they'd rushed Ben so pitilessly away. Ten days since she'd last seen him. Days of whipping out articles about Ben and his case for her paper, and of endless meetings with lawyers. The one Stephen had called in for her, the publisher's attorneys—all of whom convinced authorities not to file charges against her. And the more important meetings with Ben's new legal representative.

She and Charles had agreed to fire Ben's original attorney and engage one of the finest criminal lawyers in the country to represent him. A man whose name alone guaranteed wide media interest.

She'd hoped they'd free Ben immediately. But they kept him in prison while the legal ramifications of his situation were being worked out. The fact that he escaped was in itself a crime. A stupid charge, Kelsey thought, since if he hadn't escaped to right the wrongful verdict, he'd have remained behind bars until he was an old man.

How long until she could wake up without immediate thought of Ben raising this hard lump in her chest? she wondered. Not too long, her mind insisted. Never, her heart whispered. The days weren't too bad. They kept her busy enough—almost—to hold down her heartache over Ben. The nights were awful. She couldn't stop picturing him confined in that horrible place, anxiously pacing out that horrible cell, being subjected to God only knew what indignities.

Ten long days since she'd seen him. And she wouldn't be seeing him now if her editor hadn't issued his ultimatum: Do the interview or lose her job. So she'd shown up—along with what looked like every TV news outfit and print reporter in the country—the day of Ben's release. Parsons was crazy to think that Ben would even look at her, let alone talk to her. He didn't need her anymore.

He'd called Charles and Bonnie from the prison. He'd never called her. He loathed her. That was clear. His hurtful parting shot that she was only with him to be in on his capture still rang in her ears. She could understand why he wanted never to see her again. Quite aside from the painful fact that he evidently viewed her unauthorized story as a kind of betrayal, that story had precipitated events that almost got him killed.

The crowd suddenly started milling around its center like a cloud of hornets buzzing around a nest. Lounging camerapersons and reporters snapped to attention and vied for vantage points.

Ben was coming. A prickle of excitement crept over her. She wanted to see him. Whatever his reaction might be, whatever the cost to her hard-won composure, she wanted to see him again. Needed to see with her own eyes that he was all right.

Charles, Bonnie and Jim Whittaker sifted into the outskirts of the crowd. In yesterday's interview, Whittaker had told her he'd be here to thank his former prisoner for saving his life, and to wish him good luck.

She caught a glimpse of Ben fighting his way through the phalanx of reporters. Her heart leaped. Her throat tightened and her eyes grew misty. She grabbed a tissue from her pocket and blew her nose. Never would she let any of those probing cameras catch her tearing up.

Ben was scanning the crowd as he walked, probably searching for his brother and sister. From the way he kept shaking his head, she guessed her colleagues weren't getting much out of him. She could have told them that and saved them all a very long trip. But they wouldn't have listened.

Charles and Bonnie were heading toward their car. She got out of hers and stood so that Ben would be able to see her on his way to join them. That would let her go back to her editor in all good conscience and say that she'd tried, but Ben had refused her.

Ben searched frantically for a woman with short blond hair amid the throng. He hadn't tried to call Kelsey from prison. What he had to say to her had to be said in person. In spite of his condition to her editor that he'd grant an exclusive only to Kelsey Merrill, he wasn't sure she'd come. After what he'd done to her, why should she? He was very much afraid that he'd regained his freedom only to lose the woman he loved.

A blue dress the same bright shade as Kelsey's eyes halted his skimming glance. There she was, more beautiful than ever, standing behind a car on the other side of the road. One kind of tightness in his chest rippled into a different kind.

He made for her, trailing a gaggle of journalists hollering questions mostly of the useless how-do-you-feel variety. As he approached, Kelsey just stared at him blankly. He'd hoped she'd be smiling. She wasn't. A man shoved a microphone in front of his face. He pushed it away and pulled open the car door.

"Get us out of here, Kelsey!"

She was ready to follow Ben's orders. Her own sluggish brain wasn't coming up with any other ideas. He'd thrown her completely off center by climbing into her car instead of Charles's. She folded herself onto the seat and started the motor, leaning on the horn as the automobile edged forward. Seeing that they would come up empty with their colleague and the subject of her articles, the group rushed back to where Ben's attorney was holding court in front of a bank of microphones.

Neither of them spoke while she drove far enough from the prison to make sure no one was following, ready to pounce when they stopped. Her palms were damp, Kelsey lamented. And she had to fight to keep her lips from trembling. She felt as nervous as a teenager in the throes of her first date. Trying to prove to herself that she could handle the situation, she plunged in.

"Charles told me you had him track down the owner of the pickup and return it to him along with a generous check."

Ben nodded. "He deserved it. Taking that truck gave me the time to work things out. Evidently you didn't get your car back yet."

"Some of it. The tires were gone, and the stereo."

"I'll get you a new one."

Right. Another simple payment for services rendered and he could be on his way, free of any messy personal encumbrances like a woman who loved him. Forget it. What she wanted from Ben couldn't be covered by the gift of a new car. And no way would she let herself feel beholden to him for anything. "Thanks for the offer, but I can manage it on my own."

"Let me. It's the least I can do for you after what you did for me."

"No need for payment," she said tightly. "Any services rendered from me to you came for free."

Ben slapped the dashboard. "Blast it, Kelsey. That's not what I meant at all."

She was glad he'd turned angry. His irritation was a lot easier to deal with than his gratitude. "Let's just skip it, shall we? Where to? Fairmont?"

"I need a lift back to Dogwood Hill."

She wasn't sure she could spend that long a time with him without coming completely unglued. "That's not next-door, Ben, and I have to get back with a story on your release."

"There's a fax machine at Dogwood Hill, remember? You can get your story in that way."

Of course she remembered. And he sure hadn't forgotten. He'd probably never forgive her for that. "You could

have gone home with Bonnie and Charles. I'm sure they'
have waited while I did the interview.''

He couldn't have gone with his brother and sister, even i
he'd wanted to. They'd delicately informed him that all fou
were going to spend a couple of days in Pittsburgh, so th
house would be empty. He thought it best not to advis
Kelsey of that fact. He hoped that being there would re
mind her of the wonderful days and nights of love she'
blessed him with at the old cabin. The cabin, he reminde
himself morosely, that was now no more than a heap o
ashes.

He fell into the same silence that had overtaken Kelsey
That silence, broken only by occasional innocuous com
ments on the condition of the road or the weather, length
ened into miles. And every mile left him more worried tha
the distance between them was growing wider.

Damn! Somehow he'd gotten off on the wrong foot wit
her. He hadn't felt this awkwardness between them sinc
he'd ordered her out of the ruins of the diner at the point o
a gun. And even that hadn't stopped her from talking his ea
off. Taking her to Dogwood Hill was fine in theory. I
wasn't working out in practice. Besides, he couldn't get a
her while she was driving. And he was counting on his arm
to convince her of his sincerity if his words failed.

''I want to talk to you,'' he said. ''Pull into that sceni
overlook ahead.''

She parked at the deserted overlook. But far from offer
ing him a welcoming smile and open arms he ridiculousl
had been hoping for when they got out of the car, she wa
chillier than she'd been when they'd walked into that mote
room.

They strolled toward the low stone wall edging the spot
Kelsey, her face wooden, seemed more interested in th
gravel beneath their feet than the exquisite mountain view

ahead of them. With those damn sunglasses on, he couldn't even see her eyes to try to figure out what she was thinking.

This was going to be even tougher than he'd expected. After ten days that felt like ten months, he was ready to pull her into his arms, press himself against her captivating softness and cover her enchanting face with kisses.

If he did, she'd probably let fly with a sock on the jaw. Not that it wouldn't be worth it, but he didn't want this meeting to end without her giving him a chance to have his say.

He'd armed himself with half a dozen possible opening lines, but now that the moment was upon him, he discarded them all. Everything he thought of sounded so trite: *You're the most beautiful woman in the world to me. How could I ever live without you? Can you ever forgive me for behaving like an idiot? Can you ever forgive me for damn near getting you killed?*

How could he fault her for writing him off after what he'd said and done to her? In his painful humiliation at being dragged off in handcuffs in front of the woman he loved, and furious at himself for the selfish need of her that had placed her in danger, he'd senselessly gone on the attack.

Kelsey scuffed at the gravel with her sandal. Was Ben just going to keep on staring at those blasted mountains forever? If he didn't say something soon, she'd have to. And that posed a problem. She was supposed to be conducting an interview. But the only questions filling her mind during this excruciatingly long, drawn-out time they'd been together were personal—very personal. Very intimate.

He moved a little, and the accidental brush of his arm kicked a jolt of electricity through her. He still commanded her senses without even trying, but she had to ignore that raging desire to fling herself into his arms. What good was an embrace when it wouldn't come with what she longed for: his love. And *that* he'd already refused to give her, re-

fused on principle to give anyone. If her head kept running
down that dead-end road, the tears that lurked too blasted
close to the surface lately would surely spill over. And *that*
she had no intention of allowing.

Questions, Kelse, she reminded herself, tapping the center of her forehead with a couple of fingers. Sensible questions. Professional questions.

"So, Ben," she said with forced brightness. "How do you
feel about getting out of prison?" She grimaced and bit her
lip. Heaven help her, he'd reduced her to that.

"Fine." He nodded. "Good." He nodded again. "I'm
glad to be out."

Well, now that they'd established that a man was actually glad to get out of prison, what scintillating bit of information could she skillfully elicit next? What would his
reaction be, she wondered, to something along the lines of
*Okay, Ben, how about letting me hang around you for the
next fifty years?*

"Are you going to accept Charles's offer to head up the
company?"

The company? Ben thought. Who cares about the company? He wanted to talk about the two of them, about their
future together. If they had one. And from the closed-off
look on Kelsey's face, he knew they didn't.

"No. Charles feels that the fact Walt was able to put one
over on him means he can't really handle the business. I'm
sure he can. I'll stick around for a while to help him
straighten things out. Then—" He shrugged. Nothing held
much interest for him right now, except Kelsey. "Then I'll
move on."

Of course he'd move on, Kelsey thought. He was free
now. Free to wander where he willed, unimpeded by ties he
didn't want, exactly as he'd said he would.

"Will you go back and try to pick up the pieces of that business venture you talked about?"

If she kept this up, Ben thought, he was liable to start shouting at her. Never mind business ventures. How could he pick up the pieces of their relationship when he was the one who'd smashed it into bits in the first place?

"Maybe. Those companies I mentioned are located in the Pittsburgh area, so I'll probably wander up your way."

Yes. A sudden spurt of optimism came over him. That's what he'd do. Go up to Pittsburgh and give the woman a proper courtship. Dates. Dancing. Flowers. Of course she was cool to him. How could she be anything but? He'd do everything he could to show her he wasn't the turkey she had every reason to believe he was. "Maybe we can get together sometime for a drink... dinner...."

Kelsey managed to drag out a tight smile. "Sure...a drink sometime...." No way. She wasn't that much of a masochist.

"How about your plans, Kelsey? Did it work, your getting a big story?" He'd forgotten about that goal of hers. Maybe she was ready to cut him out of her life completely and get on with the business of making a journalistic name for herself. "Are you heading for New York... Washington... L.A.?"

The professional recognition that she once would have given her eyeteeth for had turned out not to be as exciting as she'd expected. So she'd finally decided she had a lot more to learn. And this new series her editor had suggested—how well the prison system was or wasn't working—could be interesting. Of course, she'd have to dig up a new inside source. Her heart couldn't stand being around this one while trying to view him as no more than that.

Her shrug echoed Ben's. "Maybe someday. For now... guess I'll just stay in Pittsburgh for a while."

At the sound of an approaching car, Ben tensed and whirled around. Kelsey laid her hand on his arm. The first time she'd touched him in ages. He was wearing a linen sport coat, but the solid warmth of the muscle beneath felt wonderful. And reminded her too painfully of the closeness they'd never share again.

"It's all right," she said. "No one's after you anymore." A family sedan passed them and she felt Ben relax. Two young children waved at them from the rear window. She and Ben waved back.

"I guess I'll have to relearn a whole set of reactions." She loved that sheepish grin that had come all too seldom in the past. "It'll take some getting used to. Being able to stand out here with you in broad daylight in full view even of a passing police cruiser. Being able to walk around without constantly looking over my shoulder."

"You're free now, Ben," she said, dropping her hand from his arm. "Free to go where you want to go. Do what you want to do."

Enough! He couldn't stand any more of this empty conversation. They'd lain naked in each other's arms. He knew every inch of her beautiful body, and she his. Yet here they stood, tiptoeing around each other as carefully as two strangers at a cocktail party.

What he wanted to do—what he *had* to do—was kiss her. He slid his hands up her bare arms. She curved toward him just a fraction of an inch and her hands came up between them on his chest. The thrill of it took his breath away. Her face had broken into a quick look of alarm and he could feel the tiny tremors running through her. But she wasn't pushing him away.

He had to see her eyes. He reached up and gently slid off her dark glasses. The suspicious mistiness he saw glinting over the blue completely did him in.

"Oh, Kelsey. Where I want to go is anywhere with you. What I want to do is love you for the rest of my life and have you love me."

Ben's words—the last words in the world she'd expected to hear—knocked her back on her heels. Her heart swelled with joy. His mouth covered hers, filling her with such giddy happiness that if he weren't holding her down she might just float away.

When the blissful pressure of his lips ended, she tumbled back down to earth with a thump. How could he truly mean those words of love when only a few days ago he'd so strongly condemned the idea of trust and commitment as meaningless? Maybe he was just confusing his feeling of gratitude for her help with feelings of love.

"I...I don't understand," she stammered. "You said that you didn't believe in trust, had no use for commitment. You said real freedom meant no ties, no personal bonds of any kind. That's not how I feel, Ben. I could never build a relationship with you on anything but the solid bedrock of trust and firm commitment between us."

"Oh, Lord, Kelsey. Forgive me, I'm doing this all wrong. I should have given you time to learn that you can trust me with your heart, time to understand how terribly much I love you. You have my trust, Kelsey. I'm not sure I'll ever again trust the rest of the world as easily as I once did. But I trust you. I trust you completely. How could I not, after what you've done for me?"

He was losing her, Ben thought frantically. Maybe if he held her even more tightly, so tightly she could hear what was in his heart, she'd believe in him again.

"Don't hold me to those stupid things I said before, love. I'm not the same bitter, disillusioned man I was when I walked into that diner. Those few short days with you changed me. Please believe me, my darling. There's nothing I want more than to be tied heart and soul to you forever. Having my freedom back—the freedom you gave me—means that I'm free to love you, free to spend my life wit you, if you'll have me.''

He pressed his cheek against the warm silkiness of hers smoothed his hand over the resistance he could still feel i the long, lovely curve of her back. ''I love you, Kelsey Marry me. I need you. I love you. Say you still love me.''

The desperate tightness of Ben's hold backed up his hu ried, heartfelt words. It was wonderful to feel his lips agains her cheek, but she tipped her head back a little so that sh could look at him. The handsome face she so loved was na ked with emotion, the beautiful smoky eyes burning wit love, with need. He was exposing his deepest feelings, as i he understood that to her they'd be the most precious gif he could ever offer.

She lifted her hand and stroked lovingly across the ne softness curving the firm lines of his mouth. ''Oh, Ben. O course I still love you. You've owned my heart since tha very first time you touched me.''

She offered him her lips.

The wonder of Ben's kiss, the magic of his arms, woul hold them united forever in unbreakable bonds of love an passion forged between them during days of fear and dan ger. Love as boundless as the shining blue sky stretchin from horizon to distant horizon. Passion as alive as th timeless play of sun and shadow on the enduring moun tains that brought them together.

* * * * *

Take 4 bestselling love stories FREE

Plus get a FREE surprise gift!

Special Limited-time Offer

Mail to Silhouette Reader Service™

3010 Walden Avenue
P.O. Box 1867
Buffalo, N.Y. 14269-1867

YES! Please send me 4 free Silhouette Intimate Moments® novels and my free surprise gift. Then send me 6 brand-new novels every month, which I will receive months before they appear in bookstores. Bill me at the low price of $2.71 each plus 25¢ delivery and applicable sales tax, if any.* That's the complete price and—compared to the cover prices of $3.50 each—quite a bargain! I understand that accepting the books and gift places me under no obligation ever to buy any books. I can always return a shipment and cancel at any time. Even if I never buy another book from Silhouette, the 4 free books and the surprise gift are mine to keep forever.

245 BPA AJH9

_____
Name   (PLEASE PRINT)

_____
Address   Apt. No.

_____
City   State   Zip

Fifty red-blooded, white-hot, true-blue hunks from every State in the Union!

Beginning in May, look for MEN MADE IN AMERICA! Written by some of our most popular authors, these stories feature fifty of the strongest, sexiest men, each from a different state in the union!

Two titles available every other month at your favorite retail outlet.

In July, look for:

CALL IT DESTINY by Jayne Ann Krentz (Arizona)
ANOTHER KIND OF LOVE by Mary Lynn Baxter (Arkansas)

In September, look for:

DECEPTIONS by Annette Broadrick (California)
STORMWALKER by Dallas Schulze (Colorado)

You won't be able to resist MEN MADE IN AMERICA!

If you've been looking for something a little bit different and a little bit spooky, let Silhouette Books take you on a journey to the dark side of love with

SILHOUETTE *Shadows*

Every month, Silhouette will bring you two romantic, spine-tingling Shadows novels, written by some of your favorite authors, such as *New York Times* bestselling author Heather Graham Pozzessere, Anne Stuart, Helen R. Myers and Rachel Lee—to name just a few.

In July, look for:
HEART OF THE BEAST by Carla Cassidy
DARK ENCHANTMENT by Jane Toombs

In August, look for:
A SILENCE OF DREAMS by Barbara Faith
THE SEVENTH NIGHT by Amanda Stevens

In September, look for:
FOOTSTEPS IN THE NIGHT by Lee Karr
WHAT WAITS BELOW by Jane Toombs

Come into the world of Shadows and prepare to tremble with fear—and passion....

Relive the romance...
**Harlequin and Silhouette
are proud to present**

A program of collections of three complete novels by the most requested authors with the most requested themes. Be sure to look for one volume each month with three complete novels by top name authors.

In June: **NINE MONTHS** Penny Jordan
                              Stella Cameron
                              Janice Kaiser

Three women pregnant and alone. But a lot can happen in nine months!

In July: **DADDY'S**   Kristin James
             HOME   Naomi Horton
                              Mary Lynn Baxter

Daddy's Home...and his presence is long overdue!

In August: **FORGOTTEN** Barbara Kaye
             PAST   Pamela Browning
                              Nancy Martin

Do you dare to create a future if you've forgotten the past?

Available at your favorite retail outlet.

HARLEQUIN®   Silhouette

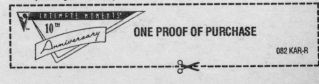